AMNESIA   NIGHTS

AMNESIA NIGHTS

QUINTON SKINNER

BALLANTINE BOOKS
NEW YORK

A Ballantine Book
Published by The Random House Publishing Group

Copyright © 2004 by Quinton Skinner

Epigraph from "The Farewell" from *Das Lied von der Erde*
by Gustav Mahler was translated by Alička Pistek.

www.ballantinebooks.com

Library of Congress Control Number is available upon request from the publisher.

ISBN 0-345-46542-3

Manufactured in the United States of America

1   2   3   4   5   6   7   8   9

First Edition: July 2004

Book design by Susan Turner

For Joyce and Richard

ACKNOWLEDGMENTS

THANKS TO: Alička Pistek for her continued good work, friendship, and belief; Liz Ziemska, who kept pushing me; Aaron Black, who made a last-second leap that improved this novel; Mark Tavani, for being a great reader; and Juan Silva and Kevan Hashemi, whose friendship in Cambridge informed sections of this narrative.

THANKS ALWAYS TO SARAH.

"He asked him,
Where he would go and also why it had to be.
He spoke, his voice was choked: Ah, my friend, on this earth, fortune
has eluded me.
Where do I go? I will go, I'll wander the mountains.
I seek peace for my lonely heart."

"THE FAREWELL" from *Das Lied von der Erde* (*The Song of the Earth*),
by Gustav Mahler (translated from German).

MONDAY

Minneapolis, Minnesota.
TODAY.

SEVERAL WINTERS AGO, YOUNG ROMANTICS IN JAPAN DEVISED AN ELEGANT WAY OF COMMITTING SUICIDE. After draining a bottle of liquor, the despondent soul went to a public park in the middle of the night, where he (it was always a he) stripped naked and rubbed snow all over his body. Soon consciousness deserted him, and he closed his eyes in a velvety hypothermic embrace. It was painless, it was beautiful.

I remember walking past Cambridge Commons, across the Charles River from Boston, with cold freezing my fingertips through my gloves and the wind insinuating itself around my exposed neck. I walked the footpath by the shadowy copses and thought about the Japanese.

In Minnesota the cold envelopes with an embrace equal parts fearful and seductive. Winter is coming.

Don't get the impression that I'm an unhappy person. Really, nothing could be further from the truth. If you met me, I'll bet I could get you to like me. I used to be very good at that.

On one of the rare occasions when she was willing to talk about him, my mother told me that my father was a construction worker. His particular specialty was industrial interiors—drywall, plaster, paint, acoustic ceilings.

Frankly, I have a hard time imagining my father laboring on a construction site, sweat collecting in the wrists of his heavy gloves. From various family members, I gather that my father's long-completed tenure on this earth comprised an un-compromising run of indolence, cheating, lying, abandonment, womanizing, and neglect. He kept those who loved him on edge with the ever-present threat of his hurricane temper. I suppose it was theoretically possible that he might have put down his beer bottle from time to time and gone to work. Everyone does things out of character.

I barely remember him. One time, when I was about five or six, he came to see me. He was angry, red, not doing much talk-ing even though he was a visitor to my mother's house. He bick-ered with her and she left the room before he felt provoked. I was alone with my father, who at first didn't seem to notice I was there. He shook his head, muttering to himself. Then he turned and fixed me with a pitying look.

"Some fucking world, huh?" he said with surprising conge-niality. This was the sum total of all the wisdom he had to im-part, but he believed in what he was saying.

I sort of knew what he meant.

I bought a house in Minneapolis a little more than two years ago. The first thing I did after closing on the property was to follow in my father's footsteps with some interior work of my own. I tore a hole in my bedroom wall, just above the baseboard. Inside it, I hid a plastic bag of photographs and almost $400,000 in cash. On top of the money, I set down a wooden truncheon bought from a martial arts store in Los Angeles. It's a nasty little club, black and hard, with a handle for swinging, like the ones the cops use on rioters.

The club was barely used. Just the one time.

It's stupid of me to keep it. I'm like an arsonist watching his handiwork from behind the police barricade, reveling in the colors of the blaze, twitching every time a detective spots my sweating face in the crowd. But I can't bear to get rid of it. I've wiped away my fiancée's dried blood and doused the thing in rubbing alcohol, knowing full well the capabilities of DNA forensics. Still, it's evidence, and if they ever find Iris Kateran's body, it might suffice to put me in prison for the remainder of my useful adulthood.

Two years ago, I thought Iris was mocking me behind my back. I was afraid of her. I thought she was going to destroy me. When I went back to her home, Los Angeles, I was poisoned by money—by my desire for it, by my new image as someone who deserved it. When everything went wrong, I was no longer myself. The John Wright I once was would never have bashed his lover's head in.

The Pertinent Facts, and Unanswered Questions, of John Wright's Life:

1. He was born poor, and his childhood could best be characterized as uneventful. He was reared by adults who lived lives of no distinction. He evinced intelligence at an early age, though he also developed a nervous disposition and had difficulty relating to others. This may have been

due to the influence of his mother's chaotic and mercurial personality. Although his occasional interactions with his father couldn't have helped much, either.

2. He never again contacted his family after high school and has not spoken to his mother since shortly after his high school graduation. Though she was a woman of many faults, John Wright was basically all Sandra Ruth Wright had in this world, and John's actions doomed her to a unique prison of her own devices. He imagines she must have begun a precipitous personal downturn shortly after his departure for college but generally succeeds in driving this thought from his mind.

3. He left his home in Indiana for Harvard University in Cambridge, Massachusetts, where he made his first and only friend. He also lucked into a beautiful and extremely wealthy girlfriend, Iris Kateran, who later became his fiancée.

4. During college, John Wright was a mediocre humanities student. His relationship with Iris evolved quickly, and he began calling himself Jack (her idea). Jack and Iris eventually cohabited in a neighboring town called Somerville. Jack's love for Iris deepened, and he began to embrace the material luxuries she provided.

5. Jack, Iris, and Jack's friend, Frank Lee, decided shortly before graduation to move to Los Angeles. Although daunted by the presence of Iris's overbearing father, Jack agreed to the move because the three friends planned to set up a small investment company, which they would run and which would enjoy the backing of the Kateran family name.

6. Things went all right for a while, but soon after their engagement, Iris and John's relationship began to deteriorate for reasons too complicated to explain here.

7. After a sudden financial and personal reversal, Jack flew into a jealous rage and tried to kill Iris.

8. Jack thought he *had* killed Iris. But the police never found her body. He waits for the police, or private investigators, to find evidence of his crime. But Iris's disappearance remains unsolved. Jack does not specifically remember killing Iris. He remembers an apartment, her being there, and deadly violence. But the actual killing? No, he doesn't remember it.

9. But, if he didn't, what became of Iris Kateran?

10. No, she has to be dead.

11. Upon seeing that his incarceration was not imminent, Jack moved to a new town.

12. Jack was involved in some very bad things. He can't explain to himself what happened.

13. It's been two years since all that happened.

I am not a financial wizard; this will eventually become abundantly clear. But I bought my house in Minneapolis just before a boom that exploded real estate values in my neighborhood by at least 50 percent. Nowadays everything is so expensive. I'm old enough now to remember a time when ordinary people could live decently. I don't know what happened, and I know I didn't think that American prosperity was going to make it impossible to live a life without competition and strife. I honestly don't know what I would do with myself if I hadn't stolen almost $500,000 from Iris Kateran's father.

My friends and I (Frank Lee, specifically, and, to justify the use of the plural, Iris herself) used to complain about how the baby boomers got in on the ground floor of everything, how they snatched up all the choice places at the table and grabbed all the goodies. But now I have obtained a few things of my own. I have my house, a car, and a comfortable nest egg hidden inside my bedroom wall. I am, by all appearances, a young man who achieved some modest success and then, when times turned lean, sensibly pulled back the throttle in favor of a modest life of relative leisure.

I'm the guy on your block whom you can't, for the life of you, figure out how he makes a living.

Morning. Orange juice and coffee. My house is quiet. I sit here at my table, smoking a cigarette. This is not going to be an important day. I fry up some bacon, eat some, and leave the rest on a paper napkin for Hero, the cat, to find when he finally comes out of his hiding place.

My neighborhood is called Uptown, although the land is flat and we're actually south of downtown. I don't try to figure it out. I don't understand this northern place. This is where I came to hide. I have been issued an exemption from involvement here.

I like to go out. When I'm cooped up for too long I start to feel frightened. I pace a habitrail through my neighborhood with the squinty-eyed familiarity of a hamster in his maze. I have become a virtuoso at killing time. My sustenance is the arm's-length interaction of commerce and service. I go to movies and bookstores. I like to eat alone in restaurants during off-peak hours. Too much company doesn't sit well with me. I don't spend much money, and it will take me at least a decade to run through my reserves.

There's a squirrel on the sidewalk at my feet, squinting over his nose as if making fun of himself for being a squirrel. I know how it is.

This city is a bastion of quiet civility. It's built around a chain of lakes, around which I walk until I have reason to hope I might be tired enough to sleep. I hate the thought of returning home to all the dust and entropy. I clean and clean the house, but I can't keep up. It's discouraging. Sometimes I wake and think I'm in someone else's home.

I arrive at the Walker Library before I realize that's where I'm going. Things like that happen, when you let them. Once I had a dream about buying a book, walked into a bookstore, and there it was—the same book. I bought it, although I haven't gotten around to reading it.

The library is two stories underground. I push the elevator button, which looks none too clean. I am developing germ phobias. I have nightmares about anthrax spores, dirty bombs, and burning airplanes. I guess this is something to connect me to greater humanity. I would like to find some other grounds for commonality.

The front desk has a washed-out, Eastern European look. It's a big room that reminds me of a scaled-down concert hall, though the acoustics are terrible—from all directions I hear murmuring and echoes. In the periodical section there is a man who may or not be extremely old. He is like an old buzzard in a nest of newspapers and magazines on an indeterminate piece of upholstered furniture.

"There's something wrong with that Don Rumsfeld," he says in the deepest voice I have ever heard.

I flash him the peace sign. Midday at a city library fails to match the intellectual environs of ancient Alexandria. Mostly we have the usual bums and weirdos, newspaper pawers, magazine chewers, book defilers. A few are sleeping, and one psychotic stares into space. My people. I prefer to huddle in a circular carrel, with books on home repair, art, Buddhism. The world comes to me.

The far end is the kids' kingdom—books, toys, some stuffed bears and rabbits with the distressed look of zoo animals. I see a toddler careening on shaky legs, on the edge of disaster. A couple of older girls, bored by their stay-at-home dad. I meet a young mother's eyes, then quickly look away. I have drifted too close, in my drifting, and now the father looks up at me. I am burdened with the tacit guilt of a single man in the presence of small children—rogue-male primate danger mixed with the deep and unthinkable threat of molestation.

But there's something else. I turn, almost sniffing the air.

Iris wanted to have children with me one day. Her childhood was cold and sterile. Her mother died young, and her father, while devoted to his only child to the point of obsession, was and is a fearful battering ram of a man, difficult at best to deal with. It touched me that Iris considered me a potential father, what with the details of my own upbringing. Iris herself was never an obvious candidate for motherhood; she wasn't one of those women who bought dogs as baby proxies or whose face would melt with unrequited love at the sight of an infant in the supermarket.

At least, I don't think she was. I can't exactly remember. I would like to change the way I think and look at things, but so far I have been unsuccessful.

Desks circled like wagons protect free Internet stations, the outposts of job seekers, local crazies, young students. There's been a lot of trouble with antisocial types loading up the most outrageous porn they can find—they're determined to find varieties capable of shocking the most jaded libertine—then leaving it on-screen for children to come across. It makes me glad not to have offspring, because I would go insane trying to protect them.

I have experienced a problem recently that is embarrassing to mention. Perhaps because my world has shrunk so, on several recent occasions I have seen people in public whom I thought I knew. In each case, the seemingly familiar person seemed to have changed his or her look—a new haircut, a radically different style of dress. One time I saw someone I took to be an old college professor of mine, another time I saw an acquaintance from my days in Los Angeles. I was wrong in both cases, and the individuals in question regarded my stares with wary apprehension. I was unable to shake the eerie impression that I had encountered an alternate universe *doppelgänger* of someone I once knew. At times I think I'm not well, mentally. I have headaches. My memory comes and goes.

So now I am in a very strange position. Because I think I see her. The most important person in my life, the one who is lost to me. But it's an ordinary Monday.

She's dead because of me.

Time telescopes. She is the same age as me, stranded directly between twenty and thirty. But I am no longer here, and this can't be happening. I cannot think of a single thing, but I am aware of everything. The only answer for what I am seeing is that I have lost my mind.

I killed her, didn't I?

She looks like a homeless person. She's dressed in a thick coat buttoned to the neck. I flash on Nixon's *honest Republican cloth coat,* but the young woman before me is no coiffed and shrink-wrapped Pat. She stares hard at the computer screen, her lips moving slightly. Her black hair is knotted and uncombed, and her eyes are ringed with purple. She looks like a woman for whom time and reality have eroded, and her lapsed hygiene and air of disorder are that of the vanquished. Her antennae have been bent. I doubt whether someone who didn't know her as well as I do would recognize her. Certainly no one who knew her as she was, as a beautiful young woman full of self-assurance and promise.

But it is her. There's no doubt about it. It's Iris.

I see her little nose, slightly upturned (she always thought it looked like a child's). Her hairline with the eccentric asymmetric widow's peak over her high forehead. I see her familiar slender fingers resting on the keyboard, motionless.

Of course, she isn't really here. So many strange things have been happening. This is just the latest, and the most vivid. Now I am going to be haunted by her ghost.

I make myself stop drifting. I'm afraid that she will look up and notice me, and then I will have to do something.

My Iris was always radiant and poised, even when she thought she was disheveled. I had fought to cast aside the hangdog slouch that was my birthright, but for Iris there was never such a struggle. She moved like an athlete, graceful and lithe, and the eyes of both genders naturally gravitated to her. Her consent to being with me, to wish to marry me, was my stunning accomplishment.

This woman at the computer, in the library, in Minneapolis, is a mockery of the Iris I remember. It can't be her.

Her shoulders are rounded and slumped under her Salvation Army coat—a garment the old Iris would have used to clean off a muddy pair of shoes. She blinks at the computer screen. Something is obviously wrong with her. But then, how is a ghost supposed to behave?

You're seeing things. Walk away.

It's hard for me to breathe. I look over at the young mother and remember the train of earlier thoughts—the sight of a mother and child evoking a memory of Iris, then the sight of this woman who looks like Iris. It's a conjuring trick.

She looks up. Her eyes focus in the middle distance, then widen. She hasn't seen me yet, but she senses something. *A disturbance in the force,* Iris used to say.

I have been waiting for word that someone finally discovered her body. Then I would finally know. I've pictured the police car, the handcuffs, the headlines about the murdered heiress.

Her head turns. Her eyes are as arctic blue as I remember them, and they reflect the fluorescence that fills this room like cosmic background radiation. Her lips are chipped and cracked. Her expression verges on stupid. Her mouth looks like the mouth I kissed so many times, the mouth that touched my body and which now comes to me in dreams and begs forgiveness for whatever she did to make me want to kill her.

She looks at me. Her face comes to life very slowly, and the corners of her mouth turn up in an unfamiliar smile. It's someone else's smile. She mouths my name without making a sound.

Jack.

My head has dropped, and my face is thrust forward. I am a big, clumsy pelican. I can't look away. I wonder if anyone else can see her or if she is a vision brought to life by my memories and my guilt.

She gets up; the chair creaks under her. She's unsteady, she has to grab the table to keep her balance. I instinctively try to help, but I pull my hand back before I touch her.

Up close, it's even worse than I thought. The rings under her eyes are actually deep violet blotches, and her skin is mottled and close to cracking. Her once smooth cheeks are traced by shadowy patches. I can smell her unclean stale odor, like something left too long in a dusty attic. I do a mental trick and see the younger Iris, the healthy Iris, but it doesn't last.

"Jack," she whispers. It's her voice. She knows me.

I say her name, and she holds out her hand and gently traces my chin. Her expression is fond but unfocused, as though she has come upon an unfamiliar object that she cannot catalog. Her fingers are rough, and her knuckles are callused.

"You're . . . really here?" she asks me. I see a flash of the Iris I used to know, the way her soul's deep ebullience would surface like a globe of light emerging from the bottom of a pool of dark water. Now I know I've found her, whatever she is now.

"Of course I'm here," I tell her.

I'm fighting back tears. A librarian is looking at us. Iris takes on a strange expression that reminds me of a Botticelli angel's. How can she be happy like this? She cups the side of my face in her cracked palm.

"You worried about me, Jack," she says. "I've been thinking of you."

This is Iris. This isn't Iris.

2

I MET IRIS AT HARVARD. I went there from Indiana, a place I never wanted to be (childhood, for me, was one long involuntary experience). I was ill at ease on campus, and I spent my first months cataloging and nursing imagined slights and insults from the students and faculty. My scholarship—a free ride—was my vehicle for transcending my roots. No one in my family had gone to college. By the time I was done with Harvard, I hoped, I would be permanently extricated in body and spirit from what remained of the Wright family.

The last time I spoke to my mother was the day I boarded an Amtrak train to Boston. By then she had succumbed to the bottle; even on her good days, conversing with her was like talking to a prisoner on the other side of a Lucite wall. If I wanted to, I could press my hand to the glass and yearn for contact. I could curse with anger, I could shed tears. I didn't do those things. I took all my things with me to college, and when my mother watched me pack, she surely understood my intentions.

It's commonly assumed that the Ivy League is an impenetrable bastion of the upper class and that a redneck kid like me would find himself hopelessly out of place. There were plenty of rich kids there, and it was indeed the first step in training to be a master of the universe. But scholarships were available, and ingrained liberalism fostered guilt money in the form of generous financial aid for a minority of poor students. My SATs earned me a shot at the McElroy Fulton Memorial Scholarship: a full pass to Harvard for an Indianapolis-area student with outstanding grades, an aptitude for standardized tests, and an ability to charm Natalie Coleman, the Fulton family trustee in charge of doling out a fresh scholarship once the previous recipient had graduated. I put on a suit borrowed from a neighbor and, to my surprise, instinctively assumed an *aw-shucks* persona that endeared me to the beneficent sensibilities of the magnanimous Ms. Coleman.

Natalie Coleman perked up considerably when I mentioned my long-term career interest in the administration of public broadcasting, and from that moment she decided that I was just the sort of promising young man who deserved the McElroy Fulton Memorial Scholarship. She was unaware that a few phone calls and a little library research had yielded the pertinent fact that she served on the board of Indianapolis's public radio and TV stations and that she hosted a Sunday morning radio show on issues in public communications. I charmed Natalie Coleman by making no pretense of my ambition; by playing the would-be sharpie, I made her feel superior and secure in her own assessment of the world.

This lesson in how to charm was one that I forgot as soon

as I arrived in Cambridge. It was as though I had exhausted my ability to connect with the outside world and required a long period of dormancy in which to recuperate. I exhibited anti-charm in the dormitory and in the classroom. These were early days, in which I shed the first eighteen years of my life. I had nothing to replace my erased memories and patterns. I felt like a single throbbing nerve ending being constantly, painfully, stimulated. But I was *in*. I worked hard. If I wasn't going to become a master of the universe—I knew how much ground remained for me to make up—then I might at least become a well-compensated lieutenant.

I was a crab in my shell. For my first two years, I hardly spoke to anyone. I can't blame the institution or the milieu. I can blame only *me*. I had no idea that *fitting in* wasn't a conspiracy that everyone else had concocted to exclude me. I thought everyone else was comfortable and that their comfort was defined by excluding me. Months passed with me in this state of delusion. The reality was that no one cared one way or the other. People there were the same sort of self-interested and vaguely benign types one finds anyplace.

With roommates (a bookish premed student my first year, a distracted theater major my second), I exchanged quasi-good-natured banter about taking out the trash and how much they hated my smoking. I stayed away from the dorms as much as I could, although at night sometimes I took out my hidden stash of photographs and allowed myself the luxury of memory. I had a picture of my parents and me taken when I just started walking. I loved it because in it my father was wearing a shirt with a collar, his hair was combed, and his expression was uncharacteristically open and wholesome. It was from a past that never happened, but which I realized I could pretend was mine.

I pursued the requirements for my Concentration, wading through Expository Writing and Quantitative Reasoning. I got through Science B15, and aced Types of Ethical Theory. I wasn't an elite student, but I considered myself more than adequate. After class and studying in the library, I wandered the streets around Harvard Square. I mapped out the trail between WordsWorth Books, the Brattle Theatre, and the Coop, usually ending up at the Garage for miso soup and prolonged browsing sessions in the CD section of Newbury Comics. Entire weeks passed without my talking to a soul. At the end of my first year, a professor took me aside and solicitously asked if I was under any kind of psychiatric care or if I had ever considered it.

"What do you mean?" I asked.

He squirmed in his chair and rubbed his belly through his blue oxford. The light through the windows was tinted with the unachievable promise of another summer.

"You sat there sort of *staring* at me the whole semester," he said delicately, as though I might react unpredictably if he were to be too blunt with me. "It was a little . . . well, a little *spooky*."

I saw Iris in November of my third year. It was at the Au Bon Pain on the corner of Mt. Auburn. She was with four or five friends, all well dressed and groomed, talking and laughing with ease and confidence. I could tell it was a well-off clique, although they weren't preppies or squares. They were what I would have aspired to be, if I'd ever come out of myself long enough to aspire to anything: hip, stylish, seemingly happy. They settled in with soup and coffee at the table next to mine, their body heat escaping from the layers of winter wear they stripped off and hung over the backs of their chairs. I was reading a foreign newspaper I'd bought at Mini's Corner, and I peered over it like a drifter at a bus station.

Iris sat closest to me. She was so beautiful that I flinched when she glanced over and let her gaze linger on me for a moment.

I treasure the moment I first saw her. It is like a masterpiece in a museum, and I view it only occasionally, not wanting to diminish its impact.

They were all good-looking, but Iris was perfect. She carried herself as though she considered herself nothing extraordinary. Her friends were arguing about going to a Nick Cave concert in Boston. Iris was firmly among the pro–Nick Cave contingent. The guy next to her—great haircut, intimidating sweater—*Her boyfriend?* I tortured myself thinking—tipped the scales by saying they could always leave early if it wasn't their scene.

I listened hard until someone called her by her name. Iris. I thought of flower stalks and a perfumed morning. She caught me looking at her again, and I buried my face in my newspaper until they left. I hoped she didn't notice my hands shaking.

I followed her with my eyes as they emptied their trays into the trash can. She wore black pants and a cropped military-style coat. I traced the lines of her thighs and the way her black hair spilled out silkily from beneath her knit hat. I had to go back to my dorm room immediately and masturbate, crying out in relief when it was over. When I was finished, I lay there and listened to the noise from the hall.

A few weeks later, after holidays spent in my near empty dorm (the only other student remaining on my floor was a Somali girl who was almost as antisocial as I was), the new semester began with snow blanketing Harvard Yard. I attended the first session of a Major British Novelists class of about twenty students. Settling in with my notebook, I looked up and felt my heart sink.

I nearly ran from the room when Iris came in and, after smiling at me with a glimmer of recognition, took the seat next to mine. A wave of acidic nervousness engulfed me, and the most contact I was able to manage was a glance at her gray wool slacks.

When the first class was over, I dared to look up at her while she was packing up her things. She was smiling back.

"I remember you," she said. "You were at Au Bon Pain about a month ago. You were acting very mysterious, like a spy or something."

I could have chewed my own face off with a mixture of delight and terror. *Mysterious? Not pathetic?* I nearly wept with gratitude.

"Uh, yeah," I said. "How was the Nick Cave concert?"

She froze for a second, processing the information that I had been listening to her and her friends. Then she smiled.

"Gothic," she replied.

"In an *Intruder in the Dust* way, or in a 'Cask of Amontillado' way?"

Her expression betrayed a trace of indulgence; she knew I was showing off. "A little of both," she said.

She got up in one quick motion, as though she had energy to spare. She wore a man's button-up shirt that revealed the lines of her clavicle under pale skin.

"What's your name?" she asked when we were out in the hall.

"John," I told her.

She laughed. "I should have guessed."

"What do you mean?" I fell over myself, ready to apologize for my name if that would prevent her from walking away.

"Anonymous, mysterious." She looked into the near distance and nodded at someone over my shoulder. "So what's the deal with you? Nice guy or serial killer? I could see it going either way."

I glanced behind me, prepared for the possibility that Iris's interest was a performance designed to amuse an audience and humiliate me. There was no one there, though, and when I turned back, Iris's icy blue eyes were open and trusting.

"Nice guy," I told her. "Definitely the harmless type."

She smiled. "We'll see about that. Just about everyone thinks they're harmless, don't they? Then how do so many people end up getting hurt?"

"Al Capone probably didn't think he was harmless," I said. "Or Mike Tyson."

"So the answer is yes," Iris said.

"The answer to what?"

She clapped me on the shoulder. "About having a cup of coffee later, stupid."

"Oh. Yes." I realized that the most beautiful and charming girl I'd ever met in my life was asking me out.

Because I was so young, I had yet to learn basic truths such as the fact that even a beautiful woman has an inner life that is not perfect and self-sustaining and that she requires companionship and love and has to take measures to obtain these things. I imagined Iris receiving affection and good fortune from all directions and no directions at once, like perfect light from on high. I soon learned that she was oppressed by loneliness. Her secret self-image, held tight and locked away, was that of a misfit. She had a knack for superficial relationships, but she saw everyone else pairing off into deeper connections of love and friendship while she played the wallflower. She needed someone, and for reasons that I still find hard to comprehend, she saw in me the person with whom she would make her stand in the search for human companionship and fulfillment.

She picked me out of the crowd. She took the lead.

3

IRIS AND I TAKE THE ELEVATOR UP TWO STORIES TO THE SURFACE, THEN WALK OUT OF THE LIBRARY TOGETHER INTO THE BUSTLE OF HENNEPIN AVENUE. When we breathe the cool afternoon air, Iris lets out a little sigh of resignation. I can smell her body odor trapped under too many layers of unwashed clothing. I'm happy when a breeze delivers a wave of truck exhaust, then a comforting whisper of green under gray metal.

There's a line of people waiting for the bus and a couple of young children playing. I breathe hard to aerate my brain. She's here next to me. I am awake. I wait for this fantasy to dissolve.

We sit on a brick wall across from the vacated tobacco shop

and movie house. Iris folds her arms and stares down at the sidewalk. I notice people giving her a double take when they pass by. There's obviously something very wrong with her.

I know what she should do. She should start screaming: *This is the man who murdered me!* She should peel off her knit hat and show the scars I must have left there.

Her hair spilling from her cap is as thick and black as ever, but it's more unkempt than I have ever seen it—even after nights when we would go to bed with our hair wet and make love until we fell asleep.

Iris looks up at me, finally, and tries to smile. She seems faintly embarrassed.

"Jack," she says.

I open up my jacket. "Want a cigarette?" I ask. We always smoked together. It was one of our great hobbies.

"A cigarette?" she asks, as though I were saying something in a foreign language. Then she brightens with recognition. "Yeah, that would be nice."

I light both of them, the way I used to, and pass one over. Her hand shakes as she raises it to her cracked lips and takes an ineffectual drag. She holds it a couple of inches from her mouth.

What are you doing here? What happened to you? Where have you been? Do you know how sorry—

"It's nice to see you, Iris," I say.

After I left her the day I hurt her, I went back to our apartment, washed off the blood, and waited for the police. By morning, they still hadn't come.

After two days she was officially missing. Her father called every night for weeks. He cried, he raged, he told me sentimental stories from her childhood, he blamed me, he demanded I tell him what I had done with her. The police found nothing.

Then came the private investigators. I was questioned by the cops, released, questioned again. Somehow I managed to keep from telling what I thought really happened.

Without a dead body, they have nothing to charge me with, although I was once told that the district attorney was considering bringing me before a grand jury. I have no alibi. I deserve to play Damocles.

I try to remember the day I did it. But I see it through a gauzy film, like a videotape with the tracking all fucked up. It was a day of grainy violence, and not even I escaped unscathed— running along my scalp, usually covered by my hair, is a long scar that I received when either my lover or my best friend was trying unsuccessfully to defend herself or himself against me. It throbs when the rain falls.

I remember some of it. Does she?

Iris pulls her coat tight. It's almost fifty-five degrees, yet she's wearing heavy wool. I see at least two sweaters through the gap in her lapel. From the sight of her bony wrists, I deduce that she's lost weight off her already thin body.

"You look sad," she says.

Doesn't she remember?

"It's . . . hard to adjust. I didn't expect to see you again," I say.

"Is it me?" she asks, her voice soft and gentle. I'm not entirely sure what she means.

She's no ghost, I think. I spend nights lying in bed, watching tree shadows on the wall, wondering sometimes if she might have deserved what she got from me.

"Ooh." She reaches for me, touches my face, and warmth floods my body. *Shit.* I still love her.

"I'm so sorry," she says, and tears fill her eyes. I reach for her and pull her very close. Her clothes are like armor. I pull her head against my chest and bury my nose in the mustiness of her wool cap.

Then I can't help it. I slip the cap off her matted hair and search her scalp with my fingers. I feel the marks, the scars, the places where she bled. Her scars are much worse than the one along my scalp, but for a moment I allow myself the luxury of hoping that our parallel suffering might somehow rejuvenate the bond between us. Then I remember the cause of all that suffering.

"Don't cry, too." Iris pulls away and looks at me. "It's all right. I'm here. I'm sorry about everything. I didn't mean to . . . go . . . leave, believe me," she says, speaking very slowly and frowning.

It's difficult for her to talk. Her brow wrinkles in concentration, and her lips falter and skip over the syllables. The shock of spotting Iris is wearing off, and I'm able to see how deeply she's changed since the last time I saw her. This is why she isn't the woman I remember. She has brain damage. I need to get her to a doctor.

"Do you believe me?" she asks.

I embrace her. Her sincerity was deep and strange when she told me not to cry. My tears caused her to hurt; it's as though her condition has rendered her deeply empathic and forced to absorb the impact of my emotions. I'm not going to hurt her again.

"Where have you been?" I ask.

"It's hard . . ." Iris's voice trails off. A passing bus muffles whatever else she says.

I take her hands in mine. I know I have no right to hold her and feel love for her, not after what I've done to her. But I feel it anyway, it's filling me up. It's shocking to *feel*.

Why aren't we talking about what happened, about what I did?

"I've been traveling," Iris says. "First to San . . . Gabriel, then San Diego for a while. I've found some friends. Really, they found me. We like to move around. We came here a day ago. No, about a month. A month ago, almost."

I blink, trying to hide my shock over her syntax and mental disorganization.

"Some people?" I repeat. "What people?"

She gives me a shy smile, almost coy. She's teasing the way a child would. Iris never behaved like this in the past.

"My friends. They . . . sort of listen to me." She shakes her head a little and executes the barest hint of an eye roll. She seems to be mocking herself somehow, but I can't understand why.

"They listen? What does that mean, Iris?"

"A lot has changed." Iris turns very serious. She balls her hands together in her lap, stares straight ahead at the display window of the smoke shop. Her cigarette has burned down to the filter, and she lightly lets it fall to the ground.

"I don't understand," I say.

"I changed." Iris bites her lip. "You can see that."

My eyes burn. "I know."

"I don't remember very . . . very much at all." She closes her eyes, and I feel her tense next to me. "I remember a lot of things, but not all the time. I can't think as well as I did. Used to. I *can't*. It's hard for me to . . . to . . . Oh, wait."

I scoot away from her as she opens up her coat. I catch a flash of moth-eaten black sweater, some fringed cloth that might be a scarf, the alabaster whiteness of her bare neck. She reaches inside a pocket and pulls out a little drugstore pad of paper and a pen.

"What's this?" I ask, reaching for it.

Iris's eyes flash, and for an instant I am positive that she is going to bite my hand. I pull back.

"Wait," she commands me.

She seals her coat tight around her neck, turns away, and hunches her shoulders. She coils with effort and concentration, writing in her book, and again I am compelled to search my memory for what she once was. There are no parallels. That was the thing about Iris: Everything always seemed to come easy for her, and even when she was performing the most complicated mental gymnastics she would appear calm, serene, untouched by the difficulty that afflicted most everyone else.

I see us reflected in the window across the street: a man in a sport coat and slacks, his brown hair combed neatly off his forehead. Next to him is a street person, a disheveled woman of the class of bus ravers, street beggars, sidewalk haunters. We don't belong together, at least not visually. More than one passerby steals a look at us. Our incongruity is so powerful that I am unable to derive answers out of her deformed, elliptical speech.

When I say her name and try to see what she's writing, she twists away violently. I light another cigarette. Iris launches into a final flurry of writing, then sits, breathing heavily. She puts away her pen and looks at me with wide eyes.

"What's this about?" I ask, motioning to the pad.

"Thoughts." Her face goes blank, and she stares at the pad. I catch a glimpse of tight, cribbed writing, and then she shields it from me. "This is how I think now . . . it's the best way."

"On paper?"

"I lose my thoughts sometimes. All the time. But everything makes more sense when I write it down."

It's shifting into late afternoon. I am astonished by what has become of Iris and me.

"You mean so much to me, Jack," she says, staring at the secret world of her notes. "And I am so happy to see you again."

She shifts a little closer, her hip against mine. I feel a tremor go through her.

"What's the matter?" I ask.

"This is very hard for me," Iris whispers, reading from her book. "I knew I was ready, but it's still so hard. Seeing you now, I'm thinking about the way things used to be. At least, I'm trying. There are so many things I can't remember."

I knew I was ready? Does that mean—

"When my friends found me, I was sick. I was hurt." Iris pauses, looks into my eyes. "I know you would have helped me if you could. I'm not sure what happened. Someone hurt my head."

"Oh, Christ," I whisper.

"Things happen for a reason. I'm not what I used to be, but that's all right now," Iris says, her voice very quiet. I strain to hear. "My friends like to talk with me, and they take care of me and go wherever I want to go. They say I'm very special, when it feels to me like the opposite is true. I know it probably sounds strange, Jack, but they're my family now. Do you understand?"

"I'm not sure."

I feel overwhelmed by her presence and find it hard to keep up with her all of a sudden. It sounds as though she's living with a small spiritual community based on (Go ahead, follow the thought to the end: Can this be right?) Iris herself. She's been transformed by her suffering; I flash back to the unfamiliar beatific expression she wore earlier. In the depths of her eyes, fear and joy intersect. In the lines of her gaunt face and desexed body is a creature possessed with an otherworldly state of being. I can't understand why I'm thinking this way. I don't usually think such thoughts. *She* is making me think them.

"What about your father?" I ask. "Have you spoken to Karl since the . . . since it happened?"

"Oh, no." She covers her hands with her mouth. "No, no. Never. You know why."

I look into the eyes I could once stare into all day. *You know why.*

"I don't see anyone I used to know. That wouldn't be good for me. No one. Just my new friends. And now you. I think seeing you again is going to be good for me."

"Did you come to Minneapolis to find me?" I ask.

Again the coy expression. She is a child with a secret, and I can see that, like a child, she is too fragile for interrogation. She is here, and she's not alone. She could be dangerous to me, but I can't think about that. I can't allow myself to become selfish again, like before.

"I live close by," I tell her. "Come home with me. We can talk more. We can—"

"I can't do that," Iris says quickly.

"Why not? I need to know more. There's so much for us to talk about. We need to figure out what to do."

"What to *do*," she repeats softly, as though learning a phrase in a foreign language.

"Iris," I say. I put my arm around her. I know what I can do: I can take her to a hospital, get her the treatment her *friends* have obviously denied her. I can confess my crime and do everything in my power to make things right again. I can save her.

"We talk about salvation," Iris says, out of nowhere. "Being hurt by life. Redemption. For what we've done and what we've thought. We were all to blame, Jack."

"What did you just say?"

"I'll call you. On the phone," she says brightly. "Can I have your number?"

"Sure. Give me that." I motion to her notebook, but she moves it out of my grasp. Instead I fish out a grocery receipt from my jacket and write my name and number on it.

"John Wright," she reads from it. "But you're called Jack."

"You were the one who called me Jack, remember?" I tell her. "I forget which name to use sometimes."

"I gave you your name?" she says, her voice heavy with emotion. Her eyes shine, and I see myself in them.

"Iris, please." I release her from my embrace but keep a hand lightly on her coat. "Don't go. I've had no life since . . . since we haven't been together. I can't go back to being nothing."

"Everyone needs help." There's strange life in her eyes, as though she's receiving a transmission. "You have nothing to feel guilty about, Jack. I'm here. You're here, too. We were with each other. I remember. I loved you. I remember the places we lived together, I remember you younger. Now we have this."

My hand tightens on the rough cloth of her coat.

"Let me go," she says.

"I can't do that."

Iris is dead, a ghost, and she's here with me.

"Do you remember Frank Lee?" I ask.

She shakes her head. "Don't make me remember too much. I get confused."

My guilt is absolute. When Iris was missing, my crime was an abstraction I shared with no one. Now the evidence of my violence is with me. Guilt has been my silent companion for two years, but now it has awakened. It speaks.

"You feel . . . responsible," Iris says, clearer now. "But forgive yourself, Jack. I left *you*. I'm so sorry I left you alone to deal with everything. It must have been so hard for you."

"Don't say that," I plead. Some people waiting for the bus are watching us.

"It will never be the old way again," she says. "But there must be a reason. You can come . . . meet my friends."

"When?"

"Do you think it happened for a reason?" she asks.

Do I? I had always thought it intellectually lazy and metaphysically dishonest to discern or proclaim a design in things, to say there is more than what is. But now, sitting with Iris, I feel my thoughts change like a jigsaw rearranged to reveal the accident of a new image.

"I might," I tell her.

"The past lives inside us." She looks around, as though to make sure no one else is listening. "Do you understand?"

"I want to," I say, and mean it.

She presses her hand to her breast. "In here," she says, smiling. "But not in my head. A lot of that is gone now. But maybe that's not real anyway."

I start to talk, but she presses her fingertips to my lips to silence me. I smell stale tobacco.

"I have to go," she says. "I promise to call."

She gets up and walks away, not looking back as she crosses the street and heads off toward the lakes. I watch her move through cars in a parking lot until I can no longer see her. She walks slowly, her head down, weaving a little.

After a while I realize I am sitting alone, my hands in my jacket pockets, watching the traffic. I could have run after her, but somehow she didn't permit me to do so. I was rooted there. *Count to a hundred before you get up.*

I get up and walk down Hennepin Avenue toward my house. I am enclosed in a bubble of impenetrability. My head aches and my vision is blurred. Without her, my days pass unseen by anyone else and, at times, even by me. The distinction between minutes and hours, weeks and days, has lately become a fine one. The world is an illusion that can't touch me. My life will resume only when I see Iris again.

4

Still Today.

WHEN I GET HOME, I BRING IN THE MAIL AND LOCK THE DOOR BE-
HIND ME. The house is silent, waiting for something to happen.
The steps creak as I pull myself upstairs, a sigh escaping me.

I sit on the edge of the bathtub. This room is barely usable;
it's a staggering mess of tile and mortar in powdered and solid
states. There are pots of gray dried grout everywhere. I've been
trying to redo the bathroom floor on my own—its surface has
shifted with the years as the old house has gradually settled into
the soil. A bulge has emerged by the lowlands near the tub, and
there's a big zigzag in the dry steppe by the door where the tiles
have gone completely out of alignment. I've chipped out the
grout, pulled up most of the tile, and exposed the decaying ter-
rain underneath. Water has seeped through, and rot has set in.

The tiles are extremely small, little more than an inch across. This floor probably once looked pretty good, a fairly elegant counterpoint to the dark wood tongue-and-groove paneling that runs chest-high along the walls. Now it's a mess.

I take off my jacket and throw it into the hall, then strip down to my undershirt. I take a couple of Advil, then I go into my office and turn on the radio loud. Sound doesn't travel well in this house. It's as though a dampening force weakens my ears. I go back to the tiles, drop down to my knees, hold one square up to the light.

Iris and I dated for a month and very quickly fell into a pattern of spending every night together and seeing as much of each other as possible during the day. She was as lonely as I was. Her friends—few of whom liked me or seemed to consider me a good match for Iris—failed to palliate a deep need within her for stability and connection. She was as hungry as I was to make a new start and to fall in love.

After our first date—a coffee that lasted four hours, until the Starbucks on Mass. Ave. closed down—we talked on the phone every day. Within a month, we were linked. Sexual intimacy came naturally between us, and I called upon the experience of a couple of brief high school liaisons for at least some idea of how to behave with a woman. I tried to attend to her every wish or need. I didn't think about what drew Iris to me, because asking that question might have snapped the spell that kept her with me. Instead, I would trace her silhouette in flickering candlelight: the upturn of her nose, the soft pillows of her lips, her dark hair tucked behind her ears. To me, all of these were objects of devotion. The nights we spent together possessed a peculiar magic, hours passing like minutes, dark and light playing on my eyes as her beauty evolved with every passing moment. Her self-confidence was no act, but when we were alone, she changed subtly. She was in a state of perpetual amusement, a laugh at herself or at me always about to form on her lips. She acted grateful to have me, as though my role were to complete a quantum unit, a counterbalancing energy to her own. I was vividly amazed that Iris wanted me, and felt redeemed, having found someone who brought out my better self.

Iris came from a rich family, real money, close to the very top of the American wealth ladder. I tried not to dwell on this fact, making sure to pay for movies and dinners and to buy her presents. Pretty soon, though, she declared that we should abandon the pretense: She had access to as much dough as she wanted, she said, and I was living off a small grant. We had total trust, she reasoned, and we loved each other. So we should be refreshingly honest and go right ahead and spend Karl Kateran's money. It would be impossible to go through it all, unless we decided to buy a small nation.

I tried not to dwell on the money, but it wasn't easy. If you've ever gone without, you know what I mean.

The Kateran family effectively comprised Iris and her father, Karl. I saw pictures of Karl, taken when he and Iris were on vacation in Fiji, in Paris, in Cairo, with Iris aging from a coltish teenager into a young woman. Karl was old, nearly bald, but he carried himself upright and stared into the camera with defiance—in picture after picture, all around the world, Karl Kateran stared into the lens as though daring it to challenge his primacy.

I joked about this and was surprised by Iris's reaction.

"What do you mean by that?" she asked, her eyes flashing.

"Nothing much," I said. "Just that your father looks like a real tough character."

"Don't say that." Iris looked meditatively at a picture of her and Karl posing close together on the architectural jigsaw of an

Egyptian city street. "My father's been through a lot. You have to be strong and on guard in his world."

"I don't doubt it," I said. "I didn't mean anything."

"I don't want you and my father to have problems with each other," she said in a tone that communicated to me that this project was to be largely my responsibility.

"Why should we have problems?" I asked.

"Just don't," she said with finality. And, for the first time, there was a crack in the perfect edifice of our love. I soon learned that when it came to Karl, Iris was uncritical, almost reverent. I was not to comment on this fact or challenge it. I was to come to terms with Karl Kateran on my own. I dreaded meeting the man for months before I actually did.

One morning, while Iris was at her Social History class, I went to the library to learn about Karl. I knew he'd grown up in Newcastle, in the north of England, but Iris had little enthusiasm for hashing over the details of his life. She took him as he was and, like most children, operated under the solipsistic assumption that his life began with her birth. I needed more because, already, I feared that Karl Kateran would be my future antagonist.

It didn't take long to unearth an intimidating lore of mythology surrounding Karl. I found admiring portraits in back issues of *Money* and *Forbes*, a long listing in a brazenly ruling-class fetishizing book called *Sketches of the Lions of American Business*, and various mentions in *Time* and *The Wall Street Journal*. Most of the straight business notices dealt with his banking interests and real estate development ventures; all regarded him as an imposing, powerful, and (reading between the lines now) shadowy figure.

His family was from Austria, but they emigrated during the apocalypse of World War I for a life as outsiders in Britain. In Newcastle, Karl's father, Jan, opened his own cobbler's shop in the respite between the wars. The family's business was arduous and demanding, and it was expected that young Karl would work in the shop and, one day, run it himself. Instead, surely to his parents' frustration, Karl left his family when he was sixteen. Here all mention ends of Karl's connection to the Kateran family. Iris had told me that her father never mentioned what remained of their relatives in England or anywhere else. Apparently the family meant little to him; maybe they represented limitations from which he strove to break free. Perhaps he simply didn't fit in with them. I never knew the truth, although it didn't escape me that Karl and I had both cut ties with our pasts in order to create new identities. It occurred to me that such creatures are destined never to reach an accord with one another.

What followed were travels so wide-ranging that—before I met him and was convinced of his capabilities—I suspected they were a rich man's apocryphal autobiography. Months later, I bore the appraisal of his black eyes, twin holes into a soul with no time or need for the soft illusions of morality or kindness, and I knew that all of it was true. I saw how everyone around him, including Iris, especially Iris, treated him with deference verging on worship. My Iris, who took no shit from anyone, became a little girl in his presence.

He spent his early twenties roaming post–World War II Europe, traveling between east and west in the interim before the Soviet bloc was consolidated and borders sealed. He was a roving entrepreneur, as far as I could tell, bartering goods and services on every available market.

> It was a time of great devastation and suffering. None of the old ways of doing business, or living life, were any longer relevant. This is when I learned that I could become successful by appraising and meeting a range of human needs.
> —KARL KATERAN, *The Wall Street Journal*, October 18, 1981

He moved back to the United Kingdom, but to London this time, apparently not interested in reuniting with his family in Newcastle. By the time he was thirty, he had set up an international corporation involved in petroleum drilling and refinement. Postwar humanity had found its bearings, and woke up with a mighty consumptive thirst that could be slaked only with oil.

I can't be sure, but I guess that by this time Karl was involved in deeply illegal and immoral transactions. Whispers and insinuations came through the dry text of profiles written about him. I know that law and justice are concepts that interest him only insofar as he can use them to his own ends. My suspicion is that Karl was involved in the weapons black market. He was one of the few Western businessmen permitted to do business in the Soviet Union during the cold war, and his primary area of involvement was the Soviet Near East. He amassed holdings in America and Europe, but he was also associated with the lawless places where violence is a crushingly pedestrian reality and where wealth is inevitably gained at the expense of suffering masses. I assumed that Karl made much of his fortune off the rapacious exploitation of the previous half century, but his secrecy was never breached. When an *Economist* reporter tried to unearth Karl's past for an investigative article in 1985, he found a trail of current and former associates too intimidated or implicated to speak on the record. One item of information seeped through: that Karl was allegedly linked to arms sales to various factions in the interminable civil wars in West Africa. It was a whisper and nothing more, but it was all that the *Economist* reporter could come up with after months of research.

I tried that afternoon at the Widener Library to imagine who Karl might really be. His entire life had been spent in a constant process of acquisition, a steady accumulation of wealth.

He cut off his family and set out to conquer the world. I cut off
my family and drifted, without a self, until I met his daughter. I
knew he should have no tolerance for me.

In 1969, Karl Kateran went to a meeting at Chase Manhattan Bank in New York, where he met a young office clerk named
Patricia Larson. I found her profiled in an old copy of *Life*. Patricia was a beauty—like Iris, her light eyes were framed by a delicate brow, and she had a bow-shaped mouth that perpetually
carried a hint of a smile. Karl married Patricia within a year of
meeting her, then moved his home and office to Los Angeles in
deference to his new wife's family ties and in anticipation of the
economic boom in Los Angeles and the Pacific Rim. Iris was
born in 1977. Patricia died four years later, electrocuted in a
household accident. Discussing what happened to Iris's mother
was the ultimate taboo, and Iris never revealed to me the details. I brought up the subject once—delicately, tentatively—
only to have her shut down and turn away. The second time I
tried, she snapped at me to leave the subject alone. And so I
never learned the truth.

I scoop up a big handful of blue tiles and splay them across the
floor in front of my bent knees. I press my hand down to the big
open patch of rotting floor. Airborne moisture and spillage from
the tub have done a real number on the layered wood. The
bathroom has no ventilation, and naturally the windows have
to be sealed shut during the frigid winter. I should tear everything out, but instead I try to banish the moisture from the dead
wood with a hair dryer. It seems to be working. Or at least I
think it is. I don't entirely trust the way I see, hear, perceive. I
wish there were someone here to be my fact-checker, to point
out to me when I'm going wrong. There are times when, to be
honest with myself, I wonder whether any of this is real. But
then the critic inside me weighs in, saying: *You are not allowed to*

absolve yourself of your guilt by doubting your past or present. You have to stay right where you are, Johnny boy.

Soon it will be winter. The very idea makes me feel frozen inside. It will be so cold here that going outside will make me desperate, all my animal self-preservation instincts kicking in and commanding me to run, to escape.

I'd never seen a father and daughter closer than Karl and Iris. Whatever happened to Iris's mother, the accident drew the survivors tight into a two-person knot. It occurred to me that Iris's loneliness at Harvard was accounted for by her father's absence. I sought a companion to fill my emptiness, to help me define who I was going to become—since, after all, I showed up at Cambridge as a newborn squinting in the harsh light of day. Iris needed someone to help replicate the binary star system of her childhood, when she and Karl floated in the ether of their hillside mansion. She found what she needed in me. I liked to think I represented an improvement on Iris's childhood model of male intimacy, but I couldn't say. We never really know our parents, not as peers, not as fallible characters with interests outside our own. In the same way, we can never know other people's parents the way their children do; we can't be another child and experience the tender moments from a stern father or the stammering desire to earn the love of a doctrinaire. I could never imagine loving Karl or trusting him, but Iris did. And she was right to, for he would have done anything for her.

Karl Kateran is without question the scariest man I ever met. He isn't physically imposing at first glance, but his short frame is all bone and muscle, a runner's build. His hawkish nose and close-set eyes are those of an accountant or a priest. He has an easy laugh and impeccable manners, and he's capriciously generous with his wealth—on his terms, by his whim. He offered to pay off the mortgage on my mother's house after Iris told him about the situation back home. He was puzzled, and subtly disdainful, when I told him that I hadn't spoken to her since I left for college. His cold appraisal of me shifted to contempt, even though he had also left behind those who shared his name when he was my age. Iris wouldn't see or acknowledge his enmity toward me. But one day, at his house . . .

Don't think about that. I force myself to snap back to the bathroom, to the tiles.

During the last two years I have feared the police, I have worried about the IRS, and I have even dreaded the abstract justice of karma. But most of all I fear Karl Kateran. The moment he learns for sure what happened to Iris, I'm as good as dead. My uneventful safety of the two years since I left L.A. has been attributable to the fact that Karl still doesn't know what happened to his daughter.

She was his treasure, his only child. *The only woman in my life,* he called her once, in my presence, with off-putting emphasis. I know about the snarling wolf beneath Karl's urbane exterior. I have dealt with the private investigators Karl has sent to Minneapolis to question me. *Just trying to get at the truth, don't take offense. Mr. Kateran has told us how much you loved Iris. If there's anything you haven't remembered until now, any piece of information that could help—*

I look down at my hands, full of tiles, then out the window. It's almost completely dark outside. I've been sitting here for hours. I glance at the clock: a quarter after seven. *How has that happened?*

This sort of thing has occurred more and more lately. I fall into recollecting the timescape of my life, always in the quiet of my house. I come up again like a deep-sea diver, sometimes gasping for air because I have forgotten to breathe. It feels as though I'm traveling without moving. I return to my body, stuck in a pose like a *tableau vivant*, and find that the world has spun and the stars have shifted in the sky. It has something to do with this house, I think. It encourages me to get lost, keeps me in timeless stasis. If it had its way, I would breathe once or twice a day, my metabolism impossibly slow, the world outside moving in fast motion like a sped-up videotape.

I think these thoughts even though they are irrational. But things keep happening. Yesterday I lost a shoe. I searched everywhere for it, it made no sense, it should have been with its mate where I left it. Finally, I gave up. Then, just before bed, I found it. It was with its counterpart, neatly arranged side by side on the mat by the front door. I know I didn't put it there. And there's no one else here to have done it. I may be haunted. Or else there's something seriously wrong with me. I may be losing track of my own actions.

"Screw this," I say. I drop the tiles. Today I haven't even bothered to mix up a fresh pot of mortar. Maybe later, if I have trouble sleeping.

I go downstairs to the darkened living room. The lights had been out when I came home, and the shades are still open to the street, where falling leaves have rotted on the pavement into brown paste. I almost lose track of myself again, then catch myself with my head nodding.

It's raining. I can't hear it, but I can see drops splash on the sidewalk. Few outside sounds filter in. Sometimes I watch people get out of their cars, talking, a mere ten or twelve feet from the window where I stand, but I can't hear their voices. I can't hear their car door slam. The action outside is reduced to pantomime, as though hearing too much would distract my attention.

From what? From remembering?

I flick on the lights and the phone begins to ring. I flash on the image of Iris taking my number in her bony hands. I search frantically for the portable handset, cursing, finally finding it and managing to pick it up before the voice mail kicks in.

"Jack Wright?" says a man on the other end of the line. I grimace in disappointment. I had hoped it would be her.

"Solomon," I reply.

Solomon Ford is the latest private investigator in my life. He is employed by Karl Kateran, like the ones still working in Los Angeles, Cambridge, and I don't know where else. Earlier investigators have followed me, watched my house, gone through my mail. Solomon is by far my favorite. His approach is refreshing: he is utterly and openly suspicious of me, he acknowledges the fact that I will cling stubbornly to my version of the truth, and, subsequently, he insists on finding humor in the essential ridiculousness of our relationship.

"How's it been going?" Solomon asks me.

"About the same," I say.

Solomon laughs. "You working?"

"Some. Not much."

"What did I tell you last time?" Solomon demands. He fancies himself a wise man and motivator, and firmly believes that I need someone to play both roles in my life.

"I don't remember, Solomon."

" 'I don't *remember*,' " he repeats. "Of course you don't. You don't pay attention. Well, I'll do you a favor and repeat myself— and you know I don't like repeating myself."

"You *love* repeating yourself," I say. "I can't think of anything you love more."

He ignores me. "I told you that the only way out of the hole you're in is to get on with your life. We're either going to find Iris or we aren't. But you need to work. You have to get involved with something that matters to you. Otherwise you're going to rot. Fuck, man, you're not even thirty yet. I wish to God I was your age."

At some point in every conversation, Solomon tells me how

jealous he is of my age. And my Harvard degree. And the fact that I'm a white man in a white man's world. Though he would deliver me to Karl if he could, I love talking to Solomon.

"So you're in town?" I ask him.

Solomon comes to Minneapolis on a random schedule, sometimes showing up at my door, sometimes approaching me on the street. In recent months, though, he's scaled back on the theatrics and simply called to tell me he'd like to meet somewhere.

"He comes in the dark of night, his footsteps like whispers," Solomon tells me. "Hell, yeah, I'm in town. My home away from home, Minneapolis. What I want to know is why you don't move to Florida or Arizona or something. You know I hate the cold. Are you trying to punish me or something?"

"Any way I know how, Solomon."

Solomon laughs at this. He has a wide variety of laughs, from the heartfelt to the blatantly contrived. This one falls somewhere in the middle.

"So you want to go out for a drink?" he asks.

I realize that if Solomon is in Minneapolis, he might have been following me earlier, and he could have seen me talking to Iris. But would he even have recognized the damaged creature I saw today as the vanished heiress whose image was broadcast across Southern California on TV two years ago?

"I was thinking of turning in early, Solomon," I tell him.

"Jack, there's something wrong, isn't there. You never turn down a drink, especially when I'm paying for it. Come on, talk to your old buddy Solomon."

"There's nothing wrong," I tell him. "I just don't feel like it."

"You got other plans?" he asks with sarcasm.

"I'm washing my hair."

Solomon sighs. "So that's how it's going to be," he says with exaggerated disappointment. "You're leaving me to my own devices. You know, Jack, I always count on you to keep me out of trouble. There's surprising variety and intensity to night-life here on the tundra. And a surplus of girls of Scandinavian descent."

"You enjoy yourself," I say. "Look. Solomon. I'll meet you tomorrow for coffee, all right? Then we can have the same conversation we always have."

Except this time, there's something new to hide.

"Coffee," Solomon says with distaste. "Fine. I'll just play on my own. You're losing your life force, John. You know that? You're sitting around that house too much."

"Tell me about it," I say.

"Last chance," Solomon says. "A fine dinner, drinks. Karl pays. If you don't want to meet any women, you can at least watch the master in action."

"No thanks, Solomon."

"Then tomorrow. Same place as last time?" he asks.

"At ten," I say.

We hang up. I turn on all the lights downstairs, the overhead tracks and the big antique chandelier in the dining room. Then I open up the cabinet, take out a bottle of Glenlivet, and fill a glass almost to the top, leaving room for ice.

Solomon is here. Iris is here. She doesn't want to see her father, and I plan to respect her wishes. *I* will be the one to help her, not Karl, and surely not the people she's been traveling with, whoever the hell they are. It occurs to me briefly that they might be after her family money.

I take a long drink, the Scotch scorching my esophagus. It burns, but it wakes me up. I haven't really eaten much all day, but I have no appetite. I take another drink and sit at the table. I remember a line from a Lou Reed song, something about alcohol making you less lucid if you're sort of stupid. I remember that old album cover, with Lou Reed in a hideous terrycloth sweater, bloated and exhausted. He didn't look like he was going to dispense any useful advice.

I put my drink on the table *sans* coaster. Fuck it, it's *my* house, my table. There's no one here but me. I can do what I want.

I sit there, waging war. I know I'm not alone. I put my head down, feeling castigated.

"All right, all right," I say. I get up, go to the kitchen to fetch a coaster. I put my drink on it after wiping up the condensation from the table with my sleeve.

I am not usually conflicted about coasters and domestic niceties. But it feels as if there's someone here, watching and judging. I'm compelled to keep the house clean, to wipe the windows and mop the floors. I don't do it for myself. I do it because otherwise there would be anger in the air.

"Are we satisfied?" I ask, and receive no answer. For the moment, I am alone again. I take another drink, too frightened to leave the room.

5

Cambridge.
THREE YEARS AGO.

I HAD BECOME SOMEONE ELSE BY SENIOR YEAR. One day Iris started calling me Jack. It was a joke at first, but then she continued because her amusement transformed into insight.

"Jack suits you better than John," she told me. "It's more a man's name. And you talk about how you've turned into a better person than you used to be. Why not take a new name to go along with it?"

I couched my conscious transformation in terms of self-improvement when it came to Iris. I wasn't sure how she would react to the truth—that I had forgotten how to be the quietly shrewd Midwestern boy who arrived at Harvard. Life with Iris gave me license to reinvent myself. Her entitlement rubbed off on me. Her wealth protected me. We never questioned the bond between us or entertained the possibility that we might not be together one day. It went without saying that each of us, in the other, had found our missing component. We socialized with her old friends, but they began to fall away. It was eventually true that we had no life outside of each other. It was also true that we were compassionate with each other, that we were honest, and that we had as healthy a relationship as I had ever seen. When I shed my old self for a new one, I felt whole and complete in a way I never thought possible. I knew my new self, and I liked him.

Iris, for a time, would still have lunch with a couple of old male friends of hers. One of them, a guy called Bill, was someone that Iris had dated for a couple of months the year before she met me. I wasn't sure how serious their relationship had been—I wouldn't ask, and I prided myself on never pressing her for details. This was another part of my new self. I would not be jealous. I would be someone I respected.

And Iris, my Iris, she was my earth and sky. The world could have made me an outcast and a pariah, and I wouldn't have cared as long as I had her faith in me. I knew every curve and plane of her body, I knew the storms of her emotions and the quiet seas. Each time I saw her was like the first, and an uplifting surge filled my chest. This was a world that wasn't going to change, I decided. It *couldn't* change.

Still I never called home, and I never wrote. My mother made no attempt to contact me. My aunts and uncles, scattered through the Midwest, were silent and invisible. They were probably relieved that I never got in touch with them. They did fine without me and, I assumed, my mother.

Iris and I moved in together in a third-story apartment with a balcony in Somerville. Iris maintained a joint checking account for us and gave me a credit card in my name. I tried to protest, but she insisted I take it.

"It's my father's money, and he has plenty of it," she said as she pressed the green AmEx card into my hand. "He gives me money because he wants me to be happy. And I'm happy when you're happy. Just don't charge a jumbo jet."

I was scrupulous about not abusing Iris's largesse. I saved receipts for everything I bought and bragged about my bargain hunting until she ordered me to stop. She'd finally had enough of the way I dressed, calling my collection of old chinos, cheap button-up shirts, and acrylic sweaters "failed mock casual." It stung to have my appearance appraised so dismissively, and part of me wondered why it had taken her so long to air her criticism of my style. I also knew she was right; I deferred to the cutting succinctness of the way she summed up my mode of dressing. This was one of her great talents, both thinking of direct and verbally dashing things to tell people and then having the nerve to actually deliver them.

So I threw myself on her mercy. "Dress me," I said, secretly thrilled. Iris knew how tense and agitated shopping made me, so she grabbed the stack of catalogs piled up by the front door and started making phone orders. A few days later boxes began to arrive from Banana Republic and J. Crew: thousands of dollars' worth of shirts, slacks, shoes, socks, and suits. One afternoon when a big shipment arrived, Iris and I unpacked dozens of sweaters and shirts and jackets and arrayed them in great heaps on our bed, feeling the texture of each item, pressing our cheeks against fine linen and wool, marveling over the colors. I started wearing suits, for no reason other than that they looked good and they were comfortable. I started getting my hair cut once a week, taming my once unruly mane of thick brown hair. I stopped looking at how much things cost. Most days, on the way home to our apartment, I stopped to buy Iris some flowers, some scented soap, some little gift I spotted in a shop window.

One day I saw my reflection in a window and had a random

reaction—that guy's got nice clothes, that guy's sure of himself—before I realized that I was looking at myself. I was tickled and titillated to mistake myself for an elegant stranger. Iris was thrilled with my transformation, and she matched my focus on externals by embarking on a buying binge of her own, purging many of her funky thrift store clothes in favor of cashmere sweaters, tailored pants, silken dresses, expensive lingerie. We started buying more things for the apartment, until it became a running joke as each of us tried to top the other, a silver salt-and-pepper set following a Persian rug, then a new microwave oven. We luxuriated in our excess and scandalized each other with our newfound passion for materialism. I loved seeing an unfamiliar spark in her eyes and, most of all, reveled in her little squeeze of my arm when we were out and she told me how good I looked. No matter how close we were drawn together, I was always intimidated by Iris's beauty; now I felt that my own appearance at last complemented hers. I was worthy of her.

It was around this time that I made my first close male friend since grade school. His name was Frank Lee. I knew Iris was happy about it; she worried that I might someday regret plunging into such a deep commitment with her and not exploring the hinterlands of life and experience. By this point we knew we would be married one day. Not until we were out of college and reasonably settled, with me making a decent living—*that* I insisted upon. If she had her way, she said, we would have already gotten married in secrecy and told her father later.

You see, she wanted to be with me *that much.*

I met Frank at the Tasty in Harvard Square. The place was as big as a generous closet and staffed by a single cook who took orders, prepared them, and slid the food across the counter in a fussy one-man-band performance. It was always packed, and it was impossible to eat there without literally rubbing elbows on either side. The cook, frenzied and grouchy, invariably got my order wrong. Eating there was tantamount to accepting an obscure dare. Next to me one afternoon was an Asian guy reading a paperback while inhaling a bacon burger and fries. He was tall, with lank black hair framing his eyeglasses. He was obviously a student, and I recognized his expensive suede jacket from the Banana Republic catalog. He dropped his book to the countertop, next to his paper plate and congealing grease. My food arrived: a cheeseburger, fries, Coke. I shifted my food toward his.

"He got my order right," I said.

"It's a blessing or a curse," he said. "See how you feel in an hour and you'll know which."

"My name's Jack," I told him, extending my hand.

"Frank Lee," he said, looking me over. "Let me guess. Law school?"

"Undergrad. Humanities," I said, pleased to be mistaken for a master of the universe in training.

Frank chewed nervously on the corner of his mouth. He wore an earring in the shape of a topaz sphere, and his complexion was flawless.

"What about you?" I asked him.

"Econ," Frank replied. He motioned again with the paperback. "Fiction is for my downtime. It's for me. The fast track to business school might not be. Or so I've been thinking."

"Who's it for, then?"

"Who else?" Frank shrugged. "My family. Chinese parents, man. You ought to try them sometime."

"I don't think it's possible," I replied.

Although Frank Lee was a year younger than me, he was on schedule to graduate at the same time because he'd aced an array of advanced placement tests in high school and entered college with enough credits to start as a sophomore. We exchanged phone numbers and met up at Tower Records a few days later, soon discovering that we both loved to haunt the dozens of used-book stores around the square. About a week later I invited him back to the apartment for dinner—steaks and fried potatoes, which I cooked.

Frank and Iris hit it off right away. They shared a sense of the world as essentially absurd, and they both liked to make fun of my innate seriousness. That first night I felt a dynamic taking shape, with Frank and Iris as satellites orbiting the sun of my affection for the both of them. Iris wanted me to have a friend so badly that she went out of her way to please Frank, suggesting almost daily that I call and invite him over and often including him when we went out for a movie or dinner. Soon he was comfortable stopping by unannounced, opening up a beer, putting his big Nikes on our coffee table.

I had no money, no family, only the fiercely guarded citadel of my self. Iris had unlimited resources and a stable home (if one populated only by her father and the domestic staff). Frank was somewhere in the middle. He was quick to laugh, and he was encyclopedic about books and music, but these were distractions from the main current of his life; I soon learned that the expectations of his family weighed upon him and drove his fidgety, almost furtive way of moving through the world. He was expected to succeed in finance, to carry on the ameliorative drive of his father, a Philadelphia bank executive and first-generation American. Frank, like Iris and me, was an only child. He was the beloved only son, talented, smart, and good-looking. His parents were intoxicated by his potential, and they had laid out for him a no-exit road to business school and then to conquering American finance.

Frank and I stayed up late drinking and talking, telling our secrets (he was the last person to whom I gave my true autobiography), even breaking down and crying one particularly besotted and maudlin midnight. Iris seemed to know when to join us, when her presence would enhance the dynamic, and when to leave us alone. I knew that Frank went on dates, but he never got serious enough with anyone to bring her to meet us—how serious that needed to be, I wasn't sure, although I sensed that Frank feared bringing a fourth into our equation that might upset the delicate balance.

Then we all had to graduate. I tried to call my mother to see if she wanted to come to Cambridge for commencement—Iris offered to buy her a ticket. But my mother's old phone number by then belonged to someone else. Directory assistance was no help. I thought about calling Uncle Ron, my mother's brother, but decided not to.

"That's that," I told Iris, gently replacing the phone in its cradle. "I'm done now. No more family."

She put her hand on the back of my neck and rubbed. "Come on, now. Don't say that."

I knew what she meant. I had Iris, so I had a family. And that would always be true.

We stayed up late one night in May and had the conversation that we'd been putting off—the one in which we talked about what to do after graduation. Everyone else in our class already seemed to have cemented their immediate futures. The future masters of the universe had already been accepted into graduate or professional schools and would start in the fall, after a summer in Spain, or Vietnam, or Australia. Other students had opted for instant entry into high-paid corporate life. I had made no blueprint, because that would have meant admitting that our Somerville days were almost over. Both Iris and I intended to work, somewhere, at something, but we were in no particular hurry.

"This is the thing. I think I want to go back to L.A.," Iris finally said over our second glass of wine. She lit a cigarette, and I watched the smoke trace curlicues in the halogen glow. She had started wearing her hair shorter, which made her look younger, her eyes bigger. She wore a sleeveless T-shirt that made her arms look long and pale.

"I have to admit, I don't have any better ideas," I replied, although I wished I did. We had spent our summers in town, with Iris flying home regularly to see her father. I had met the old man by then but managed not to spend more than a day or so around him—when I was in Los Angeles, I invented day trips to Joshua Tree (to see where Gram Parsons died), to Tijuana, to anyplace Karl Kateran wasn't. One Christmas I spent in Philadelphia with the Lees, after Frank's grandfather died and he needed backup for dealing with the uproar and drama in which his mother specialized. There would be no more avoiding Karl if we moved to L.A., though. I knew that.

"You don't want to do it," Iris said, cocking her head, exhaling smoke, and taking a sip of wine with vague irritation.

"It's not that," I said, stalling. I smelled the hyacinths I'd brought home that afternoon. It was almost summer, but the trees were late to bloom that year.

"Well, I'm open to other suggestions," Iris said. "I think you'd like living in L.A. The weather's great. There's so much going on. Maybe you could get involved in the movie business— I think you have a good screenplay in you."

Iris was so secure in her sense of self that she probably would have done whatever I wished. I knew what I wanted: to stay in Somerville, to keep things the way they were, to stay twenty-two forever. Iris had a concrete vision of moving forward. I said I wanted to get married, to share the future with her. But now I had to face my own essential immaturity—I didn't want anything to change, not ever. But I knew then that we were going.

"I have a hard time seeing myself there," I offered.

"Well, we'll live in the guest quarters behind my father's

house. We'll only see my dad during meals—three a day. And we'll have weekly status reports to tell him about our progress."

I threw the pack of cigarettes at her as her laughter pealed through the high-ceilinged room.

Then I had an idea, all at once.

"You know what?" I asked, suddenly excited.

Iris leaned forward and put her hand on my leg. "What?"

"Let's see if Frank wants to come with us."

She tucked in her chin and flashed a wary look.

"What about business school?" she asked. She puffed on her cigarette and looked away from me. "He's already been accepted. You know what he says—he's on the Lee family express train to wonderland. Going with us would be an unacceptable detour, wouldn't it?"

"Frank tends to exaggerate," I told her. "When I went to Philadelphia with him, I saw how his whole family was practically falling over with relief that Grandpa Chen was out of the picture. Frank's dad isn't nearly as bad as Frank makes him out to be. His mother kept telling Frank he needed to relax. She tried to get him to go with her to yoga class, for God's sake."

I had been surprised by Frank's family, which I had expected to be the epitome of immigrant materialism. His father was a workaholic, true, coming home from the office at seven-thirty Christmas Eve, but he also had a sense of humor and an indulgent streak toward his son. Frank's mother, whom I had expected to be a stern matron, was actually a staunch ex-hippie who burned incense and suspiciously wore sunglasses indoors. The Lees were much more with it than Frank made them out to be. Frank's father might have been disappointed if Frank put off business school, but it wouldn't be the crisis Frank liked to say it would be. And I knew I could get Frank to come with us.

I wouldn't admit why it was so important for me to bring Frank with us. Sure, I hated to say good-bye to him, to see our friendship inevitably erode with time and distance. But my real reason was transparently tactical: Frank would guarantee me an ally in my struggle against Iris's father. Frank was *Jack's friend*.

My thinking was fucked. I didn't need another ally, because I had Iris. But I had already begun to lose sight of that fact.

6

Tonight.

IT'S ABOUT MIDNIGHT WHEN I POLISH OFF MY THIRD GLASS OF GLENLIVET. I poured them strong and smoked down half a pack of cigarettes on the side. I get up from the table, swaying more than I thought I would, and go to the kitchen and piss in the sink. I think about eating something, but my stomach seems to have given up on sending me hunger signals and has gone into panicked retreat.

I go back into the dining room, ponder the half-full Scotch bottle for about thirty seconds, then pad over to the CD player in the living room. I pull out one by Elvis Costello and one by Nusrat Fateh Ali Khan, a Pakistani devotional singer Iris always loved. I put in the latter, and a high-pitched voice fills the room with devotion to Allah.

The phone is on the bookshelf. It hasn't rung. Iris hasn't called.

I lean against the doorway, let myself slide down to the floor. Music, dark, loud, rhythmic.

Iris is like a child now. She writes her thoughts down in a little notebook before she speaks. She can remember only fragments of her life. She lives with her new "friends"—how many, I can only guess.

They used to live in San Diego, a couple of hours on the freeway from Karl Kateran. San Diego. Heaven's Gate, Herf Applewhite, and black Nikes sticking out from triangular folded blankets. They ate crushed-up pills and drank vodka, then helped one another put plastic bags over their heads so they could hook up with the spaceship coming in the night sky to take them to their extraterrestrial destiny. Before that, they designed Web pages. I wonder if the last ones to go had doubts, with the house starting to stink of death, the rooms quiet and still, with the powdered pills on their tongues and the vodka stinging their throats.

I have no idea what Iris has gotten herself into. She's obviously in no condition to make serious judgments for herself. It's very possible she has gotten mixed up in some cult. Someone could be controlling her, which would account partly for her zombified state of mind. They might have found out who her father is. They might be playing it coy, waiting for the right time to make contact with Karl. Maybe they already *have* and plan to ransom her for millions. I don't know if I can trust her to discern whether her "friends" are keeping her voluntarily.

I shouldn't have let her walk away. I should have grabbed her and dragged her with me.

Sure. That wouldn't have been a problem, in broad daylight at one of the busiest intersections in the city.

There's something else. It's fuzzy now that I think about

it, but when she told me not to follow her, I *couldn't*. She had some kind of authority, some kind of spell on me. It sounds insane now.

But then, what's it *supposed* to sound like, any of it?

I decide to pour another drink, then sit on the big thick rug on the living room floor. I polish off the Scotch in a couple of big gulps, then recline. This is a major miscalculation. I have to squint and brace myself against the floor to keep the room from spinning. In the middle of my field of vision, like the eye of a storm, is a big patch of white plaster.

The music is barely audible. And now it really hits me. Iris is alive. For years I've tried not to think of the awful thing I did. I only rarely find the courage to look inside myself and try to remember what compelled me to do it, why I destroyed the only person who mattered in my life.

Sometimes I think I was possessed or that I went into a fugue state that was beyond my control. It's the only explanation—that I was inhabited, taken over. Like Iris, I can't really remember what happened. I see snippets, lights, remember a hot rage boiling inside me. It's very difficult to admit that all of it might have been generated entirely by me, by my jealousy and insecurity. It's hard to consider that such things live inside me.

I hear myself sobbing, deep and hard, but I don't really feel it. I think of how I tried to kill her, to take away her *time*. How I *hurt* her.

She's back.

I must have fallen asleep on the floor. The CD ends, but I think I hear more music, something with strings like an old big band orchestra. I sit up, breathing hard, and whisper Iris's name. She's right there next to me, caressing my cheeks and my forehead. And then she isn't.

TUESDAY

7

NOTHING MATCHES THE EXPERIENCE OF WAKING FULLY CLOTHED ON THE FLOOR, HEAD LIKE A PAIN-BALLOON, MORNING LIGHT POKING THROUGH THE SHADES. I remember sitting bolt upright during the night, terrified, sensing someone next to me, but the memory breaks up and dissolves.

I go into the kitchen, make coffee, then fetch the newspaper off the front stoop. It lies on a bed of orange and gold elm leaves. It might have rained.

The throbbing in my head doesn't really get serious until I climb the stairs to take a shower. By the time I've washed and dressed, clawed talons grip the backside of my skull and press against the curvature of bone and into the soft tissue underneath. I go downstairs and see the nearly empty Scotch bottle on the table. I nod to it, with the respect due to the vanquished in a Pyrrhic victory.

I drink orange juice and coffee over the kitchen sink while staring out the window at the big house next door. I watch a pair of squirrels skitter up the side of the stucco like spiders; they've found an open space under the eaves and plan to build a winter nest there. Making plans, getting things done. I should follow their example.

I arrive in front of Caribou Coffee in time to see Solomon Ford pull up in his rented Ford Explorer and park illegally by a short stretch of curb between two alleys. I watch what I know will be the difficult task of Solomon extricating his massive body from the car. He tosses out one leg, then another, then stops to catch his breath. He uses his giant ass to leverage himself out of the vehicle, lands with a thud, reaches out to keep himself from falling. Solomon is a giant, with a massive cinder-block head and fingers like smoked sausages. His body is all abundance, from his bushy Afro and thick beard down to his boat-size unlaced high-tops. I estimate he weighs about four hundred pounds.

Solomon fusses with his jacket, pulling it closed with no self-consciousness of his girth. People in the coffee shop window are looking at him. No one can ever help looking at him. Despite his fat, he carries himself with ursine grace and assurance. I imagine him as strong as Paul Bunyan, and I don't fool myself for a second thinking that I can trust him.

"Solomon," I call out. He stops by the coffee shop door, his floppy ancient briefcase in one hand, the other extended for me. His handshake is warm and gentle.

"Kid," Solomon says. His eyes are cast at an angle by his glasses. "What happened last night? You get your period or something?"

I hold the door open for him. "You're just not used to being turned down," I say. "I think your ego is bruised."

"I can't figure you out," Solomon tells me. "You don't want to hang out with me, fine. But I don't see you doing much else with your time these days. I mean, who are your friends, Jack?"

The word *friends* causes a cognitive echo with the people Iris is staying with, and I pause. I have things to hide from Solomon.

"What's the matter, Jack?" Solomon asks. He presses a soft hand to my forehead. "The kid doesn't have a fever. Is it all this shit with Iris getting you down again?"

Before I can answer, the girl behind the counter asks us for our order. I get a big ice water, which makes Solomon tut disapprovingly. He orders a triple caramel latte, a bottled papaya smoothie, an apricot croissant, and a big iced blueberry muffin.

"You're going to waste away," he mutters at me as I take my ice water and head for an open table in the corner. Solomon arranges his breakfast, solids on one side and liquids on the other. He takes a digital organizer and a spiral notepad out of his battered briefcase, though he doesn't open either. I sip my water, feeling better than I had earlier, and watch Solomon humorlessly attack his muffin.

"Muffins are supposed to be bad for you," I say.

Solomon looks up with an expression of delicate disdain; I have said something unspeakably gauche and naive; he will let it slide.

"Don't worry about the fucking muffin," he says. "Worry about yourself. I'm serious. You don't look all there. When's the last time you saw a doctor?"

"I don't remember," I say.

"I'm serious, man," Solomon says, giving me an odd look.

"There's nothing wrong with me."

"Okay. Then let's get our work out of the way," he replies.

"Sorry. It's *my* work, *your* life. I keep sight of that, Jack, I really do."

"I know you do," I say.

"Okay." Solomon opens up his coffee lid to let out the steam. "So what's new? Anything?"

"I'm tearing the fuck out of my bathroom floor."

"Yeah, and I brushed my teeth this morning," Solomon says. "Come on, seriously. You got anything for me?"

"Solomon, why do you think I moved here?"

Solomon pauses, swishes some coffee around in his mouth. "To get away from Karl Kateran," he says.

"Well, partly," I admit. "But it was more than that."

"Do tell." Solomon uncaps his smoothie, looks skeptically at the bits of fruit suspended inside.

"You know in a fight, when a boxer gets knocked down and the referee starts the count?" I ask. "The other boxer has to go to a neutral corner. That's kind of what this place is to me. A neutral corner. Out of the fray."

Solomon sips his coffee, nods. "But you know, Jack, the boxer who goes to the neutral corner is the one who landed the knockout punch. The kill shot. The aggressor."

I pause. "It's not a perfect analogy."

"Keep working on it." Solomon tears off a strip of croissant; his palms and fingers are pale, almost pink.

I look out the window. Solomon might know everything about my finding Iris yesterday, and still he would act just the way he is.

"Look, Jack, I'm not unsympathetic." Solomon takes a swig of his coffee, killing nearly a third of it in one go. "You know I like you. When I got hired on this investigation, the police had come up with nothing. You were my number-one suspect, and I assumed you killed the girl and ditched her body someplace. Now I'm not so sure."

"At least I've improved in your estimation," I tell him.

"It took time," Solomon says, nodding. "I've come to understand you, at least I think so. And I know what you're telling me. You moved here for a lot of reasons: to get away from Kateran, to get away from the scene of the crime, to get away from that atrocious mess you and Frank and Iris concocted. You came to Minneapolis because you don't know anyone here, and there's nothing here to remind you of your past. Am I right so far?"

I nod.

"You came here because this is a place where you can stand still, do nothing, nothing is going to happen. Which is why, when I ask you for new information, you look at me like I just sprouted titties out of my forehead. Nothing happens to you. But let's say it did. What would you tell me then?"

I sigh. Solomon has paused in the demolition of his breakfast and wipes his mouth and beard with a paper napkin. He looks at me through his glasses.

"There's nothing to tell you."

"You're sure?" Solomon asks. "Hell, if you can't talk to your big brother Solomon, who can you talk to?"

"Don't worry," I tell him. "I wouldn't bother trying to hide anything from you. You'd see right through me."

Solomon looks at me awhile longer. Too long, I think. He scans my features and gives a quizzical look that verges on recognition.

"What I've been trying to drum into your head, Jack," he finally says, "is that you have no reason to sit on the sidelines. It's *criminal*, man. If I could drop a couple hundred pounds and twenty years, turn my skin white, and get a degree from Harvard—you know what I'd be doing?"

"I don't know," I say. "You tell me."

"Shit, I can't even think off the top of my head," Solomon

says with a laugh. "I'll tell you what, though. It'd involve food, drink, and hot-and-cold-running pussy."

"As easy as that," I say.

Solomon puts his hands on the chair to redistribute his weight and looks at me again. He takes off his glasses, rubs his eyes. His face without glasses is surprisingly boyish, with small features and a child's innocence.

"You know, I feel like you're a friend, Jack, and I don't have too many of them," Solomon says.

"I appreciate that."

"You know, if I could make things right for you, I'd do it," he says.

"I know you would."

"Goddamn," he says in a tone I haven't heard before. "You still really miss her, don't you?"

Solomon puts his glasses back on, looks away uncomfortably. "Jesus," he mutters.

8

Two and a Half Years Ago.

IT WAS EASIER THAN I THOUGHT IT WOULD BE TO TALK FRANK INTO COMING TO LOS ANGELES WITH IRIS AND ME. I brought up the subject after a few days, and Frank decided on the spot that he would defer his business school acceptance. We found apartments less than a mile apart in L.A. without having to go there, an arrangement expedited by Karl Kateran's ownership of more than two dozen apartment buildings scattered throughout the city.

Iris and I were given a three-bedroom place in Santa Monica, Frank a one-bedroom apartment in West Hollywood. We would live rent-free. I assured Karl, through Iris, that getting a job would be my highest priority. I didn't plan to live on Karl's charity for long.

It was about ten days before the move when Frank and I sat out on the balcony drinking beer and watching the afternoon shadows lengthen. It was the final morsel of spring, before the summer heat set in—the best time of year in New England. We were in a good mood, the next phase in our lives still replete with undiscovered potential.

"I've been thinking," Frank said, cracking open a beer.

I lit a cigarette. "That could be dangerous," I said. I put my feet up on the chair between us. Iris was at Kinko's in the square, running off copies of her senior thesis—a theoretical exposition on female self-determination from Emma Bovary through Virginia Woolf using all the best fin de siècle analytical tools. It was by lengths more insightful and erudite than anything I was capable of coming up with.

"My family's been pressuring me about what I'm going to do in L.A.," Frank said.

"They took your blowing off business school pretty well."

"Yeah," Frank replied. "But they're not completely sold on the land-of-opportunity scenario I've been feeding them."

"You have your econ degree," I said. "You're extremely qualified to sit in a cubicle someplace and crunch numbers all day. You'll have the key to the executive washroom in a year. *I'm* the one everyone should be worried about. I'm going to end up managing a tire store."

"Very fucking funny," Frank replied with more astringency than he'd intended. I looked over at him. I realized this was a serious discussion.

"What, then?" I asked.

I hadn't thought much about what kind of work I was going to look for. I figured, vaguely, that Iris's family connections could get me something in the amorphous world of public relations—whatever that was. I had ideas for a screenplay, but so far they hadn't amounted to much more than a few pages of random notes and discordant dialogue.

I sipped my beer, suddenly nervous. I would be living on Karl Kateran's property, with his daughter, probably working at a job he would get for me. This wasn't the model of independence I'd envisioned for myself. The beer tasted funny and metallic.

"What's Iris going to do?" Frank asked.

"Take some time off, to begin with," I said. "She needs to decompress. Have you read her thesis? It's really good. She's been working like hell. We're going to Yosemite for a week."

"And after that?"

"She's talked about getting an internship with a magazine, or taking a start-up job in the movie business," I said. "I mean, you know, she can do pretty much whatever she wants."

"What about you?" Frank asked. "Are you going to continue your illustrious career as Iris Kateran's concubine?"

"Hey, man, fuck *you.*"

Frank tried to laugh off what he'd said. A cloud settled in over us. We were in new territory. Frank's handsome face and square build settled into a facsimile of amiability. We never argued, and after our initial bonding we rarely talked about sensitive topics. Having a close friend was still new to me. Having a friend probe my sensitive spots was newer still.

"Concubinage has a long and distinguished history," I said, trying to sound flippant. "You'd know that if you bothered to learn anything about culture instead of wasting your time obsessing about money."

My words clanged another false note. We both knew I had no right to talk about money and how to earn it. Where had the ten bucks I'd just blown on beer and cigarettes come from? An oil refinery in Uzbekistan? A shipping deal in Singapore?

"I need to do *something*," Frank said. He crossed his arms over his chest. "I can't just hang out, Jack."

"I'm not going to *hang out*, either," I protested. "But we just got done with college. Can't we ease into things a little?"

But Frank was right. Did I plan to take a job in the Kateran Co. mailroom? *Learn the business from the bottom up. And hey— can I call you Dad?*

"Okay. I know. I have to think of something." All my deferred anxiety bubbled up, and I lit a new cigarette off the burning nub of the last one.

Frank had been waiting for just such an opening.

"What?" I said.

"I don't want to pressure you," he said. "I know you're in a tight spot. I don't mean to give you shit about it. I'm sorry."

"Thanks, cupcake," I said. "But you've got something on your mind and you're not hiding it very well. Spill it."

Frank leaned forward, folded his arms on his knees. "All right. Here's what I've been thinking. We can go into business as money managers. We can open up a hedge fund and play the stock market."

I laughed so hard that I dribbled beer all over my shirt. I cursed and reached for a rag on the table, fixing Frank with a look-what-you-made-me-do.

"All three of us," Frank added.

"What? Iris?"

"I can do it," Frank said. He moved the ashtray away from a puddle of beer. "Shit, man, the Internet's totally democratized stock trading. You don't have to go through brokers anymore. You can do it all online. I've checked it out, Jack. You get your stock prices second by second, you make deals as the market fluctuates by the hour. We can make a fortune if we play it right."

I knew Frank read *The Wall Street Journal* and *Forbes*, and in his room I'd seen him checking out E-trade sites on his computer. The market was rising and rising, and there seemed to be no end to the spasmodic wealth creation that was going on.

"What do you mean, all three of us?" I said. "You don't need me. I'm an idiot with money. I've never had any, at least not of my own. And why would Iris want to get involved?"

Frank leaned back and gave me his drunken-froggy smile, and I knew. Iris was the key. She had access to her father's money, she bore his name, and she had his connections to the Southern California elite. Whatever field she went into—film, fashion, journalism—there would be people lining up to help Karl Kateran's daughter. Because that would draw them closer to Karl.

"No way," I said. "I wouldn't drag Iris into something like that."

"Don't be so sure," Frank told me.

It was getting darker out, and Frank's flushed face was partly in shadow. It didn't take much alcohol to lay him low, and after three beers he was already giddy.

"What do you mean?" I asked

"I floated the idea to her." Frank shrugged, as though I shouldn't be concerned. "That's all. She was more into it than I thought she would be, and that's when I started to get psyched. If she said no—which I fully expected—then I had my résumé ready to start sending out. But she said it sounded interesting."

I smoked some more. Iris and Frank had talked about our future, and neither one had said anything to me? I got a whiff of conspiracy, and I didn't like it.

"You went to her first. Without telling me," I said.

"She likes the idea of us working together." Frank smiled.

"Or maybe just working with you. You're a lucky guy, Jack. She really loves you. She'd give anything a try, as long as you were involved."

I must have been brooding, because Frank reached out and startled me by tapping the side of my head.

"Don't start tripping," he said. "Iris is into it. She said she could work on the promotional side while you manage client re-lations. She said it might be fun."

That wasn't the problem. What concerned me was Frank feeling the need to inform me how much Iris loved me. He had crossed some invisible line that I couldn't trace or define. Frank had gone behind my back and talked to Iris. I'd never known them to be alone together. I tried to tie the thoughts together in my mind, but I had been so complacent about Iris's loyalty that the threads unraveled and fell away.

"Well, what about me?" I asked. "You don't need two peo-ple to make a promotional brochure. And I don't plan to work as a receptionist. Not unless things get really dire."

My words stung some secret place inside. My mother had worked as a receptionist for years.

"You're the linchpin," Frank said. "Our secret weapon. The golden boy."

"Who the hell am I even talking to right now?"

"Think about it," Frank said with a laugh. "I've known you for two years, and you've *changed*, man. Just look at you."

I was wearing a blue cotton shirt, a pair of plain-front linen slacks, and black brogans. My gray sport coat hung over the back of my chair. I suddenly felt very self-conscious. Frank had seen pictures of me taken when Iris and I were first together, with me in my old jeans and discount store sweaters, nothing ever matching. I had shed my old skin and tossed everything from my old wardrobe.

"Your point being?" I asked defensively.

"You look the part," Frank said. He took a drink. "You've got that Ivy League haircut now, and you're comfortable in a suit. You play it off, but you've turned yourself into a natural-born aristocrat, Jack. You'll never be the most outgoing guy in the world, but you're sure of yourself now. I guess it was there all the time waiting to come out, back when you were living in the trailer park."

"I never lived in a *trailer park*."

"Whatever." Frank laughed. "It's a good thing. It's fucking *great*, Jack. You're the perfect point man. You can shake hands and charm people. The fact that you can't be bothered to act friendly half the time will just add to your mystique. People mistake your shyness for snobbish self-confidence—I've seen it. You have an *image*, Jack. And that's why you're the one who's really going to make it work."

I looked down at the burning cigarette in my hand. No one had ever talked to me like this before. I wondered if this was how Iris saw me. I had been so foolish, secure in the impermeable perfection of her devotion—as though we were above the common betrayals of lovers. I blinked, feeling heat behind my eyelids. Frank's compliments sounded like a volley of insults. He was patting me on the back for hiding who I was, as though John Wright were some sort of disgrace and something to be ashamed of.

But I guess that's what I had led him to believe.

I thought of my mother. I wondered how she would look at me now, what tone her voice would take. We could finally have a drink together, instead of me sneaking sips after she fell asleep. I remembered, for the first time in a while, the way I used to stay awake every night until she finally passed out, afraid that she would burn down the house with one of her cigarettes. Because when she fell asleep, it was like flipping a switch. On, then *off*. As a boy I was morbidly scared of fire. I used to read stories in the paper about homes burning down, children dying of smoke inhalation.

"That didn't come out right," Frank said quietly. "I'm sorry, man. I guess I fucked it up. But I think it's a great idea. It's something the three of us can do together."

"Iris said she would?" I asked. "Did she really mean it?"

"Hell, yeah," Frank said. "And I guarantee both of you that I can make money. The market's creating new millionaires every day. Give me some start-up capital, a quiet room, and a computer, and I'll get results. Shit, I don't even need a quiet room."

"I don't know anything about the stock market," I told him.

"What you need to know is that we're going to make money. It's the grand illusion, Jack. It's making something from nothing." Frank patted my knee. "Have a little faith."

"You think we can make enough to live off? That's the key. I don't want to get involved if this is a playschool adventure."

Frank smiled and ran a hand through his hair. "Independence from the old man, that's what you're talking about."

"Maybe," I replied. "Of course."

"Well, let's try," Frank said. "I don't know if I can make you richer than Karl Kateran, but let's make it a priority."

We laughed and clinked beer bottles. Frank threw his head back and sighed, loudly and theatrically. He wiped his brow.

"What are you so relieved about?"

"I was worried you wouldn't come along for the ride," Frank said. "I wasn't sure you had the guts."

I thought about it. No Jack, no Iris. No Iris, no money, no contacts. No Frank getting bankrolled for a start-up business.

It was easier than I thought it would be to talk Frank into coming to Los Angeles with Iris and me.

It was much harder to accept my first moment of truly doubting her.

"To friendship," Frank said, holding out his beer bottle again.

"All right. To friendship." I held out my bottle, but somehow we missed our attempt to toast. We didn't get it right until the second try.

9

Today.

I WALK SOLOMON BACK TO HIS FORD EXPLORER, THEN LOOK AWAY DOWN LAKE STREET WHILE HE CURSES AND STRAINS TO REINSERT HIS BODY INTO THE DRIVER'S SEAT. He slams the door shut and slides the window down.

"I guess that's it," he says, shuffling his briefcase onto a passenger seat filled with newspapers and empty coffee cups. He's managed to create about a week's worth of mess in a car he's had for—

"How long have you been here, Solomon?"

Solomon makes a confused face. "Got in last night, kid. Told you that when I called."

I glance at all the debris on the seat. Solomon looks over as well, then smiles.

"Takes a lot of fuel to keep this engine running," he tells me. "What I need is a maid. Or a manservant. You ever hear of that? It's a guy who follows you around, holds your umbrella, cleans up your messes."

"You're a natural aristocrat," I tell him.

"Glad you see things my way," Solomon says with a little laugh.

"So when are you going back to L.A.?" I ask.

"You in a hurry to get rid of me?" Solomon says, peering over the top of his glasses.

"What do you think?" I reply, although I wait a second too long, and I can tell Solomon notices.

Solomon starts up the engine. I look down the road. We're about three blocks from the library where I found Iris.

"I have an open-ended ticket," Solomon tells me. "I'll probably stick around tonight, run up some more expenses, then get out in the morning. I don't think Mr. Kateran is expecting much from me at this point. I could photocopy one of my previous dozen reports and give it to him. 'Jack Wright reports nothing new.' Hey, you don't have anything to do. Why don't you write it for me?"

"Earn your own money, Solomon," I say, giving him a brotherly slap through the proxy of the Explorer's roof.

Solomon roars with laughter, then shifts his bulk to offer his enormous hand out the window. We shake, and his expression turns serious.

"You got all my numbers, right?" he asks. "You can reach me on the cell twenty-four/seven."

"I know," I say.

"I don't know what you've been through," he tells me. "No man understands another's pain, and only a fool believes otherwise. But here's what I think you need to do: Let it go. Maybe we'll never know what happened to her. But you're still here, and you only have one life. This is no rehearsal, Jack. You're going to find yourself laid out on a slab one of these days, and I'd hate to think you'll regret all the years you wasted."

"I won't be thinking much of anything once I'm lying on a slab."

He gives me a fuck-you look and grabs the gearshift. "Might be. Might be."

"Take care of yourself," I tell him. Because, in the strangest of ways, we've become friends.

"You too," Solomon says. He flashes me the peace sign and pulls out into traffic. I wave and watch until the Explorer disappears.

The peace sign. I remember that from somewhere.

I get in my car and drive in circles around the neighborhood surrounding the library and the lakes, looking for that knit hat or that ratty old coat. But she isn't around. I won't come upon Iris by chance. She's the one who's going to find me.

And I wonder whether it was coincidence that I found her yesterday. And why she came to this town, of all towns.

I don't know if I can believe that Solomon restricts his investigation of me to our friendly little coffee chats. He is the kind of man who guards his secrets well; I remind myself, again, that he knows far more about me than I do about him.

I don't want to go home—there's too much silence there, too many chasms to fall into—so I drive south on Lyndale. On the radio they're analyzing the economy, the national hangover after the burst bubble of irrational exuberance. I wonder what Frank would make of it. I can't listen for long. The news these days throbs and thrums. I already made my disastrous mistake, and I live in the ruin it created. My people—all people—make one mistake after another, lay the groundwork for violence, and tempt themselves with the lure of self-created nightmare. I want to broadcast what I have learned: Don't do it, horror is real. But in these times the lines are blurred between self-defense and aggression, and even the kind at heart are haunted by memories of flame and bent steel, the horrible sight of jetliners crashing and people leaping to their deaths. Nihilism lies low because it doesn't care about consequences. Made weak are those who hold the line, who try to maintain sanity and order. I've heard the whispers in my mind, seen the nimbus of mayhem surrounding all things. I don't wish it on anyone. I fear there will be no one spared the heartbreaking realization that *this is really happening*.

I drive to a little one-story office box at the end of a block of houses. It's bracketed by a Laundromat and a Super America gas station. Across the street is another Super America gas station. I never buy gas at either one, just to spite them. There are three tenants in my building: a chiropractor, a marriage counselor, and me. I park and walk up, finding the front door unlocked.

My footsteps in the hall are muffled by gray twill. The paneling is old and faded. My rent is cheap—five hundred bucks a month for a small office and a walk-in storage closet in the back. I don't need much. As of this morning, I have four clients. The name of my business is stenciled on the door:

WRIGHT INVESTMENT PLANNING.

It's embarrassing, but I had to come up with something. The way things have worked out, the Wright Investment Plan is to drop a little cash with a financial adviser because his office is within walking distance. None of my clients have ever lived more than about ten blocks from here. I sit down with them and do my best. I advise them to buy long- and short-term certificates of deposit. I tell them that real estate is always a good investment. I refer them to a couple of reputable money-market funds. I generally advise them to steer clear of the stock market.

I don't give a shit about making money, which creates a shortcoming in my financial philosophy that tends to become apparent to my clients. I've apologized to the ones who move on. I'm simply not very good at this.

But I need the office and the business, because I hope it will legitimize my existence with the IRS. Karl Kateran certainly knows about the money I stole from him, but he's chosen to do nothing about it. So I pay my mortgage, and I slowly try to launder my cash into imaginary proceeds from Wright Investment Planning. The situation is a disaster waiting to happen, and like any criminal, I wish at times that the police, the feds, *someone* would come and make me pay for what I've done. At least then it would be over.

I imagine my fraudulent tax return sitting on a desk somewhere, a gaggle of short-sleeved tax investigators holding a raffle to determine who gets to pick my bones. And then the press:

LOCAL MONEY MANAGER
INVESTIGATED BY IRS;

Links Found to California Scandal,
Disappearance of Kateran Heiress

It would almost be a relief.

But no. I have something to live for now.

I open the door with a grunt—it sticks. The chiropractor next door is named Melissa, a dour woman a few years older than me. Our primary topic of conversation is the sad state of the building's amenities. I voluntarily surrendered my back-lot parking space to her, which earned me her undying loyalty and allegiance. Her other passion is an abiding loathing for Stan Garabaldi, the marriage counselor down the hall, who may or may not live in his office and who makes liberal, frequent, messy use of our communal kitchen and bathroom. Sometimes Stan comes into my office with a martini shaker and a couple of glasses in his hand. He sits across from me and lavishes invective and insults upon his clients—the adulterers, the doormats, the manipulators, the outright sociopaths. Then he chomps down a few breath mints, leaves the shaker on my desk, and goes to his next appointment. I like Stan a lot more than I like Melissa.

I grab the little pile of mail on the basket outside my office and go inside. I flip on the lights and wait for the fluorescent overheads to stop flickering. I have two windows, both glazed over with ribbed orange plastic. I have a desk, a phone, an outdated PC, and a plastic tree in a wicker pot. I have books left over from the days in Los Angeles: *Investments 1999; Riding the Curve; Diversified Stock Analysis; Solid Practices; Bold's Index.*

I sit at my desk and, after a deep breath, dial my home voice mail. It rings and I punch in my code. A woman's voice comes through, sounding vaguely irritated: "*You* have *no* new messages."

She hasn't called. It's been almost twenty-four hours.

I push the mail to the far side of the desk. The place smells stale. I haven't been here in more than a week. The answering machine blinks furious red.

A framed Edward Hopper repro hangs on the wall, a leftover from a previous tenant. It depicts a young man and woman on a front porch. She's wearing tight summer shorts and a tube top, and the guy is in jeans and a T-shirt that strains against his muscular physique. Their bodies are angled in a pose of sexual negotiation; they are young, their world is composed of only the two of them. Iris used to love this picture.

The chair lets out a farting noise when I press the "play" button on the answering machine. The tape rewinds, and I take out a pen and a piece of paper.

"John, this is Emmit Lundquist. Give me a call."

"Mr. Wright, my name is Janet Olson. I live a couple of blocks from your office. I walk by on my way home from work all the time. I think you're some kind of money manager. Give me a call if you are. We refinanced our house, and I want to do something with the money before my husband spends it."

I dutifully write down her number. Maybe I should pass it on to Stan as well.

"Emmit Lundquist again, John. Call me."

"John. Emmit. I've called you, what, two times now, and I haven't heard back. I stopped by, but you aren't in. I hope you don't mind me saying so, but this is pretty unprofessional of you. If you're on vacation or something, the least you could do is leave that information on your machine. Okay, thanks."

"Jack."

I grab the edge of my desk.

"Karl Kateran. We haven't talked in a while. I'm going to be in Minneapolis tomorrow night. Just for the day. I want to have dinner with you. Call me at the office."

"John, Emmit again. Jeez, this is ridiculous. I want to pull my money out of your company. I'm sorry, but . . ."

I am no longer listening. I barely notice when the tape ends, clicks, and rewinds. The red light goes off.

I haven't talked to Karl since he called six months ago to tell me that he had some of my things at his house and that he was sending them to me. When the box arrived, I found inside some clothes, my financial books from the old office, and the photographs Iris and I used to keep in a folder in our kitchen. It seemed like a peace offering, so I had called Karl to thank him.

"Forget it," he said then, his voice cold. "I just wanted to remind you that I'm still here."

I'm still here. And I'm still trying to find my daughter.

I pull the phone close and stare at it for a while, then light up a cigarette and get out the old Niagara Falls ashtray Iris bought for me at a flea market. I think about calling Karl, and think some more. Iris, Solomon, and now Karl. All in the space of a day.

There's a knock at the door. I tell whoever's out there to come on in. Then I regret it.

"Hey, weirdo," Kim says to me.

Kim's the chiropractor's assistant. She's about my age, maybe a couple of years younger. She has long black hair. She's skinny: kneecaps-and-elbows variety. Most of the time she is in need of a shower. I can't understand why, but Kim likes me and thinks we have some sort of unspoken personal connection. It's not that I can't stand her, but I can't give her what she wants—whether it's friendship or romance. It's like asking an amputee to run a sprint.

"I thought I heard you come in," Kim says, sliding past me to sit in the chair on the other side of my desk. She takes one of my cigarettes without asking and lights it with a match from her pocket. Sulfur fills the air. "You need to burn some incense or something in here. It's starting to reek of bachelor."

"I don't have time to talk, Kim," I tell her. The phone on my desk was called by Karl Kateran; that fact invests it with his presence, and I feel watched.

Kim drapes a leg over the chair and slumps back. She wears a long flowered dress and black tights. I can see the bony contours of her ankles through the nylon.

"What's the matter, working too hard?" she asks with a tinkling laugh. "I haven't seen you here in about two weeks. Don't you have any customers? Or have you scared them off with your scowling and skulking around?"

He wants to have dinner tomorrow night.

"John, hey. John. I'm starting to feel unwelcome here."

"What?"

"I can't figure you out." Kim taps ash into an old coffee cup on my desk. "That's what keeps her coming back, folks," she says in an affected TV announcer voice.

"Listen, there's something I have to deal with." I pick up my keys and make vague I'm-leaving gestures.

"Do you really do any work?" Kim asks. Her face is actually very pretty, although she thinks her pugnacious act is a lot funnier than it is. I've decided to call Karl from my house.

"I work at home sometimes," I say. "On the Internet."

"Oh, please," Kim says dismissively. "The Internet's a crock. Haven't you heard? You're not selling Internet stocks, are you?"

"I don't sell anybody anything."

Kim is holding her cigarette between her first two fingers with her wrist cocked back in a theatrical pose; as she speaks, she pumps the leg splayed over the side of the chair in a childish rhythm. Not for the first time I note that she possesses a real intelligence beneath her neurotic tics. She's a little spooky, and I remember her telling me that she's into radical diets and witchcraft and whatever other strangeness she can unearth. Her eccentricities have made her mannered. When she speaks, it's as though she has rehearsed the lines in advance.

"Listen, John, is this place a front for something?" she asks.

I am in the process of stuffing my mail in my jacket pocket; I look up. "Excuse me?"

"A front. For drugs, money laundering. I don't know. Stolen international intelligence?" She points the cigarette, lining me up in her sights, then starts pumping her leg again. "You're almost never here, and you don't seem to have very many clients. I don't know how you manage to cover your rent. You can tell me. I promise never to divulge your secrets."

Kim raises an eyebrow at me, smiles, and takes a greedy puff. She's being coquettish, and her entire mode of operating is to keep me on the defensive. I'm interesting to her for some reason. I think she's the first woman to be attracted to me since Iris. Then I think I'm probably flattering myself.

"Business is a little slow. It's the economy," I say.

"I guess so." Kim gets off the chair and shoots me a strange look. I seem to have unintentionally hurt her feelings somehow.

"Sorry I can't talk," I say. "Something has come up."

Kim tries to extinguish her cigarette, but it won't seem to go out. She gets frustrated, and her hair falls into her face. I suppress the urge to brush it out of her eyes for her. Then she grabs an old yellow phone message, turns it upside down, and writes something on it.

"Here," she says, pressing the paper into my hand.

"What is it?" I ask without looking.

"My phone number," she says. She looks into my eyes and I see something strange there, a tightness and confusion that startles me.

"What's the matter?" I ask her.

"Nothing, weirdo," she says. "Just call me sometime if you want to talk. Or if you get in a jam. I'll be your friend."

"Well, thanks," I say, stuffing the paper into my pocket.

Kim gets up on her tiptoes—she's wearing no shoes—and puts her arms around my neck and kisses me on the lips. It happens so quickly, so unexpectedly, that I put my arm around her waist and kiss her back. All at once I realize that my irritation with her masked attraction.

She pulls back, lets her hand linger on my neck for a second.

"That's more like it," she says. "Now are you going to call me?"

I see Iris in my mind's eye, her birdlike posture in that old coat.

"Don't say anything," Kim tells me, obviously annoyed by my failure to reply. "Just call me."

Then she's gone, back to Melissa's office. There's no one around when I turn off the lights and lock up. When I step out, I half expect someone to be waiting for me. But there's no one. I can't see anyone watching me.

10

Two and a Half Years Ago.

It was the tail end of the money boom and a period of unprecedented economic expansion. Some wondered if the good times necessarily had to end. They shouldn't have voiced their doubts. They might have jinxed it. For the good times did indeed end, although that turn of events occurred after the collapse of our enterprise in Los Angeles and after the violent end of my relationship with Iris. These were the days before the bubble bursting, before the flames and melted steel and the otherworldly physics of mass horror. Some remember it as a time of lost innocence. I don't.

We called the company Lee-Leonard (Leonard being my middle name; I unconsciously separated myself from the firm from the start by not putting my surname on the door) and rented an exceptionally well-appointed five-room suite in a Century City high-rise with a view of the San Gabriel Mountains. The furniture came with the office—a big oak table in the meeting room, tasteful desks and credenzas—and created an atmosphere of ready-made affluence for the clients Karl Kateran started sending our way.

Karl paid off the first year's rent on the office (the building was owned by an associate of his who cut him a deal) and supported our business venture with unexpected benevolence. When Iris and I flew to Los Angeles from Boston (our things en route, trucked across the country by movers), we went to the Kateran family home in the mountains north of the city and found Karl in his study, preoccupied with an international conference call on the speakerphone. Karl kissed Iris on the lips, then offered me a cold but firm handshake. I had expected Karl to greet me with his usual skepticism and ironic hostility, but instead he seemed tired and almost acquiescent. He looked shorter and more stooped than a year before, and his thinning white hair hung lank on his age-spotted head. He was, however, obviously overjoyed to have Iris back. He gave her an opalescent necklace and, for the duration of our first visit, lavished her with adoring looks and doting attention. I couldn't begrudge the old man his love for Iris.

After Iris and I spent a week in Yosemite hiking and taking pictures, we came back to L.A. and went to work. Iris took me to Beverly Hills, where I bought a dozen business suits and matching shirts and ties, all in rich colors and fabrics. My first meeting was the next day, with Leo Price. Price, tall and fat and immaculately groomed, was a real estate developer who wanted to recruit Karl into building a condominium and shopping mall in the suburbs. Karl had recommended Lee-Leonard to Price, making the call in my presence, mentioning Iris and her friend the "financial genius."

"Where's the genius?" Price asked. "Karl has told me you guys are going to be the hot thing. Just out of Harvard, right?"

Price's skepticism was apparent. He was a semi-big-time player and normally would have had no use for novices. But he wanted to make Karl happy.

"He'll be in town at the end of the week," I said. Frank's office, a quiet sanctuary at the end of the hall, was waiting for him. "His name is Frank Lee."

We sat in my office, with generic modern art on the walls and stuffed leather chairs sagging under us. Karl had chipped in a hundred thousand dollars for basic operating expenses, so we served up gourmet coffee and slices of fresh-fruit custard pie. Price launched into a slice of pie while taking my measure.

"What do you do better than anyone else?" he asked me. "What do you have that American Express doesn't?"

"We're light on our feet, unencumbered by corporate culture," I told him. "We plan to pay competitive returns on our investors' commitments—and if we can't meet those standards, we're willing to take money out of payroll in order to do so."

I had rehearsed this, and it sounded right when I said it.

Price was more interested in his breakfast than in what I was saying. He glanced over a brochure Iris had cooked up late one night, with the phone cradled between her shoulder and her ear while she typed up the financial doublespeak Frank regurgitated from his parents' kitchen in Philadelphia.

"Where's Iris?" Price asked.

"In her office."

Price rose with a fat man's sigh. "Let's go see her."

Price padded into the hall. "This way?" he asked. I nodded. Price filled the doorway with his giant frame, assumed a big smile, and called out Iris's name.

"Leo!" Iris said, quitting out of the graphics document she was working on. She wore black slacks and a man's shirt open at the neck to reveal the elegant lines of her neck. She shook Price's hand with an act of delight. "I haven't seen you in ages," she said. "I was so glad to hear you were coming in today. What do you think of our company?"

Price glanced at me, a furtive look that indicated he would play along with the fantasy of Lee-Leonard. His real business, though, was being conducted by talking to Iris.

"Very promising," he said. "Jack here has talked Frank Lee up to high heaven. I'm always interested in seeing what a start-up can do."

"So Jack's talked you into making an investment?" Iris said sweetly.

"Jack has made a persuasive case," Price said with a grin.

"You won't be disappointed," Iris told him.

We started to leave, but Price made a show of seeming to remember something. "Oh, Iris," he said. "Could you tell your father you spoke to me, and ask him to call me this week when he has a moment? There's a pressing timetable on something we discussed, and I know he'll listen if you pass on the message."

Iris smiled. "Of course, Leo," she said.

We went back to my office. Price took a big leather ledger out of his briefcase. "See what you can do with this," he said, scribbling his signature on a check, which I folded without looking at it and put in my jacket pocket. "With the market the way it is right now, it's going to be pretty hard to make that disappear too quickly."

We shook hands, and I escorted Leo Price to the door. I unfolded the check in our reception area and found that Price had bought himself an inside connection to Karl for $200,000.

I got better at my job. Frank arrived and established himself as resident eccentric genius, playing loud electronic music in his office and putting himself into a daily apoplexy with caffeine and Internet stock trades. I watched him buy a stock and sell it off within the hour, making small but steady progress through the day. Internet trading meant that investors could work around the clock, independent of the opening and closing times of the NYSE and NASDAQ, so Frank often worked well into the night. I had a calendar full of appointments with developers, traders, Hollywood executives, software moguls, and entrepreneurs made good. I flashed back to my interview with Natalie Coleman for the McElroy Fulton Scholarship and developed an easygoing, self-effacing confidence that ingratiated me with L.A.'s financial elite. It may have been an act, but it came easily. We were written up in the *Los Angeles Times* business section, referred to as "young lions." No mention was made of Iris or our connection to Karl Kateran.

Some of our clients didn't even require a meeting—they simply transferred money to our corporate account on the basis of Karl's recommendation. Very soon our fund totaled more than $4 million. I rarely looked at the statements, other than to laugh at them in amazement with Frank and Iris.

Iris worked light hours, often sleeping late while I went to work. She managed the look of our company and provided me with worksheets full of corporate lingo to toss around during my meetings with investors. She seemed generally amused by how quickly everything came together. We didn't pay ourselves salaries, though we all had equal access to the main company account. I plundered it regularly without checking the balance to buy gifts for Iris: an erotic sculpture imported from Venice, an antique silver ring to symbolize our engagement, hundreds of dollars' worth of flowers. One afternoon, while Frank was gone, we closed the curtains and made love on the big plush sofa in the conference room. Afterward, naked, I opened the curtains and we lay together, looking out on the mountains and crystalline sky. I rested a hand on the flat plain of her stomach and we decided that we should get married sooner rather than later.

At the end of our first month in business, Frank presented Iris and me with a report. He came into my office, where Iris and I were talking. He wore black jeans and an odd, militaristic tunic with all sorts of zippers and buttons.

"Rocking the Bono look today, I see," I told him. Iris giggled.

Frank shot me a look of annoyance. "Hey, preppy wonder-boy, it's called style. Look into it."

"Oh, Frank," Iris said with mock reproach.

Frank handed over his report, in which he noted he was cutting checks to clients at a rate five percentage points higher than the big investment houses.

"Nice work," I said with a whistle of appreciation.

"Why don't you take the afternoon off?" Iris said. "You look really tired."

"The markets don't sleep," Frank said, his usual jittery self. He had deep shadows around his eyes and had lost weight in the four weeks he'd been on the job. After the ebullience of our first days at Lee-Leonard, he'd taken to working with his door shut most of the time.

"No, but *you* can," I observed.

"I have to stay locked in," Frank said condescendingly. "I'm making it line up, but if I let up, next month's report might not look as good."

Iris cocked her head, her smile turning downward. "Don't put too much pressure on yourself," she said. "I worry about you sitting in that office all the time. This was supposed to be fun, remember?"

"I remember," Frank said. "Now I have to go back to work." He left us, in the inflection of his voice, with the accusation that *we* had it easy and that *he* had to shoulder the burden of Lee-Leonard. Which was basically accurate.

After he was gone, I looked at Iris. "This was his idea, wasn't it?" I asked.

"That's how I remember it," she replied.

Every day I looked forward to getting into my leased BMW (Lee-Leonard took tax write-offs on cars for each of us) and driving through the sun-yellowed streets toward the ocean. Sometimes I stopped to work out at the gym—usually when Iris was visiting her father in the mountains—but I craved comfortable sanctuary and rushed home if she was waiting for me. We had a big, spacious balcony, with a flowering hibiscus that filled the salty air with perfume. When we had moved in, we found waiting for us sets of expensive French cookware, cartons of cookbooks, linen sheets, plush towels, and preselected furniture that perfectly fit Iris's taste for expensive austerity.

It wasn't lost on me that a couple of months before I had been a college undergraduate. Now I was point man for a rising investment firm and I lived in a home that resembled a stage set for a play about the young and wealthy. Everywhere I turned was a reminder of Karl Kateran and the world he had made for his daughter and in which I lived. I didn't chafe under the conditions—that wasn't permitted under my unspoken belief system, in which Iris was all—but in the late afternoon hour after work, I saw the desert light streaming in through the kitchen window and felt I'd lost my moorings. Nothing seemed real. Maybe nothing *was* real.

One day, Iris saw me fumbling with a complicated espresso maker, cursing under my breath about how I just wanted a simple cup of coffee. She rested a hand lightly on my shoulder.

"I know we wouldn't have picked out a lot of this stuff on our own," she said. She pressed her body against mine from behind.

"It's fine," I said. I had a sudden urge to smash the espresso maker, to rip out its guts and pound it on the counter until it was junk.

"Hey, what's the matter?" she said, her mouth close to my ear. "It's not that big a deal."

"I *know*," I said petulantly. I had been in three meetings that day. Twice I had been asked about our "investment strategy," and twice I'd had to conceal the fact that I really didn't know what Frank was up to in his office, the door shut and locked.

"I wish my dad hadn't bought all this stuff for us." Iris sighed. "He was just trying to help, in his usual overbearing way. If it's any consolation, I'm sure he didn't pick it out himself. He had the housekeeper arrange it."

"Great," I said. "I'll be sure to thank her, the next time I'm up at the house."

"You're mad," she said.

"No," I said. "It's just that all this stuff seems like it should belong to someone else. I don't know. One of your ex-boyfriends, like that Bill guy back in Cambridge."

"Bill?" Iris asked warily. "You mean—"

"Forget about it," I told her. "I don't know what I'm trying to say."

"Honey, *I* don't think about Bill. Or anyone but you. You shouldn't be jealous."

"Of course not." I kissed her. I wasn't angry with Iris. That was impossible. I felt a trembling rage directed at the espresso maker, at the specters of her ex-boyfriends, at the money, at the office. At anything but her.

"I need a change of scenery," I told her. "Tomorrow's Saturday. Let's go to Santa Barbara and rent a room."

Iris's face dropped in a way I knew well.

"We can't do it, can we," I said.

"Please don't be upset." Iris seemed frightened, which made

me drop my hands to my sides and take a deep breath. "I was talking to my father before you got home. He wants us to spend the day at the house tomorrow. I didn't want to say no. He's been so happy since we moved back, and I want you two to spend time together. Maybe we can invite Frank. We never see him outside the office."

"I don't know if I even want to," I muttered.

"Don't say that," Iris whispered. "This is for us. Be happy, dammit."

I laughed. "I will try. I will try to be happy."

But I was on a losing streak. Everything began to irritate me: the apartment, the office, the BMW, the daily commute. I fantasized about living someplace else, but I knew Iris was back in her father's orbit and I couldn't generate enough gravity to pull her away.

A few months passed. I started to stay late at work and went to the gym more often in an effort to dilute my frustration with punishing workouts. Iris and I spent more time apart and less time in bed together. The clients kept coming, and I spent all day dealing with them. Frank was paying out competitive returns on investment, and he was often on the phone with Karl. I started to feel expendable. I sensed Iris's love for me dimming by a microscopic fraction each day. I blamed myself, because I was an ingrate. And I blamed her for giving me so much to be ungrateful for.

I was losing faith in her. That was perhaps my most egregious crime. Once I saw her talking with our neighbor downstairs, a guy ten years older than us who worked in Hollywood in script development. Watching without Iris knowing, I saw her run her hands through her hair in what I took to be a coquettish manner. The guy, tall, smiling, Hollywood cool, leaned his arm on the wall next to her.

As a friend, Frank was as good as lost. His success motor

had kicked in, and he turned arrogant when Lee-Leonard started paying out returns almost 10 percent higher than the competition. He started to walk past my office without even casting a glance inside. He hadn't cut his hair since moving to Los Angeles, and it had grown down past his collar. He bought an expensive Yamaha motorcycle, a real window-rattling hog, and left his helmet and leather jacket sitting on the reception desk. When we did talk, Frank described in a bored voice nights spent in clubs and hipster bars. He never invited me to join him, and I knew it was because I didn't meet his new standards of cool. I began to loathe him immensely.

Iris and I fell into a spiral. She resented me for being un-happy, and I resented her disapproval, which in turn made me more humorless and stoked her displeasure. Sometimes she didn't come to the office at all, and I would learn she had spent the day at her father's house. I was paranoid about what she might be telling him, because I knew he wanted to drive a wedge between Iris and me. I was sure the old man wanted his daughter to be with someone more suitable. For the first time, I seriously con-templated the possibility that I might lose her. I was tortured with anxiety and uncertainty, but there was no longer anyone with whom I could share my thoughts. My heart beat fast and hard all day, and at times it was hard for me to breathe. I was convinced that my heart was going to stop, that each next mo-ment would be my last, that my center was about to explode. Things were *all wrong*. I wondered if it was just me or if we all took a bad turn in the road.

I needed someone to blame for all this. I tried hard not to blame Iris. I struggled not to imagine how worthless and puny I might seem in her eyes and how attractive other men, other *lives*, might become.

Johnny and Jack, never on the best of terms, completely lost track of each other. I had a difficult time remembering what I had done on any particular day, and saw things taking place in a surreal blur. I couldn't account for why Iris was drifting away, any more than I could explain why we had become so close so quickly in Cambridge. The spell that made us never fight or doubt each other was lifted. But I still loved her. I would never stop loving her.

I could see the house Iris grew up in from Highway 1 as my eye scanned the hills. These were the hideouts of the hyperrich, and they dotted the brown landscape in a constellational tribute to their owners' will to conquer: Each estate was a kingdom, with each king denying the existence of all others. Each successive rise sprouted larger and more outlandish houses, the next more unlikely than the last. They existed in architectural fantasy—slopes of steel, pillars painted gold, walls of windows. The mansions perched in haughty defiance of physics and the laws of normality; each architectural outrage in the landscape was, to my thinking, like a jaundiced hand pressed uninvited against the small of a beautiful woman's back. I was, of course, deeply intimidated by these Ozymandian sights; in my place, in my time, I trembled without feeling mighty, and the lone and level sands stretched beneath the gaze of kings still living. This was where Iris spent her life, almost until the time she met me.

I kept my distance from Karl. He and Iris played tennis, my lover glistening with sweat and laughing at the end of rallies in a way she no longer did at home. They sat together in the air-conditioned quiet of the library, looking over old photographs and sitting close together, each luxuriating in something they had missed. I tried not to feel jealous. I sat with a book under a parasol by the pool, drinking a martini, sometimes chatting with one of the Latino servants. Dinners were strained and punctuated by silence, and Karl noted the space that had developed between his daughter and me. We talked about Lee-Leonard, though Iris had a habit of interceding on my behalf, as though she feared her father would pick me apart and expose my inadequacies. Her defense of me felt like betrayal, the latest in a long line of offenses against the once impregnable strength of our union.

Frank invited himself over soon after Christmas. It was warm and sunny, and I was swimming in the pool when he arrived. The roar of his motorcycle was like an angry dragon that eclipsed the soft music playing on the back patio.

"*Hola, hombre,*" Frank said, shaking my hand. He wore leather from head to toe, and his long hair spilled out when he took off his gleaming black helmet. As soon as we'd exchanged pleasantries, he started looking over my shoulder.

"Where's the king and the princess of the *hacienda*?" Frank asked.

"Playing tennis," I said. I motioned to the table and chairs. "Want to sit down and hang out?"

Frank ignored me, circling the patio and looking over the house with obvious admiration. It was ostensibly built in a Spanish style, with stucco and Moorish arches, but over the years Karl had added details in cold steel and gleaming glass, Moroccan tile, and Greek marble.

"And what a *hacienda* it is," Frank murmured.

The place had two full professional kitchens, eight or nine bedrooms, that big library stocked with books that only I read—Karl had remarked dryly on my "borrowing privileges." The place was full of art, most of it Russian constructivist. Iris's bedroom was upstairs in the back, with a big puffy bed and all the artifacts of her childhood lovingly preserved like a museum. When I slept there, I felt like a perverse interloper.

"Real money," Frank said, smiling appreciatively. "Nothing tacky, no false touches. I never get tired of it."

Frank didn't bother to hide his covetousness and his ambition, because he obviously didn't care what I thought. The threads of our friendship were far thinner than I had thought possible. I could read his mind. *This is for me, this is what I want and deserve. Show me how to get this, and I'll do anything.*

"So what are you doing here?" I asked, the words practically crackling. Frank's mouth curled into a knowing smile.

"The shrimp cocktail and champagne. What else?"

"That's hard to believe," I told him. "How long has it been since I saw you outside the office? Since before Thanksgiving, at least."

"Don't get your ass chafed, Jack," Frank said.

"My ass is far from chafed," I replied, feeling weak and contemptible. Whatever this enterprise, this *thing*, in L.A. had become, I was now on the outside. I was sure of it. Irritation buzzed behind my eyes, and my breath stung in my chest.

"So now I need a reason to visit my friends?" Frank asked, sitting backward on a chair.

"I haven't seen you, is all," I said.

"Not all of us are as fortunate as you," Frank said, looking at the row of hedges that obscured our view of the tennis court. "You think I wouldn't like to work light hours, then come home to a beautiful woman every night? Seems to me you're hassling the goose for not holding your hand and keeping you company after he lays the golden eggs."

"Fine. No problem. Forget I said anything."

"You know what I think?" Frank slid his chair closer to mine. His eyes were bloodshot, and his lips were a little cracked. The old affection and brotherhood between us was gone. "I think you're jealous, Jack."

"Tell me more," I said, trying to sound sarcastic but failing.

"Everyone's got something of their own." His smile turned bitter. "But you're still a kept man at heart, aren't you? You're starting to feel a little bad about yourself. Don't worry, I won't tell anyone. But I can read it on your face."

"You're being ridiculous." I stood up, and Frank did the same. I had my back to the pool, and for a moment I thought he was about to push me in.

"She's probably thinking the same thing," Frank said quietly. "You haven't exactly beat a path out into the cold, cold world, have you? You're pretty comfortable taking what she gives you, except when you get in a bad mood and decide to be a brooding, ungrateful fuck."

I remembered the college nights with Frank, the trust I had put in him. Money had changed him. It had changed me.

Dark poison flooded my mind. *How did he get the nerve to speak to me like this? Have he and Iris been talking behind my back?*

Sometimes I was alone in the office at night. Frank was gone more and more. Where? With Iris? The way they had been alone when they talked about Frank's moving to Los Angeles with us?

My heart beat with anger. Frank wanted all this: the house, the connection to Karl. And Iris.

"I'm just talking shit, Jack." Frank laughed and tapped my shoulder. "You've been walking around like someone died, and we're supposed to be riding that pretty face of yours to the top. Can't have you moping around. You're the man, the image. Don't forget it."

Voices moved closer. Iris was laughing. Karl spoke in a low, sonorous tone. They turned the corner, both dressed in tennis whites. I was standing in only my bathing suit; I felt exposed and pale.

"Frank!" Iris said, apparently very happy to see him.

Karl, short and stooped, walked over to Frank, put his arm around his shoulder, and pulled him close. Karl had never been so warm to me in all the time I'd known him.

"Frankie Lee," Karl said with a tight grin, slapping Frank's padded leather shoulder. "If it isn't the biggest bastard in L.A."

"Oh, Daddy, Frank doesn't know how you joke with people," Iris said. She glanced at me. "Be nice."

"This genius came into my life about six months ago," Karl said. "Now he's got a seat at the table and he wants to talk side business with me. Thinks he can run with the big dogs. You two know about that? I'll bet he didn't tell you."

A silence descended. Karl stared at Frank with a predatory smile, showing off his gleaming white caps. Frank physically *faltered*, taking an intimidated step back.

Iris's expression froze. Whatever Karl was talking about, neither Iris nor I knew about it. I didn't much care. I was just happy to see Frank looking so stunned.

"I guess I dropped a turd in the punch bowl. Oh, my goodness." Karl looked through me. Then he put his hand back on Frank's shoulder. "First thing you have to learn, Frankie, is how to take a joke."

Karl reached up—Frank was about ten inches taller—and tousled Frank's long hair. Frank burst out with nervous laughter.

"All right, easy rider," Karl said. "You wanted to talk. Let's go talk. Then we can enjoy the rest of the afternoon."

Karl led Frank into the house. They didn't look back. Apparently I wasn't to be included.

I put on my robe and sat down. Iris sat next to me, toweling off and stretching. "Do you know what that was about?" she asked.

"I have no idea."

"Are you all right?" she asked. She started to reach for me, then pulled back.

"I'm fine," I said.

"Well . . ." She stood up and straightened her collar. "I'm going inside to take a shower. Come with me if you want to.

Although you should know I'm not going to hold my breath. It seems like you never want to be around me much anymore."

The glass door slid on its track. I saw Iris inside, jogging up the stairs, her muscular calves flexing and disappearing. I thought about how she was getting older, becoming a woman, how one day I might not know her.

"I love you," I whispered. But I didn't go inside and say it.

| |

Today.

THE FIRST THING I DO WHEN I GET HOME IS CHECK MY VOICE MAIL:
YOU HAVE *NO* NEW MESSAGES.

I take off my jacket and loosen my collar. Hero comes out of
his hiding place, all black and furry, and rubs himself against
my slacks until I go into the kitchen and give him a big dollop of
Savory Stew. He purrs then, for the food. I picked him up at Animal Control a year ago in a bid for companionship. He tolerates
me graciously.

I sit at the dining room table with the portable phone in my
hand. I don't have to look up Karl's office number. I've committed it to memory.

In the two years since I moved here, I've seen two magazine

articles that featured Karl Kateran. The first was on big-money petroleum deals in the former Soviet Union—Karl was mentioned as one of the major players in the region, with interests and connections predating the breakup of the Soviet empire. The other article was in *Time*, a feature on prominent people who lost children to untimely death. There was Carroll O'Connor, Bill Cosby, Eric Clapton, and a former state senator from Florida. Karl was in there too, pictured in a pinstriped suit in his glass cathedral of an office, looking haunted and frail. I read the article over and over again, remembering, searching.

"This is Jack Wright returning Karl's call," I say to the receptionist. It isn't Judy or Monica, the two that I remember.

I have a very strong impulse to hang up the phone. But if Karl really wants to see me, he will find a way. There's no point in hiding.

"I believe he's on the other line," the receptionist says. It's clear she doesn't know who I am. "Can you hold for a moment?"

"Why not?" I ask. She clicks off without replying.

The day I tried to murder Iris, I saw red, a crimson nimbus over things. I was enraged. My mind was poisoned with sick thoughts that I used to justify my violence.

Strange how I haven't thought about it all that much.

"Jack?" asks the voice on the line.

When I lift my hand off the table, I leave a sweaty imprint behind.

"Jack?" Karl asks again, impatient.

"I'm here, Karl." I take a deep breath and let it out, then regret having revealed my nervousness.

"Took you long enough to get back to me," Karl says. "Is something wrong?"

"Everything's fine, Karl. Thanks for asking."

"Well, I have my reasons." Karl pauses. "You know, about a

week ago I had a funny feeling about you. Like something wasn't right."

One time I saw the real Karl, beneath the arrogance and the refinement. It was the day Frank Lee came to visit. Karl Kateran revealed himself to me as a snarling beast. Now he sounds genuinely concerned about me, but he reveals to me the real Karl to the same degree that I show him the real Jack. Or John.

"It hasn't been easy," I say.

Karl sighs. "I know what you mean, Jack."

I am in no mood for a heart-to-heart talk with the devil. I'm thinking about a day in the sauna with Karl. It was the time when—

Why am I thinking this?

"Okay, Jack," Karl says. "How about dinner?"

Sure, Karl. And while I'm at it, I'll try to get in touch with your daughter's keepers and see if I can arrange a day pass so she can join us. She's pretty odd since I bashed her head, but I know you'll still want to see her.

It's been a day since I found Iris in the library. Since then, both Solomon and Karl have dropped back into my life. I scratch my head and close my eyes. I try to connect all three people and fail.

"Jack? . . . Jack?"

"Sorry." I shift in my chair. "I'm a little surprised. I don't know why you would want to have dinner with me."

Karl makes a sound as though he's about to say something, then stops. He's silent for a full thirty seconds before he speaks.

"There isn't much left that connects me back to Iris," he says softly.

"Karl, I—"

"If you don't want to, then fine," he interrupts brusquely. "I suppose it wouldn't be unjustified for you to tell me to buzz off. I was never exactly kind to you."

Karl has changed. He sounds older, and there's a laborious rattle of phlegm in his voice. Karl is about seventy now, though the malicious old buzzard I remember would never have settled for as diluted an expression as *buzz off*.

"I'll have dinner with you." I want off the phone. Iris might be trying to call.

And I'm sure of something now. She isn't getting away from me next time. Not until I hold her in my arms and tell her how sorry I am, and promise that I am going to make things right.

"All right, good," Karl says.

I naturally suspect that Karl intends to do me harm, but I can't see how. I've lived in fear for two years that Karl would decide to obliterate me. It would be like a cloud passing over the sun; once the darkness lifted, I would be vanished and forgotten.

"Anyway, I have something for you," he says.

"What is it?" I ask. My heart thumps in my chest. *Here it comes.*

"A surprise. Listen, stay on the line and tell my secretary where you want to meet. Say about eight."

"Okay."

A surprise. I know Karl has the power and the will to have me killed, and I assume my demise would satisfy his fondest wishes. But he suspects I possess the secret key to Iris's disappearance, and that fact has probably kept me alive the past two years. I used to think that men were going to come in the night, deposit me in a burlap bag, then torture me in a basement somewhere until I revealed everything I knew. But Karl is too frightened of losing his last link to his daughter.

"Jack," Karl whispers. It's a strange noise that puts me in mind of the cold wind caressing a tree in wintertime.

"What, Karl?"

"Tell me. Have you heard anything? Seen anything? Can you give me anything to help me find her?"

I always knew it was over for me the moment Iris was found. But then no one found her. Until yesterday. She will decide for herself when and where she wants to see her father again.

"Do you even remember what happened that day?" he asks softly.

"Karl. I'm sorry. I don't know how to find her."

"I had to ask." Karl coughs. "I know you'd tell me, Jack, if anything had changed."

"Of course I would."

There's a long pause. We're playing chicken to see who will talk first. Then there's a loud bump outside that makes me gasp and get out of my chair. It takes me several moments to deduce that it was only the mailman.

"What do you think happened to her?" Karl asks suddenly. "When it's late at night, and you're alone, where do you think she is? Where do you picture her?"

In the days and weeks after Iris disappeared, Karl called me constantly. He threatened and cajoled, invoked his power and tried to bribe me. Once or twice I came close to telling the truth, but instinctual self-preservation kept me silent.

"She could be anywhere," I tell him.

Maybe I didn't really see her yesterday. Maybe she was dead and I saw her ghost. I believe in such things now.

I shake my head. I am *not* going to go crazy. Not until I know everything.

"I have to go," Karl says, his voice suddenly thick. "I'll see you tomorrow."

"Yes, Karl. All right."

I stay on the line long enough to give Karl's secretary the name and location of a restaurant near downtown. After I hang up, I realize I forgot to ask Karl what business was bringing him to Minneapolis.

A quick voice mail check. *You* have *no* new messages.

I open up the mailbox outside, irrationally hoping there's something from Iris in there, but instead I find a bill, a couple of catalogs, and, stuffed between ads for a supermarket and a tire shop, an official-looking envelope.

It's from the IRS. I tear it open and read through half a page of officious double-talk before I comprehend its contents.

I'm being audited. I have two weeks to get my financial documents together and call for an appointment.

My laughter is so loud that Hero tears himself away from his lunch to see what's the matter.

12

Two Years Ago.

I STEWED ON THE PATIO ALONE FOR ALMOST AN HOUR THE DAY FRANK CAME TO VISIT KARL'S HOUSE. I saw Iris move past a window once or twice, but she made good on her pledge not to draw me out of my shell. And I remained unable to go inside and make things right. No one spoke to me or even seemed to notice I was there. I seethed with impotent anger at Frank over the way he had talked to me and how he had insinuated himself with Karl. If they were inside talking business, I should have been included.

For what reason, though? I had never made a stock trade, and I never bothered to go over the details of the transactions Frank conducted in his office. I was a sham businessman. I was a stuffed shirt.

I put down my drink and my book and looked inside. I could see nothing. Frank was obviously trying to cut me out of the deal. It was the only reason he'd come to Karl's house—to run an end around, to go straight to the source of Lee-Leonard's power and connections. I recalled the way he had looked at the house, the way he'd stared at Iris.

He was betraying me.

The door opened. Frank came out first. He went straight for his motorcycle helmet. I joined him in the shadow of a stucco portico.

"Staying for dinner?" I asked.

"Not really." Frank looked at me blankly, as though I were a stranger. "Got other plans."

Karl stepped lightly in bare feet over cool tile. He still wore his tennis clothes. He patted Frank on the back.

"Sure you can't stay, Frank?" he asked, glancing at me.

"I hate to miss it," Frank said, studiously avoiding eye contact with Karl. "I'm sure it'll be a great feast."

"You could say that," Karl said, and shrugged. "Nothing will go wasted. You could learn a lesson from that."

Nothing will go wasted. Karl conserved and preserved everything he owned, everything he was. He was generous with some things, but he hoarded what he cared about. And his time with Iris was sacred. So why had he devoted an hour to Frank Lee on a quiet weekend afternoon?

"We'll be in touch," Karl said, shaking Frank's hand with cold precision.

Frank looked at me, then nervously stepped back from Karl. "Look, if I—"

"You explained everything I need to know," Karl interrupted. He smiled, and his eyes narrowed.

"Yeah, great," Frank muttered, and tucked a long cord of

hair behind his ear. I could see that nothing had gone as he wished. *Good.*

"Talk to you soon," Karl said. I slipped on my robe and the three of us walked slowly around the house to the big cul-de-sac in front. The center circle was planted with lush blooms and a flowering vine that wound around a tall wooden trellis. The sun shone down and baked the parched hills.

"This is yours," Karl declared when we reached Frank's motorcycle sitting in the shade of an acacia tree.

Frank nodded and smiled, too eagerly.

Karl pursed his lips and shook his head. "That's a danger-ous means of transportation, Frank."

"I'm careful," Frank replied, like a little boy justifying himself.

"Good," Karl said. "You *be* careful."

Frank put on his helmet and gloves, got on his bike. The motor roared, and exhaust spat out of the tailpipes, and Frank paused for a second to look at us through his windscreen.

Karl turned away from Frank. "Come on, Jack," he said. "Let's take a steam."

As we walked around the house I heard the Yamaha roar away. When Frank arrived, it had sounded like the heraldic fan-fare of a conquering army. Now it sounded like a bitter grumble of defeat, and it made me happy. I would never trust Frank again. Betrayal stung my tender center and made my head hum.

Karl led the way past the pool to the path by the tennis court that terminated at a sloping cabana. I glanced over my shoulder, half hoping that Iris would come out of the house and extricate me from her father's company, but she was no-where to be seen. Karl opened up the heavy door and walked through, not bothering to hold it open for me. It banged against my shoulder. By then Karl was already inside.

There was a sauna at each end of the corridor and gender-segregated shower rooms in between. Beyond those was a parlor with sofas, a bar, and a big-screen TV. For some reason, hardly anyone ever used the place.

"This one is hotter," Karl said, motioning toward the men's side. "The other one's fucked. I don't know why. I keep paying people to fix it and it keeps breaking."

Karl pulled off his tennis shirt and dropped his shorts. I averted my eyes as he yanked off his socks and walked, naked, into the sauna. The door creaked, and he glanced back at me questioningly before closing it. I was still wearing my swimsuit under my robe, which made me consider the etiquette of the moment—should I go in nude, in solidarity with Karl? Or would that seem strange? *Oh, fuck it.* I took off the robe, stripped out of my swimsuit.

Inside, steam curled around a red light bulb centered in the ceiling. Karl sat naked like a diminutive pharaoh, his face in crimson shadow, his belly covered in white down, and his little penis curled against his thigh like an emaciated snail. For all his apparent smallness, though, he was no weak, antediluvian shell. His musculature shifted under his skin when he moved, and the red skin of his shoulders was taut. I climbed up on the bench and took a seat diagonally across from him.

Right away I felt far too hot. My breath burned my lungs, and the bench burned my back and my thighs. I fought an urge to get up and leave; that would be an admission of weakness.

Then I looked at Karl. He had been staring at me the whole time. His face was reptilian, predatory, drained of affect. His mouth hung slightly slack, and his black eyes went in and out of steam clouds.

"How long have you known Frank Lee?" Karl asked in an unusually rough voice.

"A year and a half," I replied. "I met him the last year of school."

"Do you trust him?" Karl shifted a couple of inches closer to me, his eyes not straying from mine.

"I used to. Not now," I said. "He's changed, probably because of the money. Which is too bad, since we're just getting started. I'm well aware we're a relatively low-level success story, and that we're subject to factors beyond our control. Frank seems to have lost sight of that."

While I was talking, Karl blinked rapidly, pursing his lips. He continued to stare at me with rapt interest.

"What exactly do you mean," he asked meditatively, "when you say you're subject to factors beyond your control?"

"I'm under no illusions, Karl," I said, feeling emboldened by this suggestion of intimacy between us and flattered by the attention Karl was paying me. "Lee-Leonard only got off the ground because of your support. We've brought in some clients on our own, but the majority of our business is connected to you in some way."

"Are you concerned that I might pull the plug?" he asked. He seemed to have moved closer to me, which was impossible. I had my eyes on him the whole time.

"No," I said. "But I'm not going to fool myself into thinking that Lee-Leonard's success has been solely due to my hard work and Frank's financial genius."

"So you give credit where credit is due." Karl leaned back, closed his eyes, and breathed deep the hot air.

I was glad to be having this conversation—there never seemed to be an appropriate moment to express my gratitude to Karl in a manner I thought he would accept. But now that we stopped speaking, I started to feel overheated again. I tried to lean back, but the dry wooden wall burned my back and shoulders. My breaths came shallow, and a wave of nausea engulfed me with a fear that I might throw up or pass out.

"You keep your eye on Franklin Lee," Karl said.

I looked up. "What do you mean?"

Karl opened his eyes and fixed them on me. "He came here today and tried to fuck you over. He's a lightweight. A little success has gone to his head. I'm not going to continue to deal with him in any capacity."

I was stunned by the matter-of-fact way Karl delivered this news. His face hung slack, and he stared at me with an utter lack of human concern or empathy.

"He wants me to buy into Lee-Leonard," Karl said. "Which I have no intention of doing. The prick wants me to sign a paper. It's supposed to benefit me. Part of the deal would be my assuming financial liability for your little boutique business. It isn't going to happen. Playtime is almost over, Jack."

"He wanted to cut me out?" I asked.

"Of course he did." Karl put his hands over his thighs. Sweat streamed down his neck. "He says you're superfluous. I assume he feels the same way about Iris, although he isn't going to tell me that."

My head spun, and I feared that I was going to slip off the bench. I put my hands down on hot wood to steady myself. Karl seemed not to notice the heat at all.

"You kids have taken full advantage of my associations," he said.

I looked up again. Karl's face was framed in red light, and heat waves emanated from him. He seemed bigger than before, and his hands in his lap were balled into fists. I feared for a second that he was going to reach for me, claw me with his long, bony, spotted fingers.

"What do you know about doing business and working hard?" Karl asked. Before I could say anything, he spat out, "Nothing.

You know shit. Frank knows a little more, just enough to make him dangerous. Tell me, Jack, how closely have you been looking at Lee-Leonard's financial statements?"

"Close enough to know we're making money," I said, feeling the need to defend myself. The old devil was trying to undermine what we'd accomplished.

Karl smiled. "Are you? Making money?"

The question hung between us.

"Tell me, Jack. Are you making money?"

"We're . . . we're turning a profit for our investors," I said.

Karl waved his hand and snorted a humorless laugh. "I've been looking into Lee-Leonard, and I'm about to exercise a little oversight."

"We're an independent company," I protested.

Karl sneered, a little flick of his lip. "Look at the papers you signed when you took my money to set up that office of yours. You exist as long as I allow."

He meant that *Lee-Leonard* existed at Karl Kateran's mercy, though I knew the second inference of what he had said was not completely unintentional.

"Do what you have to do," I told him. I looked down and panted. The air was too hot to breathe. Frank had ruined everything somehow, and Karl was trying to take control of my life. I felt it all slipping away from me.

I tensed to get up, but Karl slid across the bench with amazing speed. He grabbed my thigh and squeezed hard, his fingernails digging into my skin. I gasped with shock as much as with pain. His touch was rough. His was the hand of someone who felt he *owned* me.

"I'm not finished with you," he said through clenched teeth. "Do you think I need this shit? You were bad enough, then you brought that Chink faggot into the picture."

I breathed hard, stunned by Karl's vulgarity and the hatred

that flashed in his eyes. I tried to stare him down, but his will was stronger than mine. When I looked at him again, he was bathed in glistening moisture and red light. I started to speak, then was rendered mute.

I thought I saw something move behind him. It was just the steam, a hallucination from my boiling brain. For an awful instant I saw a translucent form peer around Karl Kateran's shoulder, its mouth open in a ghostly oval. I looked down at the hand on my thigh, which grabbed at me even tighter.

"Where's your mother, you little fuck?" Karl hissed. "Do you even know where she is?"

"I haven't talked to her," I spat out. I was on the verge of tears, which made me hate myself. I was under assault from the heat, from Karl, and from the visions generated by my delirium. I looked away.

I yearned for Iris, the sound of her voice and her compliant sigh when she pressed herself into my arms. I was losing her. Karl would make sure of it.

"How long has it been?" Karl asked with sadistic pleasure. "How long since you abandoned your mother? About five years now?"

"You don't know what you're talking about," I said, feeling pain and tightness in my chest. Karl was right next to me, his lips bared like a predatory animal.

"She's in Pittsburgh," he said.

"How do you know that?" I didn't know I was so hungry for this information. Part of me thought she would be dead now.

"What do you care?" Karl moved his face closer to mine. The steam moved behind him, dissipating into a cloud. "You left her to die. Now you want to know how she's doing? You fuck."

"Stop it," I said, trying to pull my leg away from him.

"*Stop it,*" Karl mocked in a sissy-sounding voice. "What's the matter? Feeling weak? Are you beginning to understand how easily I can take my daughter away from you? Does that make you *jealous?*"

The shape reappeared right behind Karl. I closed my eyes tight when I saw a wispy crimson hand reach out for his shoulder. My fear was generating this vision, I knew, and the intensity of my fear was keeping it from going away.

"I didn't like you when I met you," Karl told me. "And I like you less the more I get to know you."

"I don't care," I said, my voice sounding small.

"You better care," Karl said, his hand tight on me. "My daughter thinks she loves you, you prick. You *bitch*. But she'll get over it. I'll make sure of it."

"You don't know what you're talking about," I said. The shade pressed its immaterial self close to Karl's back; I saw it put its hands on either side of his head, as though it were cupping a child's skull.

"You were finished when you let her come back to me," he said. "That was your mistake—you should have made sure I couldn't show her the truth about you. You think I'm going to let you keep touching her with your *hands?* You piece of trash. You fucking *nobody*."

"Fuck off," I said, my chest heaving.

"Keep talking." Karl slid closer to me, so that our shoulders touched. "You'll be a good meal in the desert, when you're looking up at the sky with your back broken. When your legs don't work, when the birds eat your eyeballs. You'll remember this conversation."

I grabbed his hand and was amazed by his strength; still, I had the advantage of youth, and I was able to pull away from him with a violent jerk. Karl laughed, feigned a punch at me, and laughed even harder when I flinched.

"Maybe I'll get you thrown in jail instead," he said. "I'll think of something. Just so long as I don't have to *look* at you anymore, you *pussy*. You son of a whore. You came from trash, and that's all you'll ever be."

I got up from the bench and stumbled into the wall. I looked back at Karl, afraid that he would lunge at me. Karl's naked torso pulsed with muscle beneath sagging skin. His tongue played over his lips.

"Get out of here," he said. "Get out of my sight."

When I got out the door, my breath came in harsh gasps. I dry-heaved a couple of times but managed not to vomit. I put on my robe, not bothering with the bathing suit, and staggered into the parlor. It took me about ten minutes before I was calm enough to go outside. Karl stayed in the sauna the entire time. The heat that nearly made me pass out granted him strength. The old man fed on it.

3

Tonight, and Two Years Ago.

I GO FOR A WALK AROUND THE LAKE BEFORE IT GETS DARK. There's a chill in the air, and Halloween is coming up in a couple of days. The Canada geese have vacated the lakeside, and only a few ducks remain in the leaf-strewn water. Soon the elms and the oaks will be stripped. There's a sense out here that things are grinding and slowing down. The hint of cold lends me a momentary optimism; it is always in the winter now that I feel more in touch with my thoughts and my memories, free of the intense summer heat that exacerbates the cloud in my mind.

Without really thinking about it, I walk up the street that runs behind the library. I go inside and head straight for the computer stations. Iris isn't there. It seems impossible that I found her in the first place.

What if I hadn't? Iris and the people she lives with *(kidnappers? a cult?)* apparently move around a good deal. Maybe they would soon have pulled up stakes if I hadn't found her. I never would have known she was ever here.

Unless I was *meant* to find her.

But who would plan such a thing?

Panic grips my chest when I think I might have seen her for the last time. Iris might never call. Our one meeting might be all I get to sustain me the rest of my life. At least she isn't dead. She lives a strange life now, but it's a life. It's better than oblivion.

Now, looking at the library carpet, then up at the fluorescent lights, I think that maybe I didn't really see her at all. It was a dream I had yesterday. It didn't happen. It was another ghost.

Outside, the sky is tinged with purple twilight. I go home alone.

Things were never the same after I sat with Karl in that sauna. I didn't tell Iris about it, afraid she wouldn't believe me or that she might take her father's side. I recalled flashes of his face framed in red, the infernal hallucination of a ghost. Sleep came hard for me, if I slept at all. Business at Lee-Leonard continued with languid dysfunction, and I barely spoke to Frank. We made the current month's investor payoff, and for the moment Karl failed to make good on his threats of destruction.

One night I was at home with Iris. I remember it was a Tuesday. The air was warm, with the whisper of a Santa Ana wind blowing the drapes in the kitchen. The sky was lit with a neon radiance.

"How's dinner?" I asked her. I had cooked chicken breasts with Dijon mustard, basmati rice, and broccoli sautéed in oyster sauce. The meal was intended as a gesture that I was trying.

I can't remember precisely what drove me to kill Iris, or the act of trying to murder her, but I can recollect with precision the color of the oyster sauce that night and the tabernacle glow of the city on the verge of dark.

Iris looked up from her plate. Our eyes met, and my heart quickened. We seemed to *notice* each other for the first time in weeks.

"Good," she said. Her plate was almost clean, so I knew she was telling the truth.

"I put some of that wine from last night in the sauce," I said.

She nodded. "I thought that was what I tasted."

"I also ground up some aphrodisiac powder I got in Chinatown and mixed it in," I added. "You know, to get us in the mood for later."

"You dirty man," Iris said, her feigned disapproval signaling the opposite.

I remember, back in college, we used to sit at the table until ten at night, our chairs as close as we could get them, talking and working our way through a bottle of wine until we were ready to go to bed. Now we sat at opposite ends of a table that would have filled the entire dining area of our Somerville apartment.

"Things haven't been great lately, have they," I said with a strong exhalation. Iris and I had been together for about three years, but we had never developed a vernacular of discord, any language for discussing problems between us. We had never needed to.

Iris took a sip of wine and visibly relaxed. She gave me a small smile to reassure me that I still mattered.

"Sometimes I think we made the wrong decision," she said.

I thought she meant it was a bad idea for us to be together.

"You know, coming here," she added. "Maybe we should have gone someplace else. I know it hasn't been easy for you."

"I don't know," I said. "I thought it was important for you to be close to your father."

"It was," she said. A darkening passed over her forehead. "But I don't care for the way he's treated you."

"You don't?" I asked.

"You've tried to deal with him," Iris said. "But he hasn't met you halfway. I haven't had a lot of boyfriends, you know, and I've certainly never gotten so serious with anyone. He isn't adjusting very well."

I remembered the vise grip of his hand on my thigh, the intimacy and malice of his touch.

"And what happened between Daddy and Frank?" Iris asked. "Frank barely speaks to me now."

"Frank and I have had a falling-out," I said. "I think Frank was trying to push me out of the business."

"You didn't tell me?" Iris asked, stunned.

"I haven't been able to figure out how to handle it."

Iris shook her head and let out a frustrated breath. "Well, I guess I have a confession to make, too," she said.

A confession. She had wronged me. The idea slid neatly into my mind like a peg falling into a hole. The tenor of my feelings suddenly changed. I had to realize that I was trapped, there were no allies. Not even her. Moments before, I had been willing to do anything to make things better between Iris and me. But not any longer. A switch had been flipped. *A confession to make.*

I thought of the old boyfriend, then the guy downstairs, then a cascade of images of Iris talking to other men: the way they prolonged eye contact with her, the way a few bold ones would dare a glancing touch of her forearm or shoulder. Everyone wanted her. And I was losing my grip on myself. It was apparent to me that she no longer loved me as she once did— a fact of which she herself might not be fully aware, but one which nettled me in a way that I couldn't ease. The rift was wide open now. If Iris went, all the hopes I had went with her.

Suddenly I pictured them together: Frank and Iris, in our bed with the sheets thrown on the floor. Iris on her belly, the way she liked it, with Frank hunched behind her, his muscular chest flexing as he entered her deeper. That was what he wanted. Maybe she wanted it, too. I imagined myself walking in on them, their faces leering at me.

"Jack, what's the matter?" Iris asked. "You look strange."

"Nothing," I replied. "What were you saying?"

I blinked and tried to make the thoughts go away. *Tried.*

"All I wanted to say is that Frank's been worrying me," Iris said, regarding me warily. She pushed away her plate, lit a cigarette, and took a nervous puff. "He's changed since we moved here. I think you know what I mean."

"I know."

"It's like he's become someone else," Iris said.

I pictured Frank by the pool, the way he'd sneered at me. He wanted to *do* something to me, *take* things from me.

"What's the matter?" Iris asked.

Her eyes widened. I wondered if she had already been unfaithful to me or how many times she had entertained the notion. An obscuration took form on the horizon of my thoughts. I remembered the heat of the sauna and realized much of this had begun then, on the hot bench.

How dare Frank get between me and this woman.

The thought was foreign, like a contagion.

"Did he do something you want to tell me about?" I asked.

Iris visibly blanched, and I could tell she was hiding something. "No, nothing," she said.

She was lying to me. I had been a fool to think I could keep her. She was beautiful. She was extremely rich. Every man wanted her. Frank was just one of many.

And she might have let him have his way. I couldn't be sure. She might have. And if not Frank, there would be others, an endless army of competitors exploiting my inadequacies, leaving me alone with nothing.

"Let's just get out of L.A.," Iris said suddenly.

"And go where?" I asked.

"Anywhere." She looked into my eyes, trying to find the old me. "Just us. The way things used to be. That's what I want, Jack."

I should have been relieved, but instead I felt angry and indignant. She wanted to run. From what? The world she had driven me to? I had played her game, and I had played Karl's game.

And Frank Lee's game. Don't forget him.

There was a poison in my mind that I couldn't purge. Frank had inflicted his disloyalty on me, Karl his hatred and evil. Something had to be done.

"I want the same thing. Us. Together," I told her, meaning it. I was about to add, *Maybe we can really do it,* when the phone rang.

"Let it go," Iris said.

"No, I'll answer it."

I picked up on the third ring. It was Karl. Iris saw my face drop, and mouthed the words *Who is it?*

I turned around and went to the kitchen sink. "Yeah?" I asked curtly. "What do you want?"

"I just got off the phone with Frank," Karl said. "Now it's your turn to get the news. I want you in your office at eight o'clock tomorrow morning. You're going to have a very interesting experience."

"What are you talking about?" Iris had gotten up to follow me. I turned so she couldn't see my face.

"You'll find out," Karl replied. "Just clear your calendar for the day. It might take awhile."

"I have meetings scheduled for tomorrow morning."

"Not now you don't," Karl said with a laugh. He coughed loudly into the phone.

"Who is it, Jack?" Iris asked.

"Your father," I said, still holding the phone to my mouth. "He's calling to dictate my schedule to me."

I regretted the ineffectual petulance in my voice. I knew Karl was sitting in his office, still at work. I wasn't sure how I knew, but I did—I could see a pad of white paper by his hand and his doodled spirals and squares. I saw his thin lips curled upward in a smile.

"You're scaring me," Iris said.

"Iris is there?" Karl barked. "Put her on."

"I thought you called to threaten *me*."

"Don't fuck around," Karl said. "Put my daughter on the phone."

"Go to hell, Karl."

Iris stood there watching, until she turned and left. I heard her lighting another cigarette, then the balcony door *whoosh*-ing open and slamming shut.

"Don't mistake those acorns between your legs for a set of balls, Jack," Karl said. I stood in front of the sink, but I was also in Karl's office. I watched him drop his pen on his desk and swivel in his chair.

"What do you have planned tomorrow?" I demanded. "Tell me now."

"Frank Lee fucked up," Karl said. "I have no choice but to act accordingly. It's too bad, Jack. In time I might have learned to tolerate your presence. It's almost regrettable."

I laughed. "You're too kind, sir."

"You see, Jack, the thing about you is that you have no substance," he said in the manner of a man trying to offer constructive advice. "You're like a wisp of smoke, and a stiff wind is coming. Do you even understand what I'm trying to tell you?"

I said nothing.

"Too bad you waited until now to stand up to me," Karl said. I saw him rise and straighten the crotch of his pants. It wasn't my imagination. I *saw* it. "I might have decided you were worth saving. But now . . . no, I don't think so."

I watched him walk to the window.

"You'll get the details in the morning," Karl said. "Now, if you don't mind, I have some other matters to deal with. It's called hard work, Jack. You might try it sometime."

"I'll see you in the morning, then," I replied.

"No, you won't. You and Frank don't merit my time." Karl said. I watched him scratch his chin. "You'll be meeting two of my associates. You might want to order lunch. It's going to take awhile."

Karl's expression shifted slightly to reveal a hint of regret. Now that he was about to cut into me, he found he wasn't enjoying it as much as he'd supposed he would.

I felt the phone in my hand, but I was standing in the old man's office. I saw the empty evening sky over the mountains, the grid of lights flickering on and stretching across the basin. *This can't be real.*

"We're joined somehow," I told him.

"What?" He was genuinely stunned. "What are you talking about?"

"I'm not sure," I admitted. "But something is happening."

Karl paused. "You're going down. That's what's happening."

He hung up. I watched him go back to his desk, where he sat down and gently rested his head in his hands. His fingers raked lightly through his thin white hair.

Then I was back in my kitchen. The phone emitted a dial

tone. I heard a door slam downstairs through the open window and a woman laughing.

I put down the phone and braced myself on the kitchen counter. When I walked into the dining room, my steps were light, as though I might levitate off the carpet. In a flash I saw Karl again; it had gotten cold in his office, and he pulled his suit jacket tight around his shoulders and whispered to himself.

Iris was out on the balcony, smoking and staring at the trees. She didn't look at me when I took the chair next to hers.

"Something's happened with Frank," I said.

"Doesn't surprise me."

There was a red cloud around her. I knew it belonged to me and that my feelings fed it. It was attached to me, the way it or something like it was also attached to Karl. These facts were very clear to me.

"You and my father are going to kill me," Iris said. I saw the delicate lines of her face traced with red. I thought she was angry at first, but then she turned away with an expression of deep sorrow.

I reached out for her, but she pulled away. We sat in darkness under the night and a radiant red that she seemed not to notice. I fought against my feelings, knowing that they would blossom into rage if I gave them license.

We heard a loud motorcycle engine somewhere, maybe a block or so away. I didn't know if it was Frank's or not. Looking back, I imagine it could have been.

14

THE SUN GOES DOWN ON MY FIRST FULL DAY SINCE LEARNING IRIS IS STILL ALIVE. The phone doesn't ring. Iris is out there somewhere in the city, and it maddens me not to know where. I consider getting in my car and driving around, hoping to spot her by chance, but decide to stay indoors in case she calls.

I'm staring at the phone. *Call me. Call me.*

I run hot water on a washcloth and lay it on my face. It slips down until just my eyes are showing, like a harem girl. A concubine. I drop the washcloth in the sink and step gingerly over little piles of sky blue tile. My feet crunch on the floor.

There's a buzzing in my ears and a throbbing near my scalp. I shake my head and blink, trying to come back to the moment. I'm not entirely sure what I've been doing.

In my bedroom, my eyes trace the spot on the wall behind which I hide my secrets. It isn't bad work. There's a faint line where I patched the plaster and painted over it—unnoticeable, unless you're specifically looking for it. I kneel next to the base-board and run my fingers along the wall. I won't have to open the hole up again until summer, when I'll need more cash. I have a strong urge to rip it open anyway, just to make sure everything is still there. I worry about mice chewing up my money and my photographs to make a winter nest.

The steps creak as I walk downstairs. I could fix them by driving some screws into the wood, but I don't want to. I like the creaking. It makes me feel that I'm real. The places I grew up in were flimsy, drafty, insubstantial stage sets in which nothing of consequence could ever happen.

I walk into the dining room, flip on the light, and let out a gasp of surprise.

I move slowly around the table, my breathing shallow. I am careful not to disturb the delicate improbability of this moment.

At the far end of the table, at the place where I normally sit, are my steel cocktail shaker, a martini glass, bottles of gin and vermouth, and a bucket of ice. The bottle of Tanqueray is half-full, the way I left it a week ago. The ice bucket rests on my black ceramic trivet, keeping moisture from condensing on the wood.

Everything is arranged with artful symmetry. I open the ice bucket. The cubes are fresh, and there's no water at the bottom.

I went upstairs, what, a half an hour ago? *How long did I stare at the patched-up hole in the wall?*

When I went up, there had been a newspaper and a dirty coffee mug on the table. They are gone. I do a quick visual scan of the room. They're nowhere to be seen.

I check the doors to make sure they're locked. Everything is fine, and there's no sign that anyone broke in. I double-check the locks to convince myself that they haven't been tampered with. My stereo and TV are still in the living room, so I haven't been burglarized.

Anyway, what kind of thief would lay out martini ingredients before leaving the premises?

No. I came down. I'm losing track of my own actions. Aren't I?

This is like before, with Iris, when I lost track of what I should have been doing and thinking. But now it's worse. I dig my fingernails into my palm. *Focus.* Don't let it slip away. I reach up and touch the patch of rough scar tissue on my crown.

I go back to the dining room and stare at the bottles and the shaker; I crouch down, circling the arrangement of items, watching to see if they move of their own volition. Of course they don't.

So I pour some gin into the shaker, then a little vermouth. I have to go into the kitchen for olives. I like a dirty martini. When I open the refrigerator I let out a cry and bang my knee on a cabinet trying to move away. The door hangs open.

Everything in the refrigerator has been moved. Nothing looks right. The orange juice is on the top shelf, the mustard on the bottom. The effect is jarring and unfamiliar to my eye. Then I notice the middle shelf—it's empty, save for one item. The jar of olives.

When did I take out the trash?

I reach in and take the jar out, and the refrigerator door slams. I don't think I touched it.

My head aches. The pain starts in the center of the scar on my head and moves deeper inside. It gives me a metallic taste in my mouth. For a second I have serious doubts that I will survive the hour. I'm not well. I'm not just imagining this.

I go into the dining room and let out a gasp. I don't know how long it's been, but I've forgotten to breathe.

* * *

The night two years ago when Karl called to inform me he was making good on his threats of destruction, and when I had a curious experience I later learned was known as *bilocation*, had been an evening of considerable promise. It felt as though Iris and I might break through our apathy and miscommunication. She was correct when she blamed external factors for the breakdown of our relationship. Los Angeles, the money, Lee-Leonard, Frank, Karl—they were all aspects of the same dynamic. They represented acquisition, competition, conquest, and exploitation. There were times, though, when I wondered whether I was firmly on the side of the righteous in this postulation. I took what I wanted from Iris—in the name of love, true, but it was taking nonetheless. And what I had sought was perhaps even more insidious than mere cash or a luxurious *thing*; Iris had made it possible for me to transform from John into Jack, from a tentative nobody into a confident striver. I rarely considered what ledger should have been entered into, and whether I siphoned power and strength from Iris in order to build and maintain my new self. When I did think such thoughts, I saw my world as a closed system; there was only so much energy to go around, and Iris was the best soul among us. She was the only person I knew who could have been described as *good*. Like most guilty people, I had to stop thinking in such a manner in order to continue existing.

I thought of Karl and Frank as bad people. Rarely did I consider whether they were like me.

When I got to the office the next morning (a blue-sky sunrise heralded the day Karl made good on his threat), two men dressed in expensive business suits were waiting for me. Each appeared to have been selected with a goal of providing maximum physical contrast to the other. One was tall, bald, and looked exceedingly uptight. The other was short and curly haired and had bad posture and a sardonic grin. The latter held out his hand for me to shake when I stepped out of the elevator.

"Philip Dewitt," he said. I glimpsed a gold Rolex on his wrist when we shook. "Corporate counsel for Kateran and Company. You must be Jack Wright."

"Good morning," I said, eyeing their briefcases. I held out my hand for the other man.

"I'm Richard Weaver," said the taller one, who was clearly unhappy to be there. He was immaculately groomed, and he adjusted his position in the hallway slightly to maintain sufficient space between himself and Dewitt.

"And you are? . . . ," I asked Weaver.

"I work with Mr. Kateran," he said by way of explanation.

"Good for you," I said. I unlocked the door and held it open for them. Dewitt went inside, whistling under his breath. Weaver held on to his briefcase and assessed the furnishings in the reception area.

"Where is Frank Lee?" Weaver asked. He took a couple of steps into the hall, looking at the art on the walls and glancing inside Iris's office. He had an appraiser's eye, and it was obvious that he was mentally liquidating Lee-Leonard.

I knew then that I was in very deep shit.

"Beats me," I replied. "Did he say he was going to come?"

"Karl told me he probably wouldn't show," Weaver said to Dewitt.

"Well, we all know Karl is never wrong," I told him. Dewitt blinked at me, verifying that I was mocking Weaver, then erupted with laughter.

"Karl said you were bright," Dewitt told me. He unbuttoned his double-breasted jacket to reveal a powerful, gone-to-fat torso. "Listen, Jack, you got any coffee in here?"

"I'll make some," I said. "The conference room is through there. You can get set up."

When I returned with a pot of coffee, I found Dewitt and Weaver seated at the head of the conference table. It was an arrangement that effectively made this their meeting, with me as an attendee.

"Don't be shy," Dewitt said, patting the chair next to him. "Sit close. We'll work through our business as quickly as we can."

Dewitt had his jacket off, and his sleeves were rolled up. Weaver leaned back in his chair, his briefcase open at such an angle that I couldn't see what it contained. I poured myself a cup of coffee, pushed the pot in their general direction, and took a seat leaving an open space between Dewitt and me.

"Looks like Lee is definitely a no-show," Dewitt said to Weaver.

"I'll be surprised if he's ever heard from again," Weaver said with a lemon-sucking expression. "And if he is, he'll be wearing a county jail uniform."

I stiffened in my chair. "What do you think?" Dewitt asked with a smile. "Do you look good in orange?"

"Come on, now, Philip," Weaver said. The two men exchanged a look, and Weaver smiled slightly as he poured himself a cup of coffee.

"Looks like it's just the three of us," Dewitt said. He put his hands on the table. "Jack, Karl asked me to make this relatively painless for you. I understand you're practically his son-in-law."

Weaver leaned close to Dewitt and whispered something in his ear. They both laughed softly.

"Just get on with it," I said.

"To begin with, your attitude is fucked up," Dewitt said.

"You can't blame Karl, even though I hear you two aren't the best of friends."

"What leads you to say that?" I asked.

"Certain things." Dewitt leaned back and folded his arms behind his head. "In-laws can be a bitch. I wish you could meet my first wife's family. Straight out of a Mexican soap opera. Jesus Christ, the shit I had to put up with. Pretty much broke us up."

"But this situation is your fault, Jack," Weaver interjected.

"And what *is* the situation?" I asked. I sensed Dewitt was trying to disarm me, and I didn't want any part of it.

Dewitt looked at Weaver, as though they were debating who would have the pleasure of breaking the news. I could see these two didn't much like each other, but they had found common cause in whatever they were about to do to me.

"He should have known," Weaver said. I was confused for a moment; although he was speaking to Dewitt, he continued staring at me. "This was quite a little game. I'm not convinced he wasn't in on it."

"Karl says he doesn't know shit," Dewitt countered. "How do you like that, Jack? Your girlfriend's dad stuck up for you. He said you're useless, but you're basically honest."

"That opinion will be very useful to you," Weaver said, "should we find it necessary to initiate legal proceedings."

"Get on with it!" I shouted. I was breathing shallow, and my eyes were having trouble focusing. The room blurred, and the sun shifted in the sky to shine directly in my face.

Dewitt fingered his big gold wedding band. "Here's the deal. Your buddy Frank Lee has perpetrated an epic fuckup."

Frank. Again.

Richard Weaver shook his head with disapproval. Dewitt gave me a wincing smile, as though he hated to see me in this position.

"You know what makes me happy right now?" Dewitt asked.

I fought to keep my head up. I felt sweat gathering in my armpits under my shirt and jacket.

"The fact that I'm not you," said Dewitt.

"Give him the specifics, Phil," Weaver said; his face was haloed by the sun as he glanced at his watch.

Dewitt pulled out a file from his briefcase. He opened it, peered over a couple of documents. "Karl Kateran lent Lee-Leonard around a million dollars—"

"It wasn't that much money," I said.

"Don't interrupt," Weaver said.

"The initial lease on this place was two hundred grand," Dewitt went on. "Then there was the furniture, and the personal expenses."

"Personal expenses?" I asked.

Dewitt looked down. "Yours and Frank's rent on your apartments, the car leases, the credit cards."

"Frank Lee's motorcycle," Weaver said like an impatient father.

My face burned. *Rent on your apartments.* I had assumed our apartment was free, but Karl had been keeping track of every dime.

"How does it come to a million?" I asked.

"Funny how money adds up," Dewitt said. "Frank's come to Karl on three different occasions for additional funding since your start-up, and he hasn't paid Karl back a penny. He's got money stashed in a few different accounts—what's left of it."

Frank went to Karl for more money? But why, when we were turning such a steady profit in the stock market? I never looked at the books. I was confident Lee-Leonard was doing well. Frank said everything was under control.

"You didn't know about the additional borrowing, did you?"

Dewitt asked. "Frank jacked up Karl's additional investment by about four hundred percent, and you didn't even know about it."

I rubbed my face. It felt like there was nothing behind it.

"This is serious money," Weaver said.

"I think he *knows* that, Richard," Dewitt countered. "Otherwise, why would he be willing to ruin a perfectly nice morning having his ass chewed over by a couple of bastards like us?"

I looked out the window and squinted into the sun. Slivers of light glittered on the ocean like dancing sprites.

"We'll pay Karl back," I said.

Dewitt smiled and looked in his file. "The next part was a little harder to piece together," he said. "The total amount entrusted to Lee-Leonard by various investors. Want to take a guess, Richard?"

Weaver shook his head. "Ask Jack." He nodded toward me, and Dewitt looked up expectantly.

"Come on, be a good sport," Dewitt said. "Tell me how much money is tied up in your company. Ballpark it if you need to."

"I'm not sure," I replied.

"Come on," Dewitt said, serious now.

"A couple of million," I said.

"Try six," Dewitt said. "Give or take some change."

Weaver sighed, and Dewitt gave a little whistle of appreciation.

"You had no idea, did you?" Dewitt said. "Less than a year in, and this company had taken seven million in investor money."

"How could you not know?" Weaver asked, leaning forward, genuinely curious. I ran my hand through my hair like a bashful boy.

"Talk about your postcollege opportunity," Dewitt said. "When I got out of law school—*law* school, mind you, not a bachelor's degree—I had to eat shit eighty hours a week at a firm where the partners didn't know my name. I wouldn't have minded a sweetheart deal like this one."

"Well, you surely wouldn't have screwed it up like these jokers did," Weaver said.

"What are you telling me?" I asked. "That Frank lost money? That's not true, because Frank's been paying monthly returns to all our investors. He's done better than a lot of the established companies."

"Don't strain too hard, Jack," Dewitt told me. "You're liable to hurt yourself with all those complicated business concepts rolling off your tongue."

Weaver snorted, stifling a laugh. I held on to the table, feeling as though I might float out of my chair. I felt my hands curl into fists. What had Frank done? I blinked once, twice.

Embezzlement. I looked up, and Dewitt was shaking his head at me.

"No, Jack," he said. "Frank Lee didn't steal from Lee-Leonard, at least not on a grand scale. He paid himself some questionable allowances, and he was pretty loose about accessing the company fund. But it's been pretty tame, at least compared to some of the corporate thieving I've seen in my time."

"Then what?" I asked.

Dewitt was no longer smiling. He dropped the file on the table as though it were contaminated.

"Frank Lee is a total failure as a money manager," he said. "You said you were doing better than the established investment firms. What do you base that on?"

"The statements," I said. "The money we were paying out."

Dewitt threw up his hands and looked at Weaver. "Do you believe this douche bag?" he asked.

"Now wait a second—"

"Wait a second?" Dewitt yelled, his voice thundering. He

slammed his fist on the file, got up, and stalked to the far end of the room.

"Phil," Weaver said in an admonishing tone.

"You know about all these Internet IPOs?" Dewitt said.

"I know something," I said weakly.

"People are creating money out of thin air," Dewitt told me. "Cashing in and getting rich. It's all going to blow up pretty soon and leave investors with their dicks in their hands, but for the moment a lot of people are making obscene amounts of money."

"Like us," I argued.

Dewitt laughed loudly. "Not like you," he said, circling the table. "All that money you had, you didn't do a single smart thing with it. You want to know what Frank's been up to? *Do you?*"

I felt heat all around me, red heat.

"Dipshit!" Dewitt said with glee. "He's been doing basic, numb-nuts on-line day trading. He's no better than some jerk-off working the Internet in his basement. And he's been losing money."

"Then how did we pay our investors?" I asked.

Weaver sighed loudly. "Jack, you've been paying your old investors out of the new money flow."

"You've been running a fucking *pyramid scheme*, Jack!" Dewitt said. "Your buddy's been stressed out of his mind, because eventually *everyone* was going to find out!"

"We haven't really turned a profit," I said.

"That's right, dipshit!" Dewitt moved nearer.

"Don't come any closer," I said in a hoarse voice.

Dewitt seemed surprised, but he stopped. "You know why Karl finally looked into all this?" he asked me.

"Because Frank tried to cut me out of the business."

"That's right," Dewitt said. "He wanted you out, he wanted

more money from Karl. He was going to gamble that he could turn things around. But he had no idea what he was doing."

"I told Karl not to get involved," Weaver said.

"Lucky for you, Karl knows you're basically honest," Dewitt said. "Karl let this thing play out for a while, but then it was obvious that Frank was about to flame out."

"Now we have a big mess to clean up," Weaver said.

I knew the facts now. Frank had failed, and I had been willfully ignorant of what he was doing.

Whose idea had all this been? *Frank's.* With Iris's blessing. I remembered that night in Somerville, out on the balcony breathing warm spring air. Frank approached Iris before he talked to me. This was *their* idea. Not mine. Not mine.

The office seemed tawdry and cheap. My suit was a costume for a farce. I had thought Jack Wright was capable of anything. There was no way I could lose. I wondered what was left for me outside these walls. I had no job. I had no money. I was at the mercy of two men who viewed me with contempt. A hot invisible hand pressed against the back of my neck. I worried that I might start to cry. I didn't want to be there. I didn't want this to be happening. I might have lost Iris forever.

"Now you know," Dewitt said. He moved back to his seat, and I smelled the sweet floral aroma of his aftershave.

"Frank is screwed," Dewitt said. "Karl is considering legal action against him."

"I'm advising against it," Weaver said. He closed his briefcase. "A court case would entail publicity. Karl doesn't need it."

"You're a lucky boy, Jack," Dewitt said. He lifted his arms, and I could see that he was also sweating.

Karl wanted this kept quiet because of Iris's involvement. Weaver and Dewitt weren't mentioning her, but I knew she was central to how this played out. I burned with shame.

But hadn't she approved? Hadn't she and Frank conspired behind my back?

I was scalded with anger. Iris had wanted this. Frank had wanted this. They were in it together.

Red. Red.

"A lot of money's going to be lost," Weaver said. "But we can liquidate Lee-Leonard's stock holdings for a start. The lease on your car will be canceled at the end of the day. Karl will personally contact the investors, give them a plausible explanation, and offer them an appropriate payback for their lost projected revenues."

"That means he'll pay them back with interest," Dewitt said, looking at Weaver with an expression that said, *Remember who we're dealing with. Dumb it down for the fuckhead.*

"As of today, Lee-Leonard no longer exists," Weaver explained. "Phil and I will oversee the dismantling of the company. All funds will be frozen, and this office will be emptied out and shut down."

"I recommend you clean out your desk," Dewitt said. "Once you're out of here, you're not going to be allowed to come back."

"All right," I said.

"This is the important part," Weaver said, leaning forward. "Karl doesn't want Iris implicated in any way."

"Of course not," I said angrily.

"This might really fuck things up with your girlfriend," Dewitt said with a complete lack of sympathy.

"Karl *assumes* you will cooperate," Weaver said with more force than anything he'd said all morning. "Is he correct in that assumption?"

I looked up, startled. Weaver was asking for assurances that I wouldn't drag Iris into this dark mess.

"We're supposed to get married," I said.

Weaver's mouth dropped open, and he gazed upon me with pity. "Maybe things will work out," he said quietly.

Her sweetness, gone. She could take it away.

I saw Dewitt with his sharpened teeth and playacting rages, and Weaver with his doleful disapproval. I felt like a child who had been told nothing was true.

I had loved Iris since before I knew her name. I never meant to take anything from her. I accepted what she gave me.

"Maybe, maybe not," Dewitt said. "The best thing for you might be to get out of town."

"We can help you," Weaver said.

"We can and we will," Dewitt agreed. "Karl said he'll give you money if you quietly disappear."

"It's a good offer, Jack," Weaver agreed.

I fed the crimson rage inside me. I never wanted this.

15

I'VE JUST POURED MY SECOND MARTINI. The house has been quiet, the light golden. I have smoked two cigarettes and waited quietly.

Then the phone rings.

When I rise, my knee pops and complains with a burst of fleeting pain. I've been sitting down too long. I swear and limp toward the phone, knowing I have to catch it before the fourth ring or the voice mail will pick up.

It's not Iris, but it's someone who's with Iris. I know this; my reckoning is connected somehow to the afternoon in Karl's sauna and my afternoon of bilocation two years ago. I think of the missing shoes, the nighttime visitations, the ghosts serving me drinks, the cloud that once fell over my mind. That's how I know answering the phone will bring me closer to Iris. I don't know if any of this is real or if it means anything. There's no other way to explain it.

"Is this Jack?" asks a youngish man. "My name is Zeke Bailey. Sorry if I'm calling too late."

I look at my watch. It's almost ten at night. *Jesus.* I have no idea how long I've been sitting at the table. I haven't eaten all day.

"No. It's not too late."

"Great, man," Zeke says. "I'm calling you about a friend we have in common. Misty—sorry, I mean *Iris* gave me your number."

"What did you just call her?"

"Oh, nothing." A chuckle. "Just a silly joke."

"Share it with me," I say.

"Listen, Jack . . ." Zeke pauses, choosing his words. I have a generally favorable impression of him, based on the last thirty seconds, but I'm not going to hang up with anything less than the promise of another meeting with Iris. "Iris asked me to call you. She's not real comfortable talking on the phone."

"I see."

"Don't take it the wrong way," Zeke adds. "I know Iris cares about you a lot."

"Who are you?" I ask.

"I'm her friend," he replies. "She's a very special person. Any friend of hers is my friend, too."

I flash on those triangle sheets and black Nike sneakers, the bunk beds and pills crushed in applesauce and washed down with vodka. I wonder if they had to fight not to vomit while they waited for the spaceship's running lights to appear in the sky.

They rejected the evils of this world. I do, too. Although I have also perpetrated my fair share of them.

"You don't have to tell me how special she is." My voice sounds finicky.

"Of course I don't," Zeke says. "Sorry, man."

"Where are you keeping her?"

Zeke laughs softly. "No one is keeping anyone. If anything, Iris is keeping us. She keeps us sustained."

I hear a muffled laugh in the background. Zeke has an appreciative audience. Iris? *No. She's somewhere nearby, but not in the room with him.*

"I have to see her," I say. "Immediately."

"You will," Zeke says.

"You can't keep her from me," I tell him. "And if you try, I'll have you arrested for kidnapping."

"Now, Jack," Zeke says in a tone of approbation.

"I don't know what you've done with her," I say. "But she needs to see a doctor."

"Slow down, Jack," Zeke says, sounding genuinely distressed. "You totally have the wrong idea about the situation."

Shit. What is Iris mixed up in?

"We're a household," Zeke tells me. "It's nothing more or less than that. We help each other out. We're all free to come or go as we please. It's not what you think, Jack. We're just a few friends living our lives with a spiritual focus."

"Prove it," I say. "Let me see Iris."

Zeke sighs. "Jack, the only reason I'm talking to you is because of Iris's comfort level."

"And do you determine what she's comfortable with?"

"Damn, man, give me a break," Zeke says. "I just spent the day behind a desk, temping at the electric company. If Iris wanted to see you right now, I'd walk her over."

This is not what I expected. Zeke doesn't sound like a mind-controlling guru at all; if anything, he strikes me as a low-key slacker.

"Okay, I get it," I tell him.

"Look, I don't mean to give you a hard time, Jack. I know how much Iris means to you."

"Do you?"

"I think so, man. She's talked about you since I first met her. It sounds like you two had something really special together."

Had something really special. Is Zeke Iris's new lover?

"She wants to see you, but it isn't easy for her. Give her some time."

My hopes have been so high the past twenty-four hours. If I can help Iris, maybe I can be redeemed. Then my life will continue, and I will be set free of this limbo. *With her.* What a thought.

There's weird static on the line.

"You hear that?" I ask.

"What?"

"Nothing," I say. I move to the window, look outside. All's normal.

"Look, why don't you and me get together and have a beer or something?" Zeke suggests. "We can talk better in person."

Be careful, Jack, a voice whispers.

"Yeah. Why don't we do that," I say.

"Cool," Zeke says. "I get off work tomorrow at three. Why don't we meet at the Green Mill on Hennepin at three-thirty?"

It's a five-minute walk at most from my house; Zeke knows where I live.

"Need a lift?" I ask. "I can pick you up at your place."

Zeke laughs. "Nice try, Jack. Don't worry, we'll have you over soon."

We hang up, and I am enveloped in silence. It feels warm, even though the nights are getting colder and I have yet to go down to the basement to ignite the pilot in the boiler.

A strange feeling comes over me, like the sensation I felt in

Iris's presence yesterday. She was disheveled and dirty, her mind scrambled, but—and it pains me to think it—the change in her was not entirely regrettable. She had an unfamiliar grace, a deep ocean of compassion that suffering must have bred in her soul. She is diminished, but this is not, I think, the prevailing aspect of her new reality. I want to be with her to save her, but I also want to hear more from her and to understand how she now sees the world. Sitting here in my house, on the floor leaning against the wall, I want to be with those people who care for her and pursue mysteries with her.

What are you thinking, John?

I jerk upright and look around. That was a real voice.

The hairs on my arm stand on end. I get up, pace to the window. It's quiet and still outside. No one is out there to say my name.

It seems at this point that I must admit, at least to myself, that I have been exhibiting considerable mental instability for quite some time.

But I must keep my sanity until this is over.

I cook a bowl of noodles in the kitchen, then feed Hero and start upstairs. My headache is back. I pause in the living room, looking back at the table with the martini shaker. It's all still there. It really happened. I still can't remember putting those things out.

In bed I lie in the dark, looking at splinters of streetlight coming in through the blinds. I begin to slip away, surprised by the depths of my exhaustion.

Then I wake up. I don't know what time it is. It's late.

A woman is standing at the foot of my bed. She's small, with a sensual curve to her hips. Her head is turned, so I can't see her face.

Iris? I try to ask, but it's no use. I'm paralyzed, and I gurgle loudly as I struggle to breathe.

Turn around, I think, knowing she can read my thoughts. *Let me look at you. Let me see your face.*

She starts to, then thinks better of it. She folds her arms tight around herself. She's so tiny.

It's not Iris. Iris would never scare me like this.

Is it you? I try to ask. Or something else. Something . . . *I lose the thought* . . . something I need to figure out.

Then she's gone, and I'm asleep again. I hear the floorboards creak in the hallway as I sink into blackness.

WEDNESDAY

16

The Next Morning, and Two Years Ago.

I WAKE UP FEELING MUCH WORSE THAN I SHOULD. For the first half an hour, I'm oppressed by the paranoid fear that whoever set those martinis out for me also poisoned them. But after a shower and a few minutes trying to regulate my breath next to the bathtub, I'm convinced that my lack of caloric intake has contributed to my state.

I sit cross-legged and naked on the bathroom floor amid the tiles and buckets of mortar. I arrange a few tiles on the hole in the floor, fitting them into a jagged rectangle, then scattering them with the back of my hand before I start over again. I stare at tiles until my vision starts to blur. Then I realize the morning is slipping away from me and that in a few hours I have to meet Zeke Bailey. After that, I also remember, I have to see Karl.

It's going to be a big day. Folded up in the pants pocket of my brown suit is a stack of assorted papers—dry-cleaning stubs, movie tickets, grocery receipts. And a pair of scribbled phone numbers: Solomon's and Kim's.

I light a cigarette, grab the phone, and put on my pants. I return to the bathroom, where I arrange another handful of tiles into an irregular trapezoid.

Someone was in my bedroom with me last night. Unless I was dreaming.

The last forty-eight hours weighs down on me. Solomon, Karl, Zeke, Iris. She came out of nowhere, within a day of Solomon and Karl contacting me. I think of all the coffee cups and fast-food wrappers in Solomon's car and wonder whether he was really in town just for a quick interview.

I unfold the piece of paper with Solomon's cell phone number on it and dial without thinking. It picks up on the first ring.

"This is Solomon. Leave a message."

"Solomon, this is Jack Wright." I pause to slip a blue tile into the slot created by a torn-out section of floor. "Just calling to make sure you got back to L.A. all right. Call me next time you're in town."

I hang up. I find a tile stamped with an odd imperfection, a small crimson blotch that spreads out from the center to one border. I've never noticed it before.

When I try to think about the strange hallucination in Karl's sauna, the memory dissolves and floats away. I recall the rage that flooded my mind my final day with Iris, the day that began with my meeting with Phil Dewitt and Richard Weaver. Everything went red. Iris suffered. It made her what she is.

I unfold the piece of paper with Kim's name and number on it. I don't really know why I think to call her, maybe because she offered to help. She has a witchy sort of presence. Maybe she's the person I need to talk to. I dial her number quickly and pick up another handful of tiles.

"Kim?" I ask through a fog of static.

"Yeah, who is this?'

"This is Jack Wright. Where are you?"

"I'm at work, weirdo. Where you should be."

"Is this your cell phone?" I ask.

"You ought to be watching the detectives, Elvis."

I put the tile with the red imperfection in the center of the floor, then begin to work outward.

"Hey, are you still there?" Kim asks. Her voice sounds deeper than in person; I would think she was years older than she really is.

"Sorry," I say. "I'm working on something."

"Okay." Kim pauses. "Want to tell me why you called me, then?"

"Sorry," I apologize again. "See, the thing is, I'm not sure why I called you. I was thinking about some things."

"Why don't you come over tonight," she says. "I'll cook you dinner. Do you know where I live?"

"I can't," I tell her.

"Why not?" she asks, irritated. "Got other plans?"

"Sort of," I say. "Yeah."

"Then what do you want?"

It doesn't work to arrange the tiles from the center outward; by the time I reach the edge of the hole, the spaces between the pieces don't work, and I'm too far over the edge.

"Do you know anything about . . . . I don't know what to call it. Inhabitation, maybe?"

"Inhabitation." She gives a nervous laugh. "Like you visiting me at my apartment and bringing over a nice bottle of wine?"

"No. Like . . . I don't know. Something that comes from the outside and, and, makes you do things."

Kim is silent. Then she says, "Hold on a second."

I hear muffled sounds. I stack the tiles to one side of the hole.

"I'm back," Kim says. "I wanted to go where Melissa couldn't hear me, if we're going to talk about this. All right. I'm going to tell you straight off that there's something spooky about you, Jack. I get the feeling you're in trouble."

"I might be," I admit.

"I know you probably think I'm a flake or something, but you give off really strange energy."

I unconsciously finger my sparse chest hair and shift my position on the floor. "I don't think you're a flake," I tell her. "Strange things have been happening."

"What kind of strange things?" Kim asks.

"I feel like I'm not alone," I tell her. "It's been going on for a while. I've done things I regret."

"What kind of things, Jack?" Kim asks.

Don't tell her. Don't trust her.

"Things that weren't so good," I tell her.

"You might be interested to know that the highest aspiration of my life isn't to be a chiropractor's assistant," Kim says.

"I'm sure that's true."

"What made you call to talk about this?" she asks.

"I don't know," I admit. "You offered to help."

Kim is silent for a long time. I am about to apologize and find a clean shirt when she lets out a strange humorless laugh.

"I knew there was something weird about you," she says.

"Maybe so."

"Well, I majored in folklore in college," Kim says. "Which is probably why I can't get a decent job."

"I didn't know that."

"I've also been into alternative spirituality. I have some ideas about you," she says.

I drop the tile from my hand. "You do?"

"Don't be dense," Kim tells me. "Every culture has stories of spirit possession. From Australian aborigines to *The Exorcist*. The pattern is always the same: An outside force invades the individual and controls his or her will and actions."

"Maybe that's not what I had in mind," I tell her.

"Well, there are more subtle variations," Kim says. "There are some really spooky stories from Tibet and Nepal—free-floating malevolent Buddhist demons that attach to people in states of emotional distress."

I stand up. "Tell me more."

"We would call it temporary insanity," Kim explains. "But I see it a little differently. These spirits are supposed to feed on negative emotions—for the Buddhists, it underscored the need to think right thoughts that lead to right actions. The dharma, basically."

I remember the jealousy growing more terrible by the minute, my heart trying to leap out of my chest.

"These spirits basically attach themselves to people who have negative tendencies, or who are in a state of identity flux."

"Identity flux?" I ask.

"Impressionable people who don't know who they are," Kim says. "One of these spirits finds someone and basically whispers evil thoughts in his ear for as long as it takes until he does something really bad."

"Do these spirits ever manipulate objects?"

Kim pauses. "That sounds more like a poltergeist or a straight haunting, Jack," she says. "You know, I think you're spending too much time alone."

"You're probably right," I say, my mind several places at

once. I finger the scar on my head and scrape off a little fragment of tissue with my nail.

"Come over tonight," Kim says. "Don't make me embarrass myself. I'm normally pretty hard to get."

"You still want to see me after what I just told you?" I ask her.

"I've been through worse," she says. "Anyway, what's a haunted house or a couple of bad decisions between friends? I've got my head together. That nasty old cloud couldn't influence me."

"What did you just say?" I ask her.

"I said I don't care if you think you're being haunted or whatever. In fact, it's kind of attractive."

"Not that," I say. "You mentioned something. A cloud."

"Oh, that's just something I read about one time. Some Himalayan mountain myth about a cloud that preys on men and makes them harm their daughters and wives. It's basically a folkloric justification for misogynistic violence. Come on, you're not that kind of creep, are you? Don't tell me I got you all wrong."

"I don't want to hurt anybody," I say.

"Good," Kim says. "Let's keep it that way."

I left Phil Dewitt and Richard Weaver at the Lee-Leonard office—it belonged to them now. I took my keys to the building and tossed them on the conference table. Dewitt was on the phone and didn't even bother to look up. Richard Weaver gave me a weary nod as I left.

I can recall only vague impressions of my drive home through midmorning traffic. The sun shone bright in the cloudless sky. I remember driving very fast, almost daring someone to collide with me.

There was a note taped on the front door of the apartment:

Iris,

I want to tell you my side of the story before you talk to Jack and your dad. Maybe something good can come out of all this. There are a lot of things I want to tell you. Call me as soon as you can. I'll be waiting.

Love,
Frank

I read the note over and over again, then folded it neatly in half and tucked it inside my shirt pocket. When I went inside, the radio was playing in the kitchen, but Iris wasn't there. I looked in the bedroom and on the balcony, but she was gone.

Love, Frank.

I went into the bedroom and opened the closet. All her things were still there. She hadn't left me yet.

Then something happened to me.

Slipping into the new skin of Jack Wright had been a by-product of my love for Iris. It was an act of hope to become the better man that Iris deserved. But Jack Wright was dead. I was a man who answered to no name.

I knew with unshakable certainty that I had lost Iris. I also knew that if Frank and Iris weren't lovers, they would soon consummate their complete betrayal of me. The note on the door was tangible confirmation.

My head dropped, and I sobbed loudly for several minutes. Then the tears stopped. I went out on the balcony, lit a cigarette, and tried to cry some more. The sound I made was more like laughter.

I ripped off my jacket and threw it over the railing. Then the tie went; it stuck in the branches of a tree and hung there like a party ribbon. I had an urge to throw everything over the edge—the furniture, myself, the whole fucking world. But I didn't.

Still my mother's son, I opened a bottle of Scotch and poured a big glass, which I drained quickly while retching and fighting to keep it down. Then I poured another and turned the radio up loud.

I drank more and chain-smoked cigarettes, putting out the butts on the carpet and the linoleum, forming black craters and burned spots. I knew the sky was about to open up angry red and suck the world up into its maw.

"Fuck it!" I screamed. I was pleased by the idea.

Then I thought of that fucker Frank Lee.

My only friend, my old buddy, my confidant. With his leather jacket playing with all that money money money money.

I called Frank's house, reaching over to turn down the radio when it started to ring. I felt so *strong*. I pressed my hand against the cabinet, knowing I could punch through it if I wanted. I watched its blond-wood surface move, undulate, turn deep bloody red.

They don't know who they're fucking with.

Iris.

Iris answered Frank's phone on the third ring.

"Who is this?" she asked. "Jack? Is it you?"

I hung up quietly and sank to the floor.

Oh, I thought. *This is where the tears went.*

17

This Afternoon.

I HALF EXPECT ZEKE BAILEY TO LOOK LIKE A RELIGIOUS FREAK, SPORTING A SHAVED HEAD OR THE HIRSUTE JESUS LOOK WITH A BEARD AND WHITE TUNIC. I wonder if he will be insane, this man who might be controlling Iris and bending her weakened will to his. I wonder whether I could physically overpower him.

Now someone calls out my name from the other end of the bar. The place is nearly empty, save for a few guys gathered under a TV showing a replay of last night's Gophers basketball game. Most of the tables are unoccupied, but there's an air of anticipation for the dinnertime rush. Zeke doesn't get up, but he smiles and shakes my hand. A half-full bottle of Bass Ale sweats on a coaster in front of his place.

Zeke is about my age. He has tidy black hair that looks

freshly cut and a well-manicured goatee. He wears Dockers and a nondescript short-sleeved dress shirt. His long forearms are hairy and muscular. He could be anyone.

"Nice to meet you, Jack," he says. He has a firm handshake.

I sit on the stool next to him and glance around. It occurs to me that he might not be alone.

"This is pretty great," he says with a warm smile. "Don't take this the wrong way, but I've always been curious what kind of guy Iris would fall in love with."

The bartender comes and I gesture at Zeke's beer. "Two of these," I say.

"Hey, thanks." Zeke takes a long swig. "Look, let's not get off on the wrong foot like last night. Everyone at the house really wants to meet you. As soon as Iris says she's ready, we want to have you over for dinner or something. There's really no reason why we shouldn't be friends."

"You do what she says?" I ask.

Zeke gives a little shrug. "You know what?" he says. "This was my last day at a shitty temp job I really hated—they had me inputting numbers all day on some resource allocation project. I didn't even know what the numbers meant. It's been that kind of gig, but at least it's over. I don't think I'm going to let you harsh my mellow."

"What's this?" I ask. Next to his coaster is a photo, turned facedown on the bar.

Zeke smiles and holds it up for me to see. It's a picture of me in Los Angeles, standing in front of our apartment building. I'm dressed in slacks and a button-down shirt, and I'm smiling. I remember the day it was taken. Iris and I had gone to Venice to walk along the beach. We had gotten in a fight on the way back about something I can't remember now. Iris used to keep the picture in her wallet.

"Iris gave me this so I would recognize you," Zeke says.

"What did Iris tell you about her past?" I ask.

Zeke glances up and down the bar, then swivels his jaw in a pose of thoughtfulness.

"She doesn't remember much," he tells me. "The general picture, sure. But the details come and go."

"Does she know what happened to her?" I ask.

Zeke's expression is unreadable. "I was hoping you could fill me in. You remember when I called her Misty? Well, that's just a silly name we have for her. It's short for Mystery. We had to call her something when we found her because she couldn't remember her name at first."

"Mystery," I say. "That's pretty fucking corny."

"Well, at the time we didn't know we'd have to live up to your high standards of wit."

The beers come. I take a long drink of mine, feeling a smoldering fire in my chest and gut.

"Where did you find her?" I ask.

"Outside of Manhattan Beach, where we were staying for a while. I took a walk one night by the water and found her huddled up in some old blankets under an empty lifeguard station. No one was trying to help her or anything. They must have thought she was just some crazy homeless person."

"So you helped her?"

"She didn't want to go to a hospital. She freaked out when I mentioned it. She said she wasn't safe, that someone was trying to get her."

My forehead feels cold against the back of my hand. "How bad was she?" I ask.

"She had a very bad head wound, Jack," Zeke tells me. "She could barely talk, and when she did it didn't make much sense. We had a big argument about what to do to help her."

"Did she ever go to a doctor?" I ask.

Zeke shakes his head. "Like I said, she was too afraid to go outside for a while. We figured out pretty quick that she was going to make a run for it if we didn't just keep her quiet and try to help her get well."

I look outside the window at the ordinariness of a Wednesday afternoon. An old food wrapper blows in the breeze. Traffic moves slow in front of a big four-story apartment building. I imagine Iris wandering south along the coast from Los Angeles, injured and nearly dead. Somehow she managed to travel that far on her own. No one helped her. Until Zeke came along.

"Pardon me for saying it, but this is really exciting for me," Zeke says. "This is the first time I've had the chance to talk to someone who knew her, you know, *before*."

Zeke *has* to know.

"You and your friends were already living together before you found her?" I ask. "These are the same people you live with here? And you all take care of her?"

Zeke nods. "We're just a bunch of misfits. We work to pay the rent, but in a way Iris gives us something more important. She's given us a focus. Do you know what I mean?"

I light a cigarette. "Maybe I do, maybe I don't."

"I grew up in Orange County," Zeke says, as though this explains everything. "A big-time Christian family—Bible readings at dinner, antiabortion rallies, the whole thing. That's where I got the name Ezekiel: the prophet, seer of visions."

Zeke seems to wait for a response. "Well, at least you got a cool name out of it," I say.

He laughs. "My parents thought I'd be into their trip, but by the time I was a teenager I was smoking dope and doing crystal meth. I hung out with my aunt and her girlfriend a lot—they were into *The Celestine Prophecy* and channeling and all that shit."

"California," I say.

"Yeah. But that doesn't mean it's worthless," he retorts with a smile. "It's just that it wasn't right for me. But I was pretty heavy into the whole spiritual seeker trip. I got deep into Zen for a while. I joined the Hare Krishnas for about six months, until it got too regimented."

"Couldn't take the food?" I ask.

"The food was *excellent*," Zeke tells me.

I am suddenly very jealous of Zeke. He is no one to be feared. He has no obvious excess of intelligence or charisma. He's religious driftwood, the kind you find anywhere. The fact that he defines his life as a religious autobiography is, in itself, utterly tedious to me. But he gets to spend his nights with Iris, and I don't.

"Iris says you lived in San Diego for a while," I say.

"One of us got a job down there that pretty much supported us all," says Zeke.

"How many of you are here now?" I ask.

Zeke pauses, sips his beer. "Six right now, including Iris."

"Why did you come here?" I inspect every nuance of his reaction for prevarication or evasion but see no tics or false notes.

"Iris said we should," Zeke says with his little shrug.

"And you do whatever Iris says?"

Zeke swigs his beer and gives me a condescending look. "She hasn't told me to do anything," he says. "I consider her an instructor, Jack. She's tapped into something very heavy."

I allow that one to sink in.

"Iris has taught me about focusing my energy on compassion. She needed us so much at first, but pretty soon that image of our relationship started to shift. She showed us, without ever coming out and saying it, that we're all damaged in some way."

"Speak for yourself," I say, unkindly.

He gives me a look that tells me he's speaking for me, too.

I fold my hands on the bar and remind myself not to take Zeke at his word. I decide to operate under the assumption that Iris is a prisoner. The Iris I knew would never be involved with anything like this. She used to say she had to stay away from churches because she might spontaneously combust if she went inside.

"I can imagine what you're thinking." Zeke strokes his goatee.

"What's that?" I ask.

"That I'm nuts," Zeke says good-naturedly. "And that I'm somehow a bad influence on Iris. I know she isn't the person you remember, Jack. This has to be really hard for you. I see her as this perfect person, man, this . . . *angel*."

I can't help but think that Zeke is basically a nice guy. Fucked up and deluded, sure. But I don't see him as a sinister puppet master.

"We should clear the air," Zeke says, suddenly serious.

I think he is going to tell me he knows what I did to Iris. I grab hold of my beer bottle but don't drink from it.

"I know you think we're a cult or something," he says. "Talk a little spiritual growth to most people and they think you're a fanatic."

"Now why would I think that?" I ask, relieved.

Zeke smiles. "You have every reason not to trust me. But you know something? You haven't thanked me for taking care of her. It gives me the chills, man, to think what might have happened to her if I hadn't found her."

"She might have been found by someone else," I say. "And returned to the people who love her."

Out on the balcony that night, she said, *You and my father are going to kill me.*

"Iris definitely doesn't want to see her father," Zeke says. He looks around. "She won't even talk about him."

"You know who he is."

"Yeah," Zeke says. He scans my face. "I know about his money. So what? I make money. I spend it. I don't care."

"Then you're a unique individual," I tell him.

The place is starting to fill up with semiprofessional types; I halfheartedly check out their tentative mating rituals as I light another cigarette.

"Don't be so condescending," Zeke says, making me look at him.

"Excuse me?" I say.

"Look, you're a nice guy, I can see that." Zeke shifts closer. "But you obviously aren't taking me seriously. You think I'm a loser."

"The thought crossed my mind," I say with a shrug.

"Cults. Protesters," Zeke says pointedly. "All the crazies trying to destroy the world of *good* people. Not to mention the *terrorists*," he adds.

I touch the scar that exists in my mind, the one beneath the one under my hair; this one is the witness to the deaths of innocent men, women, and children, the nightmares of millions, the drumbeat nihilism, and the physics of modern engineering perverted into satanic horror. I put a hand to my temple and press hard. The headache returns.

"You look down on me, you think I'm insane," Zeke says. He sounds angry, although he keeps his voice low. "That makes you normal, right? That makes you neutral, like everyone else?"

"I really couldn't tell you," I say.

Zeke finishes off his beer. "I live in a house full of close friends, with someone we look to for guidance. What do you call that?"

I should eat something. Zeke's exposition is making me feel giddy. "A slumber party?" I ask.

Zeke's tension dissolves, and he smiles at me. "Might as well call it that," he says. "Sure. A slumber party."

"Zeke, I would like to believe that you have Iris's best interests at heart," I say, speaking slower now, making sure that I am clear. "But from what I've seen, you could easily be controlling her."

"I understand that," Zeke allows. He strokes his chin. "And I respect your protectiveness and your genuine feelings for Iris."

I almost laugh. Zeke respects my feelings. This is becoming very upsetting all of a sudden.

"You see, this is my problem," I continue, feeling a moment of mental clarity that I know I must exploit. "Call it what you will, but no matter how you might use your rhetorical tricks to put me on the defensive—and I liked the one about the *terrorists*, by the way, that one had me on my heels for a second—you're still talking religiosity. Most of what we're talking about is blind belief."

"What's wrong with that?" Zeke says.

Where to begin? With the Crusades, the Inquisition, the witch trials, Jonestown, al-Qaeda? This was the world of God, with its stifling of intellectual inquiry, its hardening of whole societies' arteries of thought, its perfidy, hypocrisy, and depthless cruelty writ large and small in the name of speaking for holy authority on earth. And, in the moment that I remember, the weight of suffering suddenly chokes me, and I am no longer at all certain that I can connect the madness of belief with the insanity of history. I cannot be sure that all the actions from the grandest to the smallest, each bearing in common the signature imprint of denying another's humanity, would not have happened anyway, had God's name never been evoked. Perhaps the filthy memories of our species, the battlefields and infernos, are our deepest truth. My crimes were committed in the name of no God or transcendent ideal. What better solution can I be credited with devising?

"It's . . . it's played out, Zeke," I say. "Nothing good comes of it, no matter what anyone says."

"I feel sorry for you," Zeke tells me.

"I'm having dinner with Iris's father tonight," I blurt out.

Zeke's smile drops. It takes him a moment to compose himself, and I see a flash of fear in his eyes.

"Don't tell him you've seen her," he says. His hand twitches, and for a second I think he's going to reach for me.

"I don't plan to," I say. "Because apparently Iris doesn't want me to. But I'm not going to maintain the status quo much longer. I want to see Iris."

Zeke is clearly shaken by my invocation of Karl. I drop ten dollars on the bar and put out my cigarette.

"Tell her to call me," I say.

"Will do." Zeke looks down at the bar, thinking his own thoughts. I leave him without a handshake or a good-bye.

8

Two Years Ago.

WHEN I CALLED FRANK'S HOUSE AND HEARD IRIS'S VOICE ON THE LINE, I DROPPED THE PHONE. I remember a loud noise in my ears and objects around me blurring and shifting. I see images of drawers opened, closets turned out, as though I were looking for something.

My thoughts were not my own. I went outside and got in the car. I felt as if I didn't need to breathe. I had already died and there was nothing left for me on this earth but a final piece of business.

I stopped at the bank before I went to Frank's house. The building's glass facade shone. Every noise was amplified to the threshold of aural torture; still, I walked slowly, and my manner was calm and confident when I asked to see a manager.

In my wallet I had a card and a password that gave me access to Lee-Leonard's accounts. I was ushered back to a desk, where a man with coiffed hair and thick glasses looked up from his computer monitor.

Lee-Leonard's money was locked up in a series of accounts. I passed across the desk a slip of paper with all their identification numbers. The bank manager's eyes widened as he ran them through the computer. "These accounts are frozen," he said.

My hands went numb. Dewitt and Weaver had beaten me there.

"Wait a second, this one is still liquid," the manager said, tapping on his keyboard. He looked over his glasses.

"How much is in it?"

Without looking back at the screen, the manager informed me that the account contained more than $400,000.

"I'm closing it out," I said. "I want cash. Large bills will be fine."

The manager leaned back and exhaled deeply.

"Is there a problem?" I asked.

"That's a large amount of money to withdraw," he said.

"My business is having liquidity problems," I told him. "As you can see, we're suffering short-term difficulty that has resulted in frozen accounts. I have to access whatever capital I can to stay afloat. My creditors will only accept cash payments. I have the proper password, and I'm a signatory on the account."

Dewitt and Weaver had missed one of the accounts. I didn't care who the money belonged to. I was taking it.

The bank manager nodded. "All right," he said. "Come with me."

In a small back room behind the tellers' stalls, the manager paged an assistant. They left and came back about ten minutes later with four thick manila envelopes. He pulled out hundreds and thousands bound in little strips of paper.

"Your account is now closed," he said to me after I took the envelopes. "Good luck."

Two blocks away, I slammed on the brakes and made a U-turn when I spotted a martial arts studio on La Cienega. They didn't want to sell me the black club I saw in the display case, but they got it out for me when I dropped two hundred-dollar bills on the counter. I tossed the money in the back but kept the club wedged between my seat and the door.

I don't remember walking up the drive to Frank Lee's apartment.

My eyes blazed with red.

I was not myself.

The musculature of my body was tense and wiry. My foot-steps were soft on the warm pavement.

That bitch and that fucking traitor. My friends. I trusted them, and I have no mother. They want me to pay for what they did, fucking behind my back while Karl carves me into pieces. Frank wants to take my place, and Iris is going to let him. I'll go to prison while they fuck on my bed. She'll press her face into the sheets while he sweats and moans on top of her. They'll laugh at how stupid I am. I'll go to prison. I have no mother and I can't even cry, and this is what they did to me. She's ripped me open and left me bleeding. This is what she does. She takes it all away from me.

Frames failed to coalesce into anything that made sense. The fire in my head raged. The entire world collapsed into the painted rectangle of Frank's front door. I pounded on it.

When it opened, I punched Frank in the face. He was bigger than me, but I knocked him off his feet and closed the door be-hind me. I grabbed at his hair and hit him again and again.

"Get off me," he moaned. "You fucking psycho."

I got on top of him and pressed the side of his face deep into the rug. I moved his head from side to side, tearing his skin. I put my hand over his mouth as he tried to scream. I looked around and saw no sign of Iris. I punched at him, grabbed at him, tried to disfigure him with my hands.

They schemed behind my back. Frank lost the money and wants to pin it on me. So he can take her to her father's house high in the mountains and fuck her hard. She blames me for not making her happy. They're going to make a family and leave me with no one.

The room exploded bright red, vibrant, undulating with the rapid-fire beat of my pulse.

Feels like my heart's going to explode.

"Where the fuck is she?" I screamed.

Iris was hiding from me in the bathroom. I left Frank limp and moaning and smashed in the door as she tried to lock it. Her face turned pale with fear as I denounced her; my voice lowered to a hissing whisper, and I laid my hand on her neck.

I pulled her out. She put her hand over her mouth when she saw Frank lying on the rug. I told her not to worry about *her new man*.

"I'm taking care of everything," I said.

She asked me what I was talking about, begged me to listen to her, told me I wasn't making any sense. I would hear none of it. I was like a pillar of flame, a bolt of raw electricity. The walls were about to catch fire from the heat I was giving off. Iris wore all black: jeans and a short-sleeved top that showed off her breasts. All dressed up for her man.

You take away the mothers and leave the baby boys to the dogs. You bitch, you bitch. Never lie together on that bed again. The things you've done to me, I was never the same. You killed me.

Iris fell back against the wall, both hands over her mouth,

crying. She looked at me, *through* me, so shocked that she could only stare.

This is what I am now. Look at me. Look at me. Look at what you did to me.

She told me she loved me and pleaded for me to say I loved her. She said she wanted things to go back to the way they had been. She knew about the money, and her father, and she didn't care about any of it. *She was lying to try to save herself. She lay under Frank and laughed at me.*

She cried and reached for me, calling my name over and over. My words came out in orgasmic torrents, and she kept saying stop it, stop it, don't say those things. I had the club in my hand. There was blood on me.

The next thing I remember was darkness. I was sitting in my car a couple of blocks from our apartment. I went home and picked up the ringing phone. It was Karl, wanting to talk to Iris.

I didn't know where she was.

I had bruises all over, and my clothes smelled of sweat and violence. There were spots of blood on my shirt and hands.

I changed out of my clothes and disposed of them in a garbage can on a side street near Venice Beach. I put the money and the club in a pillowcase and deposited them in a locker inside the Santa Monica Greyhound station. Then I went home and waited until dawn. The hours passed slowly. Motes of dust hung suspended in sunbeams that shone through cracks in the curtains.

I stared at the curtains for hours. Any precise recollection of my actions ended with me dragging Iris out of Frank's bathroom. I could hear her voice, panicked, begging, shrill with fear. I could remember the immense strength I had possessed, the way I had been able to overpower and physically humiliate Frank with no effort at all. I thought Frank was still alive; it didn't seem possible that I had beat him badly enough to take his life. As for Iris . . .

I remembered the feel of the club in my hand. I found more blood, pooled in the collar of my clean shirt, and realized that at some point I had been injured. I went to the bathroom and ran water on my head until I located a long bleeding wound on my scalp. Frank, I realized, had landed a defensive blow that I hadn't remembered. By morning it swelled up to a lump that I had to arrange my hair to cover.

It seemed prudent to assume the worst. My mouth was dry as the desert, but I vomited every time I tried to drink water.

The voice in my head was gone. I was angry with Frank for letting Lee-Leonard go to hell without telling me, and I wondered what Iris was doing at Frank's apartment yesterday afternoon. But I no longer felt the burning betrayal that drove what I did.

It was, I knew, too late. I stared at the curtains.

By nightfall, Karl was calling every hour. I tried to sound appropriately anxious. I told Karl I didn't know where Iris had gone. Apparently, Frank hadn't called the police after I left him on the floor of his apartment; I watched for the red-and-blue fireworks display of an approaching squad car, but they never came. Karl called through the night, demanding answers I couldn't give him.

After two days, the police finally showed up at my door. I answered their questions in the kitchen. *No, I don't know where she is. No, we didn't have a fight. No, she didn't seem depressed.* It was easy to lie to them. I figured any minute someone was going to discover Iris's dead body, and I would be charged with her murder. Deflecting the detectives' questions was a means of passing the time until then.

But they never found Iris. Karl posted a reward and hired

dozens of private investigators. The story was widely reported in newspapers and on the TV news. One night on the TV in the kitchen I watched myself duck cameras as I made my furtive exit from LAPD headquarters after hours of grilling by homicide detectives. I wore a linen suit, and I was clean-shaven. When I turned off the television, I closed my eyes and tried with all my might to *will* her back. *Come on. Come back to me.*

Within a couple of weeks, most of the furor had withered away. Iris Kateran had vanished. The police told Karl that she was probably dead. Frank was gone, too, although before his disappearance he mailed a letter to Karl begging for amnesty and apologizing for his fiduciary irresponsibility. I returned the BMW and received a letter in the mail from Karl's real estate company telling me to be out of the apartment by the end of the month. I was surrounded by Iris's things but unable to touch any of them. I managed to pass entire days without thinking or feeling. Remembering, living: it was impossible. There was no longer anyone who knew Jack Wright. There was no use for him.

I paid cash for a Suburu at a used-car lot in Westwood. I informed the police and Karl that I was moving. Because the investigation had stalled, the police let me leave California with a pledge to forward my address when I reached my destination. I drove days and nights until I finally reached the desolate wastes of the Dakotas, then the plains of Minnesota. There was a chill in the air. Everything I owned was packed in the trunk. I followed the highway to Minneapolis, where I found a hotel room downtown.

It was as good a place as any to live—a city somewhere between Cambridge and Los Angeles, isolated by harsh winters and, to my thinking, shielded from the rushing main. When the first snow fell, I signed the papers to buy my house. I furnished it from discount and secondhand stores, then sat back and waited for someone to come. I thought the next knock at the door would be by a killer hired by Karl. One day soon, I assumed, they would find her body. I imagined Iris alone, decomposing, waiting to be found. In the winter the snows piled high, and I captured mice in my pantry and tossed them outside. I waited in quiet—it was always too quiet—for something, anything.

At night I tried to recollect what I had done to Iris, but even in solitary meditation the memories eluded me. I wanted to relive the moment when the truncheon struck her skull, to find some meaning in it, but it was blotted out. I entered the dark spot of my mind and settled there, waiting for a release that rejected me.

Until the day I walked into the library and found her.

9

Today.

THE INNER LIFE OF A SOLITARY PERSON CAN GET VERY WEIRD INDEED. Ask anyone who's ever lived alone. The mind shuts down for hours at a time or, conversely, shifts into modes of hyperactivity. Waves of anxiety break on the shore with no one around to anchor the self.

I'm alone when I get back from having a beer with Zeke Bailey. It's a very windy afternoon. Leaves blow in funnel formations, scattering and falling to the pavement before rising and swirling in the opposite direction. It's a churning, unsatisfied wind. It presses against the window and makes the casement creak.

A familiar bald man with a distended belly walks past my

house. He's carrying a plastic bag, through which I see the out-line and color of two cartons of Marlboros. He's a lonely man slowly killing himself. He's always in a hurry. I imagine what his home must smell like: the stale sweat and nicotine, the acrid odor of pointlessness.

He glances up, sees me watching.

I have the phone tucked in my pants pocket in case Iris calls. I wonder what Iris and her people are doing this very moment. I imagine candles, incense, Iris moving slowly somewhere in the city. I picture her pressing her fingers gently against the scars on her scalp, through her unwashed and matted hair.

Rubbing my eyes, I reach for the phone. It's no longer in my pocket. I don't remember taking it out.

I stand very still and remember the martinis last night and all the other things I have relegated to the periphery of my consideration. The way my shoes go missing, only to be found arranged neatly side by side by the front door—that's happened twice in the last month. My constant searching for my wallet and keys—hunts that always end when I discover them in plain sight in a place I had searched two or three times already. I remember the woman standing over my bed, the hands that had caressed me the night before as I passed into oblivion.

I don't think I'm really alone.

It's hard to keep hold of the thought. The hallucinated figure in Karl's sauna, the bilocation experience when I was on the phone with him the night before my life exploded—these memories, too, escape me when I try to fix them in my consciousness. It's as though I have a crossed circuit.

I think of Kim. *Identity flux.*

I take her number out of my pocket and call it. Maybe she can tell me something more. But then I get her voice mail. It's almost impossible to get through to anybody these days.

* * *

I meet Karl at the address I gave his secretary—a crowded Mexican place. I arrive first and take a table. Picking El Mariachi was, I realize now, an act of unconscious aggression against Karl. It's noisy, full of children, packed with Mexican immigrants— just the kind of environment from which Karl takes pains to insulate himself. I see him come through the door, in a suit and overcoat, and I smile when his expression sours with distaste. He comes to the table and offers his hand to shake.

"Charming place," he says.

Karl sits and opens up his paper napkin. I'm stunned: he looks as though he's aged a decade since I last saw him. There's empty space between his neck and his collar, and his hands shake before he plants them on the table. His temples are mottled with constellations of age spots, and he sits as though maintaining an erect carriage requires constant effort.

Look at him. He's dying.

"You don't look good, Jack," he says.

"Don't try to flatter me, Karl," I tell him.

"I mean it." Karl pushes aside the menu the waitress brings. "It's not an insult. You simply don't look well."

I consider pointing out the same about him, but it seems an excessive cruelty. I no longer have the moral authority to hate this man.

"I wish you'd picked someplace quieter, Jack," Karl says. He leans forward; his shoulders have narrowed, and the skin around his mouth has lost tautness.

"Maybe I don't like to be in secluded places with you, Karl," I say. It's the first time I have ever alluded to the sauna. Karl nods, slightly, with an air of sadness that completely disarms me.

"I was hoping we could talk," he says. "After all this time, it seems the least we can do is have a conversation like two men."

"We can talk. No one here cares."

Karl looks around at the young families and bachelor laborers. The mood here always buoys me.

"I guess no one here is concerned about us," Karl says with a bitter smile. "They have their own lives to lead."

"Unlike you and me."

"That's what I was thinking," Karl replies.

We both know it. It's what binds us together now: Without Iris, we're completely lost.

"It's been hard recently." Karl sighs. He fingers his lapel and regards me with an almost paternal look. Gone are the malice and scorn he reserved for me in the past.

"I know," I tell him.

"I never imagined it would come to this," Karl says. "Two years, and still nothing. I no longer delude myself hoping she's alive. If I can give her a decent burial, if I can just bring her home, then I'll be satisfied. I worry about her being alone."

She isn't alone. But I won't tell Karl.

"I know you loved her," Karl continues. "No matter how I ever felt about you, I know your feelings were genuine. And she loved you, too. The thing is, Jack, I wanted more for her."

"You made that clear," I say.

"I'm not trying to insult you, dammit." Karl balls his napkin in his fist. "I thought you would limit her. I thought she was too young to get married to any man."

The room swells with music, soccer on TV, voices talking in Spanish. A little black-haired baby at the next table is trying to get my attention from behind Karl's shoulder.

"What I'm trying to say is . . . ." Karl pauses; his icy black eyes seem clouded. "What I'm saying to you, Jack, is that I'm sorry. I was wrong. I'm also . . . I'm sorry for what I did to you."

"You don't have to—"

"The Frank Lee thing wasn't really your fault," Karl

interrupts. "I could have dealt with it differently, instead of using it to drive a wedge between you and Iris. It also wasn't right, the way I let Weaver and Dewitt work you over like that. It wasn't fair. I want to apologize, Jack."

My expression must be one of utter shock, because a dark humor flashes across his face and I see a glimpse of the old Karl. But then he smiles gently, or tries to, and I can see how much he needs for me to accept his penitence.

"Well, all right," I say. "It's over now, anyway."

I want to apologize, too, but I can't. I can never tell him.

"What are you doing here?" Karl asks.

"What do you mean?"

"You know what I mean." Karl gestures to encompass everything with a spectral expression of aversion. "You don't have any family in this town, do you?"

"I don't have any family at all," I say. Karl must know that.

"You're not really working, are you? Your little investment company, that's just a tax dodge, right?"

"Maybe not for long," I say. "I'm being audited."

Karl lets out a snort. "That's all you need," he says. "I'll talk to my people, see who's a good tax attorney here."

"All right," I say.

"Your living here alone doesn't seem right," Karl tells me. "You're still young, Jack. You're not like me. You can't grieve forever."

"I . . . I think I will, though."

"She wouldn't want it." Karl exhales with a little rattle. "She wouldn't want to see you like this. She loved you, Jack."

"I'm not ready to give up, Karl. She's—" And I stop myself short of saying, *She's still with me. She's here.*

The waitress comes back. Karl looks away. I order a couple of specials and beers. It's been too long since I ate. When the waitress goes, Karl looks down at me over the bridge of his nose, as though he has reached some kind of conclusion.

"You can come back to Los Angeles," he says. "You don't have to be here all alone."

I run my hand along the edge of the table. For the first time this night, I sense some hidden motive behind what the old man is saying.

"You can work for me," Karl says. "I've been loosening my grip on the business. I'm just a figurehead now. Richard Weaver's running the show, you can work for him. I'll get you an apartment, whatever you want, Jack. I know how much Iris wanted you and me to have a relationship of some kind. You can come back to the family, Jack."

Back to the family. As though I were ever part of it.

I picture myself with a suit and a briefcase, showing up to work for my old tormentor Richard Weaver. Karl has to know I could never do it.

"Thanks," I say. "I appreciate it, but this is my home now. I think I could have loved living in L.A., but I was never able to escape the feeling that it was Iris's city. *Your* city. I went there because of her, and it's impossible for me to imagine living there without her."

Karl nods. This is the reply he expected.

"Don't worry about the money you took from me, then," he says. "It's not a concern. At least I can grant you that."

"What money?" I ask.

Karl frowns.

"All right. Thank you," I say.

"I left that one account liquid on purpose," Karl says. His expression is unreadable. "I thought you might take it and go someplace where Iris was hidden. I had you followed as soon as you said you were leaving."

"I figured as much," I say.

"After you took the money," he says, his eyes turning cold, "I could easily have had you arrested."

"I know."

"I'm glad I didn't." Karl's thin lips carve a rueful smile. "I don't give a damn anymore. I'm sure Iris would have wanted you taken care of."

Iris *would* have. She was never selfish, unlike her cadaverous old man and her hypocritical ex-lover. I flash on an awful image of Karl and me carving up her body at a banquet, two grinning carnivores deriving their sustenance from prey.

The food comes. Instead of eating, Karl stares sullenly at the table. I eat with surprising gusto. Karl looks away and sips his beer. We fall into a silence that is not particularly uncomfortable. There's isn't much left for us to say, and Karl's mood of proclamation and apology has passed.

I blink. For a second I see a face superimposed on Karl's— almost Iris's, but different. The restaurant blurs, my perspective turns fish-eyed. There's no sound, no sight other than a blurry face tinged in red.

"Iris's mother," I say before I have time to think.

"What about her?" Karl asks, surprised.

"How did she die?"

Karl sits back, folds his arms, and looks at me for a long time. His old contempt for me is replaced by an enervated curiosity. He is trying to *see* me, and finding it difficult.

"A kitchen accident," he says.

"What exactly happened?"

Karl coughs, thinks, comes to a decision. His chair scuffs the floor as he moves closer.

"I've never talked about this with anyone," he says quietly. "Not even Iris."

"She would never tell me," I say.

"I'm not surprised." Karl stares at his hands. "The three of us were in the kitchen. It was morning. I was about to leave for work. I remember it was hot, but Patricia would never turn on the air conditioner. I was in a bad mood because I was sweating through my shirt already, and it was only eight in the morning."

I continue eating.

"Iris was a little girl, not even in school yet," Karl says. He reaches for his beer. "Patricia and I got in a fight about something. You know, the kind of fight you can't even remember what it was about."

I know.

"I got very angry. I had a terrible temper when I was younger. And don't bring up that business in the steamroom that day. I was just trying to scare you off. I was worried about you and Frank Lee dragging my daughter down, and I was right to defend her. I'm talking about a *real* temper, *real* anger."

I picture Karl at about forty-five, with more hair, even more strength.

"This time, for some reason, I got angrier than I ever had in my life." Karl takes a drink of his beer. "It was strange. It was like I wasn't myself."

I drop my fork. "What do you mean?" I ask.

"I lost control," Karl says in a manner that implies this was something he never did.

"You weren't yourself. Did you hear voices in your head that didn't necessarily sound like your own?"

"Don't get fucking weird," Karl says.

"All right, sorry. Please. Go on."

"Patricia was telling me to lower my voice, to calm down. Iris was crying. But I wouldn't stop. I *insisted* on something, I don't even remember what. I had been *wronged* somehow, I know that was what I was thinking."

"What happened?"

"I . . . Patricia backed up against the counter. I was yelling, Iris was crying. And I . . . I grabbed Patricia's arm, and I pulled her. When that happened, I knocked a big pitcher of water on the floor. There was broken glass, and we were standing in water, and Iris was crying."

Karl stares into space, lost in the memory of that moment—one among countless billions. I almost don't want to hear this.

"She pulled away from me, and I backed off, because I was *trying* to control myself. Patricia was making waffles for Iris, and the machine made that noise to say that the waffles were ready, and Patricia was trying to make Iris stop crying and telling her that she could have a waffle with extra syrup, and—"

There are tears in his eyes.

"And she reached for the waffle iron, and right away I knew what happened. She started to convulse, and her eyes rolled back in her head, and there was this god-awful burning smell."

"Iris—"

"I was yelling at Iris to *stay away*, to *stay away*, because I knew we couldn't help her. Then it was over. Patricia fell face-down on the floor in that puddle of water she'd been standing in."

"Jesus," I whisper.

Karl's lips curl back, the face of a wounded animal.

"I have something for you," he says, handing me an envelope. "This is the surprise I told you about. Don't open it until I'm gone."

Karl stands up and starts to put on his overcoat.

"Wait, what are you doing?" I say.

"I have to leave," he says. He motions at the envelope. "Consider that a gift from me."

I get up and shake his hand. "Take care, Karl."

His handshake lingers. "All right. You too, then."

I watch Karl's back recede and think about the rage that once engulfed him, a moment he couldn't back away from and which stained the rest of his life. So I wasn't the first.

Karl is halfway to the door when he stops, pauses, and turns. He comes back to the table and leans over me.

"One last time. Tell me where you think she is," he says.

"I don't know where she is," I say, somewhat truthfully.

"Do you know what happened to her?"

"I don't," I say, lying to his face.

"Then do you know what happened to you?" Karl asks.

I watch a bulge in his throat expand and contract, then look up at his sagging eyes. He is close enough to me that I can hear the sound of his breathing, sense his entire being inclined toward mine in a posture of expectation and querulous curiosity.

"What happened to me?" I ask.

"You really don't know, do you?" he asks with a fleeting expression of sadness and a brief revisit to a flash of penitence. "You *have* to know. You really don't remember, do you?"

"I—I remember what I need to remember," I say slowly.

Karl straightens, buttons his coat, and looks at me for a long time. He puffs out his cheeks slightly, and I can see him wandering the dark corridors of his memory.

"Good luck to you, Jack. I hope we all know the truth someday."

He nods, then leaves.

I seem to have given him the answer he expected or somehow required. If he knows what I did to his daughter, he is doing a supreme job of hiding it.

THURSDAY

20

I SIT AT THE TABLE UNDER THE ANTIQUE FIXTURE THAT KEEPS FLICK-
ERING AND BLOWING BULBS. I've gotten up early, and a gray mist
hugs the lawn outside. I look at the newspaper and, with some
surprise, see that it's Halloween.

When I returned home from my dinner with Karl last
night, there was a message waiting for me on my voice mail:
"Solomon here. I'm back in SoCal. Nice of you to call. Let me
know what's up. I'll see you eventually, but I'm probably going
to stay away until after winter's over. You deal with the wind
chill. Later."

There's a pen in my hand. I look at the margins of my
newspaper and see that I have been writing unconsciously. It's
odd to see an unfamiliar thought in my own handwriting:

If my actions are who I am, then who am I?

Next to this, in another hand, I see:

You are the ignorant soul.

I feel as though someone is watching. Beneath the floorboards something scuffles in the basement. I look again at what I wrote without thinking. *If my actions are who I am, then who am I?*

"I am John Leonard Wright," I announce. I begin to add, *And I am not an ignorant soul,* but I stop. I fear what will happen next if I acknowledge this is real.

If my actions are me, then who am I? I pretended to be someone I was not. Is that what I'm being punished for?

No. I'm being punished for what I did.

I shake my head. I have blamed the violent thoughts for what I did, but my thoughts have always been my own, and my deeds constitute all that I can claim to be. But again the headache begins, a cloud in my vision, and it's so goddammed hard to think straight.

"Who's here?" I ask. The floor creaks next to me. I feel my mouth drop, and all the hairs on my arm stand on end.

"Don't tell me," I say.

Karl's parting gift—the sealed envelope—is on the table in front of me. It crackles with static electricity when I tear it open. Inside are two small typed sheets of paper. The first is a note from Karl on his business stationery:

Jack,

I hired an investigator to procure this information. Go to her. Neither of us has family, and we have to make the most of what's left to us.

Karl

The second sheet of paper bears the letterhead of something called Advantage Investigations. I scan down the page until I find an address in Cincinnati for an assisted living facility called Tree Hill and a name: Sandra Ruth Wright.

My mother. Karl found my mother for me.

The phone rings, and I am relieved beyond description. I move to it through a thick miasma, but I can feel myself getting better. I will knock back a couple of aspirins and soon will feel well again.

"Jack," says Zeke Bailey. "Good morning."

It takes me a couple of seconds to shift back from wherever I have been.

"Jack, are you there?" Zeke asks.

"Yeah. Yeah." I stand up and begin to pace.

"Iris wants to see you." There is a strong hint of beneficence in his voice. "Now, if you're not too busy."

I almost laugh. *Well, I had hoped to do a little more automatic writing and commune with my ghosts, but there's always time later.*

"You sound strange, Jack," Zeke says warily.

I don't bother to explain. How am I supposed to sound?

"Walk down Twenty-fifth to the lake," Zeke says. "Then turn left and go down the path until you reach the first bench. We'll see you there."

"We?" I say. "No. Just Iris."

Silence on the line. I must acknowledge that I am not negotiating from a position of strength.

"All right, whatever," I say. "I'm leaving now."

It's chilly out, and I have to button my jacket and stick my hands in my pockets. By the time I reach Hennepin, I'm sweating. I walk as quickly as I can without breaking into a run. My mind chatters to itself. The houses get bigger as I near the lake, and maybe I could afford one if Iris comes back to me. There's one up for sale, a Victorian with a big porch.

We could sit out there together, side by side, talking about the future.

My hands pump as I walk. I reach up to wipe wetness from around my eyes. *Asshole*. Here I am, fantasizing about her coming back to me. She won't even tell me where she lives.

I cross the parkway and walk along the path until I find the bench tucked away beneath two old elms. There's no one there, so I sit. The island in the middle of the lake is shrouded in mist. I trace its outline through my condensing breath. The gray sky unfolds like an umbrella over the curving shoreline.

I wait. A couple of joggers go by, then a woman with a baby in a stroller. A man goes past with a big golden retriever; the dog watches me as it passes, a quizzical expression on its face. I shrug at it. *I know. What are we going to do?*

They come around the corner. Zeke is taller than I remember, dressed in a bright orange windbreaker and faded jeans. He has his hand on Iris's back, supporting or guiding her. She's wearing the same old coat as last time, along with a long, heavy dress, stockings, and thick-soled black shoes. There's a multicolored handkerchief tied around her head. From this distance, she looks as though she might be an arty eccentric. With every step closer, she appears more and more like a bag lady. She walks with her head down, staring at her shoes, and it's Zeke who spots me first.

I get up. I can't help but smile at the sight of her. Zeke runs his tongue along the inside of his teeth.

Iris says my name and, before I can react, envelops me in a crushing embrace. I close my eyes and feel the familiar contours of her body beneath all those layers of clothes, my hand tracing the shoulder blade that protrudes from the narrow line of her spine. I have to hold my breath when I'm assaulted by a wave of musky body odor.

"Nice to see you," Zeke says, shaking my hand. He holds my

gaze longer than he should, and right away I know something is wrong.

Iris and I sit beside each other, and Zeke takes a place at the end of the bench, facing away. He stuffs his hands in his windbreaker and looks up and down the parkway. *Looking for what?*

Iris looks out at the water, her lips parted slightly, eyes focused in the near distance among the dead reeds and the water's gentle undulation.

"This is a beautiful place," she says quietly, almost to herself.

I ask her how she is, and she smiles and puts her hand on my forehead.

"You're sweaty," she says.

"I was in a hurry to see you."

"That's sweet," she replies, a hint of confusion confounding the relative clarity in her voice.

"What's the matter?"

She opens her mouth, but only an ambiguous consonant comes out. She looks at Zeke; he taps on Iris's coat pocket, then resumes his monitoring of the parkway.

"Did I say something—" I begin, but Iris shushes me. She pulls out a pad of paper as worn and faded as the one I saw the other day. She flips through, and I spy page after page of notes in pencil and pen in tight script. I suppress a grimace when I spot a few lines written in blue crayon. I start to say something, but Iris shakes her head irritably and finds an empty page near the end of the book. She gets a pencil from her pocket and begins to write.

I know I shouldn't disturb her, so I monitor the parkway with Zeke. I count twelve cars passing by before she's finally done. She folds back the notebook and holds it out for me.

"You want me to read this?"

She nods, rocking her body and chewing on her lip. I can

see how much effort it took her to commit her thoughts to paper. Zeke glances at the page, but she hands it to me before he can read it.

> *Since the acident it isnt easy for me to talk about things. How I feel. What hapened yersterday or what will hapen tomorrow. Im sorry. Its somethign I have to live with, and it helps me to write things out or else I get furtrstaed. I want you close again, but things are very different now. We've both been through so much hurt. I can read it in your eyes. I'm getting better all the time and I know you are too. We wont have to run forever.*

I read this, then read it again, then a third time. My legs feel hollow. My eyes water, but I stay steady. Tears might bring me comfort I don't deserve.

"Everything's all right, Jack." She moves closer and puts her arm around me. This small gesture of comfort is too much, and a sob erupts from somewhere beneath my breastbone.

"No," I manage to say. *It isn't.*

"I know . . . you want to help." Iris moves her face close to mine, and for a second I think we are going to kiss. But instead she locks her crystalline blue eyes onto mine, and I am unable to blink.

"I wish . . ." I feel Zeke watching. "I wish none of this had ever happened. I wish . . ." *I wish we were still together. I wish rage hadn't come over me and taken you away, like it took your mother away. I wish I never had such a terrible sickness inside me, that I could even think about hurting you. No one should ever have hurt you.*

Iris cocks her head, studying me. "I got pulled out of . . . my life," she says. "Into this. I know you have a lot of questions. I'm happy now. You should understand that. I'm not worried about anything in the whole wide world. Really."

She is *here*, my Iris. She's shattered, but it's her. I want to leap out of my skin and dive into those eyes.

I say her name. She smiles at me.

"Come home with me," I say. I take her hand. "Zeke can come, too."

Iris's mouth forms an O, and she looks down at her hands. Perhaps she can be medically treated. Zeke and his friends are probably smothering her with their devotion, deepening her confusion and isolation. We can check her into a neuropsychiatric hospital. I can stay by her bedside and never let her get away. I believe there are quantum universes in which none of this happened, where Iris and I are married and happy. But I am stranded in this one, with its particular branch of causation and circumstance, and I can make it a better one than it has been. There is always choice, volition, the opportunity to cheat an unkind fate. I can help her. She can help me.

"No." She shakes her head, then glances at Zeke.

"Why did you look at him first?" I ask.

"We look out for each other," Zeke says. He seems more nervous. "I told you, man."

"I didn't ask you, *man*," I tell him.

"Jack," Iris says. She suddenly sounds very tired, and I can see how much work it is for her to interact with such intensity.

"Please," I say. "Just come with me."

Iris hunches her shoulders; it's as though the bench has turned to liquid and she's sinking into it. Zeke gives me an apprehensive look that is surprisingly devoid of hostility.

"What do you think?" he whispers to her.

"Not now," Iris says in a childish voice. "I'm not ready."

I pull out my cigarettes and give one to Zeke. I have to back off. I mustn't frighten her. I light one of my own and sit back. A couple of old women walk past, ready to smile at us until they see Iris's ragged dress and the look of consternation on her face.

"Would you like to come to where we stay?" Iris asks. I hold out a cigarette, and she accepts it.

"Iris," Zeke says. "I don't know."

He puts his hand on hers, but she pulls away. *Good.*

"You obviously know where I live," I tell Zeke. "So let's get on equal footing. We're all friends, right?"

He gives me a pinched smile. I know Zeke is anxious, but I don't think I'm the cause of his worry. Something has him preoccupied.

"You're asking for a lot of trust," Zeke says.

"Well, you've had everything your own way until now."

"Stop," Iris hisses; Zeke and I are both caught off guard. She looks at Zeke, then me, with a grievous hurt. "I can't stand for you two to fight . . . this fighting. I can't stand it. It tears me in half."

In the fractured cadence of her voice, I hear the pain I caused her when I sparred with her father. I have to break this pattern. Whether or not I am worthy or disagreeable is beside the point; Iris is the only person in my life who has looked out for my interests. With the possible exception of my mother.

The thought creeps in, and I am defenseless for a moment. This is the effect my mother has on me. This is why I try never to think of her. *Cincinnati.*

"I'm sorry," Zeke says. "I don't want to get into some macho *thing* with you, Jack. If Iris wants you to come over, then great. I'd love to have you. You can see for yourself that Iris is in a good place."

"I had dinner with your father last night," I tell Iris.

She looks at me with shock, glances away, then locks on to my eyes. Her lips move a little before she can speak.

"My father?" she asks. "Daddy? Here?"

"He called me. We ate and talked. We . . . we decided not to be enemies anymore."

She wrinkles her nose, digesting what I've said.

"He's still looking for you," I tell her. "He hasn't given up on you."

Iris's mouth drops, and I'm afraid that I might have over-loaded her circuits. I don't know why I told her. Maybe it's the least I can do for Karl. Perhaps I'm simply trying everything that comes to mind to bring Iris back to her old life.

"How . . . does he look?" Iris asks.

He looks like he's dying, but I can't say that. He looks spent, as though losing Iris has left him withered and exhausted. *The way I might look one day.*

Suddenly something changes. A screw turns. I tried to kill Iris, and nearly killed Frank, because I thought they were con-spiring against me. *Fucking behind my back.* How do I know they weren't? She was at Frank's apartment that afternoon two years ago. How do I know that I hadn't been right to protect myself? Iris might be working against me again, right now. Iris, Zeke, Solomon, maybe even Karl. Maybe I'm being set up for the punishment I eluded when I slipped out of L.A. I can *feel* it com-ing closer to me.

Iris says my name and puts her hand on my cheek. "Come back," she says. "You went away."

My heart is beating hard and a bead of sweat slips down my back to the waistband of my underwear.

"We should go," Zeke says, sensing a change in the air.

"Why haven't you contacted your father?" I ask Iris.

She shakes her head with adolescent vehemence. "I can't—" She halts, struggles to formulate a thought.

"Enough, Jack," Zeke says.

"I stay away," Iris says slowly. "You should, too. He isn't bad, Jack. But bad things . . . happen around him. You should know that as much as anyone. People get hurt. Like me. And you."

And your mother. "All right," I say weakly. She still doesn't blame me. She still can't remember.

Iris blinks, and tears fall from her eyes. I wonder whether she remembers what happened to her mother. Her clouded eyes run red with teardrops that trace the blown-out blood vessels on her cheeks. She puts her face in her hands, and I see that her nails are long and chipped. The nail on her forefinger is blotched with purple.

Zeke reaches for her, but I get there first. I take her in my arms, and the cloud that threatened to engulf me goes away again. I pull her closer and breathe deep of the malodor from the scarf covering her hair. I whisper that I'm sorry.

When they leave, they promise to call. I watch them vanish around a bend in the trail and consider following, but I've done enough. And I have extracted a promise that they will allow me into their world.

When I get home, my front door is unlocked and open. I go inside slowly. I don't remember closing the door when I left, but I must have. I go from room to room, searching for signs of a break-in. Of course no one is there. I go downstairs, close and lock the front door. Everything is in its place; I find Hero asleep on my bed, so sprawled out and otiose that he doesn't even notice I'm here.

When I go into the dining room, I see the newspaper I had been holding when Zeke called, the obscure messages still scribbled there. Then I look down at the envelope Karl gave me containing my mother's address.

There's something written on it, in my handwriting.

Every boy loves his mother.

I look at it for a while, then decide to try to cry. But I fail. I'm all dried up for now.

Instead, I take a handful of Advil and lie down on the rug in the living room. It's hours before I remember where I am.

21

Several Hours Later.

A LITTLE BEFORE SUNSET I LOOK OUTSIDE AND SEE SMALL BANDS OF CHILDREN WALKING THE STREETS WITH THEIR PARENTS. They look strange somehow, and it takes me a minute to realize they're dressed in costumes—a preteen Darth Vader, a princess, a Teletubby.

The newspaper said it was Halloween.

I flash back to when I was ten, when I dressed up as a *bandito* in a comically massive sombrero my mother had lying around the house. I added a plaid shirt, a beard of mascara, and a Lincoln Log that resembled a textured, gnarled brown *cigarillo*. I collected a bagful of Snickers bars and quarters, careful to avoid the razor-blade-spiked apple that city kids were taught to dread. At one house, a drunken, laughing man called me inside

to show his girlfriend my costume, then gave me an extra helping of candy. I was flattered and vaguely terrified. My mother
waited for me on the sidewalk.

I jog off to the gas station for a bag each of peanut-butter
cups and Mars bars. When I get back, Batman and the Little
Mermaid are knocking on the door. Although I don't watch
much TV, when I flip on the set I usually locate the cartoons—
so I know many of the characters coming to see me. Their parents eye me suspiciously as I rip open the candy bags and dole
out a couple of pieces for each child. One kid thanks me, the
other doesn't. The guilty party is promptly sent back to express
proper gratitude.

"Happy Halloween," I say, smiling and waving beneficently
at his parents. I can tell by their expression that I am not suc-
cessfully pulling off the role of benign local home owner.

I leave the front door open and the screen unlocked, then
pull up my rocking chair. It isn't long before the next crew shows
up, four young black kids trawling the higher-rent neighbor-
hoods in search of better loot. I don't disappoint them; I empty
about a third of my stash into their bags. A dinosaur roars at
me in appreciation. The oldest kid gives me an it's-cool nod.

Pretty soon I decide this will be even more fun if I sit on the
stoop. I light a cigarette, hastily balancing it on the edge of the
step when the next group approaches. By the time the sun goes
down, I'm feeling better than I have in months. I remember being happy on Halloween when I was a child, and a flicker of
that old self inhabits me. When the sun goes down, the flow of
kids slows to a trickle. I eat a couple of candy bars and go inside.

I'm just about to close up shop when there's a knock on the
screen door. I rummage through what's left of my candy, hoping I have enough to dole out and wishing I hadn't dipped into
it. But I pull up short when I get to the door and see who's there.

At first I take him for a very large child, but that can't be. It takes a moment to process what I'm seeing: a full-grown man in a tan suit and shirt open at the neck. He is wearing, improbably enough, a ski mask covering his face.

"Trick or treat," he says in a comic book voice.

I reach to lock the door, but he's quicker than me. He's got the screen open, and he pushes his way into the house. He's a little bigger than me, and I'm no great fighter. *Fight?* But a moment ago—

He stands on the threshold and slams the door behind him. I back off, looking for a weapon. He laughs and, with a flourish, bows deeply at the waist.

"I don't care what you want," I tell him. "Just get the hell out."

He straightens. He reaches up and tugs at the ski mask. He teases me for a second, pulls it back down, and laughs. Then in a flash he rips off the mask and throws it on the sofa.

"Well, Jack, aren't you glad to see me?" asks Frank Lee.

A knock at the door behind Frank startles him. His smile disappears. I motion for him to let me by—for some reason, it is very important right now that I give the children their candy. I give Mars bars to a SpongeBob and a Power Puff Girl, then close the door again. The house is silent, and I feel us sealed inside.

I motion toward the dining room. "Okay," I tell him. "Come on. Come in. Can I get you anything?"

Frank takes a place at the head of the table. "A beer," he says.

I go into the kitchen and bring back two. I sit across from him. It takes awhile for me to overcome the monumental bad timing of his showing up in my life again.

"Okay," I finally say.

"Okay," he says back at me. He looks over my shoulder out the window, as though thinking that someone might have followed him. Or else he's brought someone with him.

"Here's an idea," I tell him. "You go first."

Frank smiles without much warmth. "Nice house," he says.
"That's not what I had in mind."

Frank pulls on his beer and his eyes narrow with hostility. Until now, I have seen him as I remembered: good-looking, strong. Now the memory has faded and I see him for what he is. His face is patchy with stubble. His hair is cut short, with the texture of dried-out straw. His suit is wrinkled, worn, with a stain on one lapel.

"I see you stopped wearing leather," I tell him.

"I dropped the bike about a year ago," he says. "As in dropped it on the freeway with me on it."

"Bad?"

"Bad enough." Frank puts an elbow on the table and winces with recollection. "A broken leg. Skin grafts on my elbows and my back."

In the golden glow I spot a mottled patch on the back of Frank's hand where it apparently met pavement.

"I hope you were wearing a helmet," I tell him. Frank nods, and I add, unnecessarily, "I may have told you that thing was dangerous."

"Not as dangerous as being friends with you," Frank replies.

His affect is flat, weary. He has aged in the two years since I last saw him. Though he has lost weight, the boyish angles of his face are lost in bloated thickness around his eyes and mouth.

"That may be," I say.

Frank laughs. "Fuck, Jack. Are you burnt-out or something? Last time I saw you, you were a lot more *animated*. Maybe you need to see someone. I'm serious. You seem really different."

"If you want an apology for beating you up, then fine. I'm sorry. I don't know what came over me," I say. I wonder how long it will take me to be rid of him.

Frank gives me a thin smile. I scramble to think. I've spent two years with minimal contact with my old life; now, in the span of three days, everyone has returned. Whether or not it's a coincidence is strangely irrelevant. What matters is what happens to Iris.

"Apology accepted," Frank says.

"Where have you been?" I ask.

Frank makes a slightly mocking face that informs me he will dispense information at his own pace.

"I found out later about what got you started that day," he tells me. "You know, how Karl's lawyer and his hatchet man worked you over at the office. They were supremely pissed I wasn't there, and so they took it out on you. That was rough. Still, you know, you did a pretty good job of making sure I felt your pain."

I say nothing.

"You should have seen yourself, Jack. I thought your eyes were going to pop out of your head. Screaming about your mother and all kinds of crazy shit."

I flash on Frank's face in my hands; I squeezed his head, the muscles in my forearms straining, while he begged me to stop.

"What's the matter?" Frank asks. "You don't want to talk about what happened?"

"Talk if you want," I say, staring at the whorled grain of the table between us.

"You know what was funny?" Frank drains a third of his beer in a single swig. "You were *crying*. You beat the living shit out of me, but you were the one crying."

Frank's foot taps the floor, slowly at first, then quicker.

"You landed a good shot of your own," I tell him, thinking of the bloody lump on my head the next morning.

"I should have gone to the hospital," Frank tells me. "But I didn't have the fucking luxury. Karl wanted me out of town or else he was going to have me arrested for fraud."

"Charges that would have been justified," I say.

Frank bites his lip. "I was in over my head without any help," he says. "You and Iris sure didn't want to hear any bad news about how the business was going."

"I apologized for beating you," I say. "But I'm not going to apologize for the fact that you ruined the company. Lee-Leonard was *your* idea."

Frank's face falls flat. I try to remember the last time we spoke without these tripwire defenses. Things were never the same once Lee-Leonard entered the picture; money's presence corrupted the delicate balance of our regard, called into question what could be gained and lost from an interaction that had been free of avarice. It had been easy before to live without the shadow of greed. Iris had insulated us—or at least me—from striving, from using.

"You wanted to change so badly, Jack," Frank says. "Maybe you don't want to remember. You wanted to be a rich boy. You wanted *class*. You wanted to forget every damned thing about where you came from and how you grew up. I saw you. I was there."

So what. I shrug.

"It must have been a real shock for Iris to see her best boy, her pet project, turn into a snarling animal," he says. "I heard her screaming for you to stop beating me. But you wouldn't. Not until you had to."

I feel a swirl in the air of the dining room, though the windows are shut. I hear a rush of air in my ears, like the wind that insinuated itself through the faulty casement of the window in the room I used to stay in when I visited my grandmother's house as a boy. The memory pops into my mind, vivid, almost sweet, and obscures whatever I was trying to think. I reach up to touch my forehead, find it cold with sweat.

"What happened to her, Jack?" Frank finishes his beer. "Where did she go that day after she left the apartment?"

"I don't know," I tell him.

"You don't remember it," he says, and gives me a long, calculating look.

"No, I don't remember." I pause, thinking. I remember striking Frank, feeling almost possessed by my fury, then—

"Where is she?" Frank folds his arms over his chest and looks at me with genuine curiosity. "And why did Karl let you get away? You were the perfect suspect. They had you. I followed it on the news. How did you manage not to get thrown in prison?"

"Karl wanted the Lee-Leonard fiasco kept quiet," I say. "And as for Iris, I don't know what happened. They haven't found her."

"Bullshit you don't know. Bullshit Karl doesn't know."

"Why are you here?" I ask.

"Go, ahead, ask me," he says.

"Ask you what?"

Frank tries to laugh, but instead manages only a hateful sound somewhere between a cough and a sneeze. His cheeks pulse, and he spreads his hands flat on the tabletop.

"Was I fucking Iris?" he says.

I am silent.

"Do it, Jack. Ask me."

I look down at the table.

"*Ask me.* Maybe *you* don't remember, Jack, but it was certainly on your mind when you were pounding my head. Iris heard it all. So go ahead and ask me. Give me a little satisfaction here. I was a raw nerve ending for a month after you were done with me. I rode my motorcycle from one town to the next, figur-

ing there would be a warrant issued for me, all the while coughing up blood and waiting for the cuts to heal. That's no joke.
You apologized, but you know what? I don't forgive you. What
do you think of that?"

Now Frank stands up and, with a hurried motion, pulls a
black pistol from inside his jacket. He clicks it and points it at my
chest.

I find myself nodding. *Sure. Why not?*

"I can't see why you think you need that," I tell him.

"In case I decide to shoot you. It depends."

"Depends on what?" I ask. My chest feels tight and hot.

"Ask me!" he shouts.

"Fine." I flinch, despite myself. "Did you sleep with Iris?"

"I'm glad you brought it up." Frank's hands are shaking. I
calculate whether he could really kill me and decide that he's
capable. He has the furtive look of the hunted. I quickly recast
his old cynicism as an absence of empathy, his swagger as de-
rangement. I can see that I knew Frank at the fulcrum of his
life—between being a man with a conscience and being a man
without. He probably should have gone to business school after
all. But the balance has been tipped, and probably permanently.

"Well, come on, Frank. I'm dying to know."

Frank laughs, a brief flash of his old self. "You were convinced she was cheating on you," he says. "It all came out that
day. She was going to leave you for me. Or at least for someone,
and I was the surrogate. We were conspiring to make you take
the fall for Lee-Leonard. Do you at least remember that?"

"I remember."

"That's all you remember?" Again Frank gives me a slightly
sideways look, trying to see if I'm putting him on.

"I don't remember much more," I tell him.

"Maybe I should have tried to fuck her. God knows she was
lonely enough that she might have gone for anyone who paid

her some attention," Frank says. "It didn't really occur to me. But I don't mean to torture you, Jack. Look at your face—you're starting to relive the old jealousy. Look, man, she never would have done it."

Through my fear, through my rush of conflicting emotion, I am compelled to listen.

"She was faithful to the end, Jack," Frank tells me. "Don't ask me why. You got cold, and you neglected her. You didn't have your shit together, Jack. When things got tough, you went into a shell."

"While you handled everything perfectly well," I say. "With so much grace and loyalty."

Frank closes one eye and looks down the gun barrel, right at my heart. I put up a hand, my eyes watering.

"I went a little off the rails," he admits. "But I still cared about you and Iris. You're right. I fucked up with the money. I got so uptight that I thought I was going to have a heart attack. I sat in my office for hours, trying to get my breathing to slow down. Not that you would have noticed, Jack. You're so wrapped up in yourself that you can't see beyond the end of your nose."

Seeing as how he's right—and pointing a gun at me—I opt to say nothing.

"You idiot," Frank says, moving around the table. "You thought I asked Iris over to my apartment that day to make a play for her?"

"I . . . I guess I did."

"I asked her to come over because I needed *help*," he tells me. "I knew Karl was going to go for my throat. I was the odd man out, and I didn't want to go to jail. I was begging her to talk to the old man, to try to get me out of trouble."

"You weren't—"

He moves a little closer. "Jack, you don't even know that I started seeing men when we were in L.A., do you?"

I must have a particularly dumbfounded expression, because Frank laughs and throws up his gun-free hand as though to say, *What am I going to do with you?*

"Why didn't you tell me?" I ask.

"Jack, I really didn't want to have the conversation with you where I told you I thought I was gay." Frank laughs again.

I knew almost nothing about Frank's life in Los Angeles; when he became secretive, I backed off. I can see how much this hurt him.

"I'm sorry," I say.

"Well, it's only sex," Frank says. "And in case you're wondering, I was never attracted to you."

I have to laugh. "Seeing anyone nice?" I ask.

A trace of amusement plays in Frank's eyes, but then it disappears. The light flickers, and the floor creaks.

"You got to the bank before me," he says. "Cleaned it out. You should have seen them when I showed up. I half expected them to reach for the panic button and have me arrested."

"I took what I could," I say. "Karl froze almost everything."

"I went home for a while, but it didn't work out," Frank says. "I did get a little money after my dad died."

"Your father—"

"*Don't.* Don't say anything about it."

"All right."

"I went to Vancouver for a while. About a year ago, I got in touch with Karl and tried to negotiate a truce." Frank leans on the table but keeps the gun up.

"I had a little leverage on him, too," Frank tells me.

"Leverage?" I ask.

"You know what he said? He didn't give a damn about me

anymore, but I wasn't allowed to come back to L.A. Classic Karl, man. Like the city's his personal kingdom."

"That's Karl's view of the world," I admit. There's a thread of something going through my mind, but it turns into wisps of smoke when I try to follow it. *Leverage.*

"Then he told me something really interesting," Frank says, blocking my fragmented thoughts.

"I'd love to hear it." I sigh. "Why don't you uncock that gun first. If you twitch, you're going to be talking to yourself."

"Karl made me an offer," Frank says. "Five million in cash if I told him what you did with Iris. He was *sure* you knew."

"What did you say?" I ask.

"I told him I had no idea where she was." Frank's stare turns glacial. "Karl said that if I gave him *closure*—one way or the other, Iris dead or alive—I'd get the money. And there'd be another million if I was willing to testify about seeing you hurt her."

By then she was in San Diego. Or Riverside.

"I had nothing for him," Frank says. "But at least he said it was over as far as I was concerned. He was going to leave me alone, and I didn't have to worry about being charged with anything. It was a real load off."

I know what he means. Now Frank is scrutinizing my face again, and I slide my chair back a couple of inches.

"So you're free," I say. "Why this?" I motion to the gun.

"Like I said, it's for shooting you."

He stands in full view of the window, and I wonder whether anyone passing by will see that I'm being held at gunpoint. Maybe they already have, and they don't care. Nobody around here knows or cares about me.

"Guess what?" Frank says. "I think I might be sick."

I notice dark rings around his eyes and an unhealthy sheen to his skin. He's less muscular than he used to be, on the edge of gauntness.

"AIDS?" I ask.

He frowns. "Not yet. Not as far as I know. But something's going on. This ain't just the aging process, baby."

I feel for Frank, but I'm also aware that I might precede him by several years in learning the secret of the great unknown.

"Mind if I get us a couple more beers?" I ask.

"Yeah. Okay." He seems thrown off; he points the gun away and moves to the window, where he parts the curtains and looks outside.

I go into the kitchen, watching carefully out of the corner of my eye to make sure he hasn't followed. I open up the fridge and get out two more beers. When I go to the counter for a bottle opener, I take a deep breath. There, on the cutting board, is a bread knife. It isn't big, only about five inches long, but it's serrated and very sharp. I feel a slight tingle on my neck, as though someone is touching me.

"Are you hungry?" I call out.

"Don't worry about it," comes Frank's sarcastic response. He's still in the dining room.

I open a beer then, with a furtive motion, grab the knife, and stick it in the waistband of my slacks, pressed against my spine. I am sweating, and my vision is slightly blurred. *Concentrate now.* I untuck and fluff out my shirt to cover the knife. I feel the blade, cold and sharp, although for the moment it doesn't cut into my skin. I open the second beer. Frank is still in the other room.

I hand Frank his beer and move around to the other side of the table. He raises the gun and says, "Sit."

"Sure thing." I lower myself. The knife pricks my skin. "You know, you have a beer in one hand and a gun in the other. You look like an episode of *Cops*."

"That's pretty funny," he says.

In the yellow light, for an instant, I see Frank's features

transform grotesquely—his black hair fallen out in clumps, his teeth missing, his skin mottled with a geography of broken capillaries and spots. Then everything is as it was. My headache is moving in again, a cloud on the edge of my physiological topography.

"Let's talk about what matters," Frank says.

"Love and beauty?" I ask. My voice shakes.

"Don't," Frank says. "Get up."

I do as he says, trying not to wince when the blade pricks the skin above my tailbone. I maneuver to keep facing him, so he doesn't see the knife's outline through my shirt.

Frank comes over and puts the gun to the side of my face, pressed hard against my cheekbone. My knees decide it's time to buckle, and I have to grab a chair back to keep from falling.

"I want the money," Frank says with a little smile.

"What money?"

Frank presses the gun harder; the metal is surprisingly warm.

"Here's a little secret," he says. "Karl told me where to find you."

I take a deep breath, then another. "When?" I ask.

"A year ago," Frank tells me. "He told me you got to the money."

"And you waited until now?"

"I didn't need it until now."

A year. And he shows up now.

"There isn't much left," I say. "I bought this house, I paid for a car. I don't know what you're thinking, Frank. It's not like you're raiding Fort Knox."

Frank angles the gun up, so that the bullet would go through my teeth and into my brain.

"You got away with almost half a million," he tells me. "I don't see too many big-ticket items around."

He's right. "I don't have that much money," I say in a hoarse whisper. I think of Iris. I can't die now. And I think about the knife. I sharpened it about a month ago.

I close my eyes. *If I get a chance, can I do it?*

He's trying to do it again, trying to take everything away from you. He doesn't even hide his greed. You put him down once, and now you're going to have to do it again.

Wait, that isn't quite right. He didn't conspire against me before, did he? *Of course he did. Fucking liar.*

"Where is it?" Frank asks. "Don't tell me you deposited it in the bank. Even *you're* smart enough to know that would have raised too many red flags. It's in the house somewhere. Get it for me."

You didn't finish the job last time. You left him on the floor, you left the slut with her head knocked in and bloodied, but they both got away. Now look. A gun at your head and the girl playing games with you. Makes me sick, how weak you are.

I am vibrating. The floor pulses beneath my leather shoes. Frank taps the side of my face with the gun, not hard, but enough to make me look at him.

"Come on, Jack," he says. "Just hand over the cash. Then we're finished. I won't even shoot you."

"What a great deal," I tell him.

"Fuck you," he says, and spits on the floor. He pulls the gun a foot from my face, aims it across the room, and shoots.

I cry out; the retort is harsh next to my ear, leaving it ringing and feeling wounded. I smell something burning and hear a sharp whine as the bullet hits the living room sofa, passes through it, and imbeds itself in the wall behind.

Frank and I are breathing hard in unison. I smell his fear like a citrus tang.

"It's upstairs," I say.

"Where upstairs?"

"In the bedroom wall." I'm panting. "I tore out a piece of wall and hid it inside. That's where it is."

"Do you need tools to get it out?"

"Yeah. From the basement."

I click on the basement light and we trudge down the creaky stairs together. Frank is behind me, but the light is dim enough that Frank doesn't see the knife.

"Get everything you need," he says when we go into the tool room.

It's dark and cool down here, with sawdust and plaster on the floor. The overhead bulb makes the sweat on Frank's forehead sparkle. I pick out a hammer, a chisel, and a crowbar. Frank takes a step back.

"Put them in here and give them to me." He nods at a wet old grocery bag on the bench. Into the bag go the tools. I hand it over to Frank, who takes it with his free hand while leveling the gun at my chest. We move back up the stairs. The bad lighting saves me—Frank fails to see the blade. I think I can do this.

You can do it. Cut him.

The knife feels hot and alive against my skin. The muscles in my arms and shoulders feel taut and strong.

When we get up to the second story, Frank looks inside the bathroom and turns on the light. Tiles and mortar are everywhere.

"Jesus, Jack," he says. "Hire a professional."

"It's my hobby," I tell him.

We move down the hall to my room. When I flip on the light, I slip the dimmer switch down. Frank doesn't seem to notice that we're in murky half-light.

"Where is it?" He looks at my austere mattress and box springs on the floor, the prefab dressers and the pile of half-read books stacked next to my pillow. He seems momentarily distracted. "You know, you should have spent some of the cash on nice things."

I shrug. "I've been trying to make it last." I look at the gun. "So much for that idea."

"So much for that," he agrees.

There's a plain wooden chair between the dresser and the closet; I give it a nudge, and without saying anything, Frank sits. I turn so he can't see my back.

"Get to work," he says.

I kneel carefully on the floor and trace my hand over the plaster above the baseboard. "It's in here," I say.

"Pretty good," Frank says. "I wouldn't have suspected a thing."

"My father used to work on walls," I mutter. I motion for him to kick the bag of tools over to me. Frank watches as I hold the chisel to the wall and give it a hard whack with the mallet. There's a loud noise, then big chunks of latex patch splinter and fall to the floor. I toss them behind me and begin to pry at the wall with the crowbar, tapping out plaster and gouging hard. I make a big mess very quickly, and I stop to cough when I inhale old dust.

"Come on," Frank says impatiently. "Don't make a big production out of it."

But I can't stop coughing. I sit back on my haunches, put both hands over my mouth, and let loose a cacophony of lion roars and canine wheezes. My lungs feel dangerously inflamed.

The dust settles. I pry away a little more and open up the hole. I peer at the darkness inside.

"Get down here," I say to Frank. "Help me pull it out."

"Get it out yourself," Frank tells me.

"There's a weapon in there." I point at the hole. "I'm not planning on using it. But you should know."

"Hold it." Frank shifts off the chair and crouches next to me, the gun to my head. "What kind of weapon?"

"A club," I say.

"The one you brought to my apartment?"

"The same one," I answer.

"Why didn't you use it on me?" Frank asks.

"I didn't think to," I tell him, honestly.

"You did fine without it," Frank says dryly. "What, were you saving it for Iris?"

I don't answer. I almost want to give him the money. Let it cause him as much grief as obtaining it caused me. But *no, no, no. Can't let him get away with it. He made me lose my mind, and he got between me and Iris. The girl who did nothing wrong but to love me. It was my hand that struck her down, but it was Frank who caused it. Don't fool yourself, Jack. Without Frank it would have all worked out. You'd be happy.*

"Move over." Frank kneels next to me. The gun is pointed in the vicinity of my chest. I imagine a single bullet piercing skin, nicking a rib, embedding itself in the delicate muscle of my heart. Blood, blood, blood, and Frank standing over me. I slide over and put my hands over my mouth to stifle another coughing attack.

Frank kicks the mallet, chisel, and crowbar to the other side of the room. His gun smells of crematorium ashes. He cranes his neck and looks into the hole, rolls up his sleeves, then reaches inside and pulls out a bundle of bills.

"Hundreds. Thousands," he whispers. "Very nice."

A bag of photographs comes out with the money, and a few of them spill; I see a shot of me and my mother in the backyard of one of the houses we lived in, a long-gone morning with the two of us and a puppy she bought for me. I get up on my knees.

"Take it," I say. "Take it and go."

Frank reaches in with his free hand and gropes for another

bundle of bills. It's a hell of a lot of cash, and there's plenty more inside.

I look inside the hole and see clouds roll.

Frank's eyes are wide, his forehead shines with sweat. He looks intoxicated. *He'll have to kill you, you know. How else can he be sure he's rid of you, and how else can he pay you back for what you did to him?*

I groan and arch my back. I reach around and feel sweat soaking through my shirt above my belt. Then I press harder and feel the handle of the knife.

"I see what you were talking about." Frank pulls the truncheon from the hole and throws it across the floor. It clatters and joins the tools on the other side of the room.

I grimace. "I wouldn't have been able to hit you with it," I tell him. "The same way I know you won't be able to shoot me."

Frank looks at me wide-eyed. He has the money, and he has me on my knees. This is his moment. I can read his thoughts: *Yes,* he decides. He hadn't been sure before, but now he is.

He glances down at the hole, unsure how to proceed. The gun drops a couple of inches, and I slide over a couple of feet and reach both hands behind my back.

I pull out the knife. Frank lingers on the hole a moment too long, then moves the gun again. But it's too late. I slash hard across his exposed wrist, feeling the resistance of his flesh give way.

I'm doing it again.

Frank lets out a guttural howl of pain and surprise. He looks at me with an expression so infused with hurt that I pause a second.

The gun goes off. I put my free hand to my chest, prepared to find there a galaxy of pain and damage. I look over at the bed, where a neat hole has been blasted in the side of my mattress.

Frank drops the gun because he can no longer hold it. I

slice again, deep into the tendons of his forearm, and this second wound makes his fingers twitch like the musculature of a hooked fish. I rise up and hit him square in the middle of his face with the knife handle. The skin of his nose splits. He bends down at the waist, moaning, then falls awkwardly to the floor.

I grab the gun and point it at him. *Bang bang.* But instead of shooting him, I switch on the safety and tuck it in my pocket. Blood is gushing from Frank's shattered nose down the front of his shirt. The skin of his forearm has peeled back to reveal gristle and bone. Frank rocks back and forth, making an unusual sound.

I know this feeling from before.

I push Frank down on his back and straddle him, my knees pinning his arms. His eyes open up in shock.

I am panting. Everything's *so* red.

Finish him.

My hands clench into fists.

I shake my head violently, feeling as though I'm trying to throw something off my back. I see Frank. His breathing is ragged, and he moans.

"Hold still," I tell him. I reach over to the bed and pull a case off a pillow. I grab Frank's injured arm, which makes him scream and try to twist away.

"I told you to fucking hold still," I hiss at him. I pull his arm straight and wrap the cloth around his biceps, then tie a simple knot that I pull as tight as I can with my teeth. Frank whimpers and goes limp. The wound is about three inches across and has exposed several layers of his anatomy. I wonder whether he'll ever regain full use of the arm. I get up and tell him to do the same.

Frank stands, shakes, and nearly falls. I support him by pushing him against the wall. Then I bend down and grab a single handful of bills, which I shove into his bloody jacket pocket. "Take this," I say. "Use it to get away."

I half lead, half carry him down the stairs. "How did you get here?" I ask, elbowing him in the ribs.

"Car," he gasps.

"Can you drive?" I demand.

"I can't—"

"You're going to fucking have to."

I grab Frank's mask off the sofa and pull it over his bloodied face. He lets out a shriek of protest that almost immediately dies away.

"Where's your car?" I ask.

"Down . . . down the block."

Frank makes a gurgling sound as though he were underwater. I open up the front door and look around. There's no one, save for a couple of people half a block down the street. I push Frank out the door and tell him to lead me to his car. We step out into the cool night air, our footsteps muffled by fallen leaves, until we reach a dark Toyota. I open the door and help him inside. All I can see of his face through the mask are his eyes, glazed and staring.

"Take what I gave you and go," I tell him. "I don't ever want to see you again, Frank."

I flinch in surprise when I hear him sobbing. He says my name, then his chest heaves.

"I know," I tell him. "Just forget it."

He fishes for his keys with his uninjured arm and is surprisingly adept at starting the engine and turning on the headlights. He looks with hollow eyes at the cones of illumination his car carves into the darkness. Then he's whispering something. I lean in close.

"I could have helped you," he is saying over and over.

"There's nothing you could do for me," I tell him. "We fucked it up."

In his suit and bloodied mask, he could be mistaken for a macabre Halloween party guest. The arm I cut lies limp by his side.

"There's a hospital downtown," I say. "Go there and get your arm fixed. Make up a story. Then get out of town."

He looks up at me through teary eyes. "You're not innocent, Jack," he says with sudden clarity.

"I never said I was."

I watch Frank's lights turn the corner, then disappear. My hands clench at my sides. *Damn. Damn.* The rage is still inside me. At least this time I didn't do what it demanded. I didn't kill him.

FRIDAY

22

Later.

W HEN F RANK HAS GONE, SLEEP IS IMPOSSIBLE. I lie down on the couch, but instead of drifting off, I go into a state of hyper-awareness. I consider calling Karl or even Solomon, asking them if they knew Frank was going to come after me. But I decide against it. I can't expect honest answers from them.

After about half an hour, I get up. There's blood every-where in the bedroom and red spots trailing down the stairs to the front door. A jolt goes through me when I realize there might be a trail of blood leading to where Frank's car was parked. I part the curtains and see a timely drizzle is falling, hopefully enough to wash away the blood.

I go outside. Just to be safe, I plug in my garden hose and wash off my front step and the sidewalk. Then I point the hose at the dogwoods below my front window. If anyone is watching, they'll figure I'm out for a little night watering instead of erasing evidence of an assault I perpetrated an hour ago.

When I'm about to go inside, a police car passes slowly. It doesn't stop. Even now, they won't come for me.

I lock the door quietly behind me. I get out a mop, bucket, and sponge, then head up to the bedroom after a stop-off for some Advil. I make sure the blinds are closed before I turn the light up all the way.

Jesus. Blood is smeared everywhere, the slope of the floor creating bloody rivulets that have coagulated into black pools by the closet door. Chunks of plaster and powdered patch are mashed into the wood where Frank and I stepped on them. I decide to patch the hole tonight. I have a strong need to make everything as it was before the sun comes up.

I choke and gag when I start cleaning with the sponge and rinsing it in hot soapy water. At first the blood expands and smears on the floor, but pretty soon I begin to make headway. After about fifteen minutes, something occurs to me. *Frank said he was sick.*

I drop the sponge and kick myself away from the mess. I hold my hands up to the light. I search for nicks, abrasions, cuts—anything that might serve as an entry point for Frank's infection.

There. Right there. On the webbing between the first and second fingers of my left hand is a small wound. I remember working on the bathroom tile a couple of days ago, how I had been chipping some dried-up grout. I had gotten frustrated and started banging with a screwdriver. That was how I cut my hand. And then I had gotten Frank's blood on the cut. *It's probably fine.* There's no blood on the area right now, although the skin around it is wet and sudsy from the bucket.

"Shit," I say aloud. My hands are shaking too much now to examine them properly.

The weight of this . . . Iris and Frank reappearing within days of each other . . . the rage again descending on my mind . . . the envelope downstairs with my mother's location . . . Frank's blood everywhere in my room . . .

I stamp down to the basement and search around until I find a pair of rubber gloves. I grab a bottle of bleach, which is what I should have been using from the beginning. While I'm there, I get out the bag of plaster patch, a trowel, a mixing tub, and the synthetic mesh I need to close the hole in the wall upstairs. I'll have to come back for the sander and the paint. I don't know what time it is, but morning is coming. I feel a presence around the back of my neck like a finger tickling my ears.

"Fuck off!" I shout. "Leave me alone!"

I look at the basement wall—something is jarring to my perception. There's old wood paneling put up by some prior owner. It's a half-assed, unfinished job. Wispy tufts of yellow insulation poke out the top. I look down at the concrete floor beneath and see a little pool of water.

Tinkling on the casement window. It's raining harder.

I notice plastic sheeting between the insulation and the foundation wall. *Never noticed that before.* It's idiotic—the plastic is trapping moisture against the foundation. The unsettling realization kicks in that this dampness has been trapped against the foundation wall for as long as the paneling has been up.

I grab a chisel and drive it into a section of paneling. I pull hard, and the wood splinters and groans. I hear a soft hissing sound, which I immediately identify as pieces of decayed wall falling against plastic.

One strip of paneling goes, then another. More hissing and crumbling. The paneling runs along the entire front foundation wall facing the street. I begin to panic as I tear away the biggest section yet; big chunks separate from the wall and fall to the floor in clumps. In the process, a loose nail hooks itself into the back of my hand. I might have tetanus to contend with before the main event of Frank's infection.

I light a cigarette and stare at the partial ruin of the foundation. The old paint is faded and blackened with necrotic-looking fungus. The wall looks as though it might give way while I am standing here. I have a vision of the entire front of the house caving in, me in my bed sleeping, falling into a ruin of building material, the money and the club falling out and landing in the street for everyone to see.

Tobacco smoke mingles with the acrid tang of disturbed construction: dusty wood, filaments of insulation, powdered concrete. The place is going to rot out from under me.

I drag in the dehumidifier, switch it to its highest setting, and let it hum away. Maybe it will desiccate the rot. I can't think of anything else to do. I crush out the cigarette, grab my tools, and switch off the light. It's too much to even think about.

The sun is peeking through the bedroom blinds when I finish restoring the wall. I have stacked all the money into a few neat piles on the dresser. Next to it are my photographs and the black truncheon. The hole is closed now, and there's nothing hidden inside. I follow the trail of blood down the stairs with my bleach and bucket. Traffic has picked up outside by the time I pour the bloody water down the bathtub drain and scour the porcelain clean. By nine I'm running the electric sander, and by ten I have finished painting the patch. It looks the same as before, painted mustard with only a little bulge to indicate that the wall was ever anything other than whole.

At eleven, I am out on the front stoop smoking a cigarette and having a cup of coffee. Hero presses his face against the screen door and calls out to me. I look around, finally satisfied that my late-night watering and the rain got rid of all of Frank's blood. It's as though he were never here.

I go inside when I hear the phone ringing. I curse and spill coffee on myself, racing to pick it up before the voice mail kicks in.

Zeke Bailey wishes me good morning.

"Good morning," I repeat back to him. "I want to see Iris."

Zeke pauses. "Man, Jack. Let's not waste time on chitchat."

"Is she there?" I ask. "Put her on. I need to talk to her."

"You're wearing me out, Jack." Zeke sighs.

"Tough," I say. "Maybe I should call her father and see what he thinks."

Silence. "You shouldn't be talking that way, Jack."

"Karl is pretty resourceful," I say. "If he knew Iris was in Minneapolis, I doubt he'd waste time before coming after her. You might get arrested on a kidnapping charge."

"I'm going to pretend you didn't say that." Zeke lowers his voice. "Keep it up and you'll never see her again."

"So you really are controlling her."

"Hold on," he replies. "Let me switch phones."

I hear a shuffling, then twin clicks as one extension is picked up and the other cut off. Zeke is breathing a little harder when he gets back on the line.

"I'm not kidding," he says in a near whisper. "If Iris heard you talk like that, she'd probably have us out of town in the time it took us to pack our things. She's really freaked about him, and about your saying that you saw him the other night."

"You're not keeping her from Karl," I say with sudden clarity. "She's the one avoiding *him*. You'd let her go home if she wanted."

"It's not my place to *let* Iris do anything. She makes her own choices."

This time, I think I believe him. But still I don't trust him; I remember his furtive manner on the bench by the lake yesterday, his scanning of the parkway for cars. He might not be controlling Iris, but he isn't telling me everything he knows.

"She asked me to invite you to dinner tonight, Jack," Zeke says. "Dinnertime is when we touch base. We want you to join us."

I stop short of accepting right away, part of me fearing that I might make some misstep.

"It's just dinner," Zeke says. "We'll make you feel welcome."

Now I hear a voice in the background. I switch the phone to my other ear. It's her.

"Someone wants to talk to you, Jack," Zeke says.

I listen to the phone being transferred. I remember how it felt to wrap my arms around her, my fingers tracing her neck. When she was a student, she often wore a hand-knit blue wool sweater that she bought in Portugal. She was wearing that sweater the first time I touched her breasts, her thin torso twisted toward mine, her breath warm against my ear.

"Jack?" Iris says.

"It's me." Once she left her sweater in bed when she went to class; I pressed it against my face and slept that way an hour after she left. "It's so good to hear your voice. Every time you walk away I wonder if that was the last time I'll ever see you."

"Well . . ." I hear her falter, trying to compose her thoughts, and I can tell that I've confused her.

"None of that matters," I break in. "It's just nice to talk to you."

"It makes me happy, too. Really happy." There's a smile in her voice now. "Are you coming to dinner?"

"Of course I am. If you'll have me."

"If I will have you," she repeats, delighted, as though she has just heard the most clever thing ever uttered.

I hear some more shuffling, and then Zeke is back on the line. "You there, Jack?" he asks, then gives me their address.

It's not far from the library, close to Lake Calhoun. She's been so close all this time. I agree to come over at seven.

"Should I bring anything?" I ask.

"How about a decent attitude?" Zeke laughs. "And maybe a bottle of wine."

"Red or white?"

"Make it white," Zeke replies. "We're having chicken."

23

This Afternoon.

I GO DOWN TO THE BASEMENT AND FIND A 1992 NAPA CHARDON-NAY FROM THE REMNANTS OF A RAID I MADE ON A WINE SALE LAST YEAR. That day I optimistically bought two bottles of white wine—which I never drink—in case I eventually had someone over for dinner. They've been untouched until now. I head up-stairs, judiciously avoiding even a fleeting glance at the rotting foundation I exposed earlier. The wisdom of emperors: if I pre-tend it's not collapsing, maybe it won't.

When I'm upstairs I jump up and down on the floor. *Ha!* The house doesn't fall down. I jump some more, like a boy, say-ing to myself, *I'm going to see her I'm going to see her I'm going to see her.*

I haven't slept, but I'm too charged up to rest. I make a bowl of instant oatmeal, feed Hero some cat food, and work on the bathroom for a while. I mix up a fresh pot of mortar and wedge about a dozen tiles into a particularly daunting corner of floor that I've avoided dealing with. Each time I've worked on it in the past, I've screwed up the spacing between the tiles, leaving me forced to jam them together in the final stage. Without room to grout, the tiles won't hold in place, so I've had to rip up my work every single time. But now it works. It fits perfectly. I stare in amazement at a perfect grid of robin's-egg blue, straight and geometric, a vision of order.

I'm getting better.

I commemorate my achievement by going down the hall and collapsing into bed. Sleep comes, albeit of the fevered and delirious variety; at one point I sense I'm not alone, and I refuse to open my eyes even when I feel a light tickle of fingers on my chest. Another time I hear the phone ring, and I don't so much as stir.

When I wake, the blue sky is streaked with orange and gray. I start, gasp for breath, and scramble for the clock. It's only six. As I surface, my breathing starts to regulate and my blurred vision begins to focus. I think I feel pretty good.

But it's when I stand up that things go wrong. I have a hollow feeling in my ears, as though I'm falling. My head feels hot someplace deep inside. The middle of my chest feels constricted. I put my hands out to the wall. Outside, it's a regular day: cars going past, a girl walking her mutt. But for me it's all grainy and out of focus. My ears ring with silence even when I open up a window.

I wonder if anyone down there would hear me. So I yell through the dirty screen: "You down there! Look up here! Can you hear me?"

She doesn't seem to hear, so I wait for the next pedestrian and try again. It's a young guy sporting a goatee, heading for his standard-issue black Jetta. He doesn't hear me, either.

I close the window and turn. Something has happened to my eyes. I see floating lines in the air, abstract squiggles like great luminescent spermatozoa. On the floor I see ocher streaks where Frank's blood was. When I look at the wall, I can see paint peel away to reveal layer after layer of plaster and wooden wall beams underneath. I put my hands over my eyes and moan when everything starts to turn dark red. *Not now.* I hear a rustle behind me, a touch on the nape of my neck.

I feel the room fall away, but I'm still standing. I peer into a depth so dark that it verges on black. I realize my eyes have rolled up into my head.

What you did to Iris was wrong.

"No shit," I say, although I can't be sure I'm really talking. I feel as though I'm being held up by invisible hands. Things are moving around me. The sound in my ears is a seashell roar.

"I know," I plead. "I can't fix it, not completely. I can't live with it. But now maybe I can do something."

They're very close to you now.

"Who?" I ask myself, panting.

You'll never escape from what you did.

"I know. I know."

But you have a chance to redeem yourself.

I have finally gone crazy. I have totally and irrevocably lost my mind. I blamed the crazy thoughts for what I did, I thought I sensed ghosts. But maybe I was just completely delusional all along.

Wait. That's not true.

"Leave me alone!" I yell.

With that, I drop. My chin hits the floor and I feel spiky warmth that has to be blood.

I lie with my face pressed to the floorboards, my eyes blurred and my cheeks soaked. I feel the weight of the harm I have done, the charred place I've left in the lives of the few who have cared about me. I have done nothing but spread hurt. I have played with lives as though they were thin and insubstantial things. My mind has stubbornly refused to acknowledge the souls of those near to me—the most damaged among them, Iris, has finally taught me that. What did I think was going to happen, toying with the world, then hiding in this house with the walls falling around me? I have to open up in the middle and take it into me, grasp the elusive pulse of reality beneath the veneer of illusion. I know I must *wake up*.

No one has come to punish me. The police, the government, Karl—any of them could have. But they let me stand. I've been granted the freedom to shape my own penitence.

When I get up from the floor, I see a woman sitting on my bed. She's about forty and she wears a plain dress. A blue miasma pulsates around her, coloring the sheets and the walls. Her expression is blank. I think she looks like Iris.

"You're not here," I tell her. "Something is wrong with my mind."

She purses her lips. This isn't a malevolent visage. Her human contours are defined, though she looks slightly out of focus.

"I don't know what you want from me." I stare at her, and she disappears for a second before coming into hazy focus, like a TV image in need of severe rabbit-ear adjustment. Her expression shifts to one of pity.

"Just go away," I say. "I'm going to do something to make things right."

I grab the money and the club, then go out into the hallway and lean my forehead on the wall. The house is completely silent. It's getting dark. I have to leave soon.

Two quick steps and I'm back in the bedroom doorway. *She'll be gone, she'll be gone. I'll have my mind back.*

I crane my neck around the doorway, one hand gripping hard the glossy trim. I paint a picture in my mind of the empty bed, then look.

She's still there.

She looks at me, and I hear my own words inside my head: *They're all around you.*

She gives me a look of grave seriousness. I gently close the door and leave her inside. My vision is blurred, and I fight against the part of me that beckons the hallucinations to intensify. There are things for me to do.

24

Evening.

I PARK BY LAKE CALHOUN, A COUPLE OF BLOCKS FROM THE ADDRESS THAT ZEKE GAVE ME. I shaved, showered, and dressed in extreme haste—and without returning to my bedroom. I was able to cobble together an outfit from the laundry basket in the hall—wool slacks and a blue button-up, topped off by an old blazer from the closet in the spare room. I figure wearing a tie will be unnecessary.

I stop for a cigarette. The wind carries a sobering bite. People are walking the paths in jackets and sweaters. The small boats anchored at the lake's north shore are covered with tarpaulins; they look like ducks with their heads sunk under the water in search of food. The earth has tilted, and there will be a lot of dying before the freeze. The gray sky has begun to

conspire with the water to dim all the violent shades of sum-
mertime. I stamp out my smoke and head back to the car.

I retrieve the bottle of wine from the passenger side, then
feel around the floor under the driver's seat until my hands
touch what I was looking for: the black truncheon, retrieved
last night from the hole in my wall. It feels cold and hard. I jog
over to a trash can across the street and throw the truncheon
inside. I should have gotten rid of it years ago. I rid myself of it
because after last night I realize that, in some fashion, I have
been expecting to use it again.

I double-check the address as I walk—in the process discovering I still have Kim's and Solomon's cell phone numbers in
my pocket—until I find a two-story wood-shingled duplex. The
flowerbeds on either side of the front porch are covered with
dead leaves. The street is quiet, save for a man raking. A car
passes, its headlights on.

I ring the bell and look around at the screened-in porch. I
see a couple of sleeping bags, some U-Haul boxes, an old vinyl
beanbag chair.

The door opens with a clatter, pulled with a grunt by a tiny
woman. She's barely five feet tall and has a dense mane of hair
and thick glasses that make it impossible for us to make eye contact. She wears jeans and a sweater about five sizes too big.

"Yes?" she asks, wary.

"I'm Jack Wright," I tell her. "I've come for dinner."

"Jack Wright." She folds her arms.

"Zeke and Iris invited me," I say, converted into a convincer.
I hold up the bottle of wine.

"They did?" She glances over her shoulder with uncertainty,
one hand still on the door as though ready to slam it shut. She
mutters something, then opens the door all the way. Zeke comes
down the hall dressed in one of those Foreign Legion sweaters,

along with a pair of ostentatiously distressed painter's pants. He looks over my shoulder at the street.

"I came alone," I say. "Don't worry."

He shakes my hand absently. I already feel like an over-dressed yuppie. The decor, such as it is, leans toward thrift store shabby, with a worn-out sofa and 1970s-vintage coffee table in a living room off to the side. It reminds me of the student apartment I never lived in.

"This is Leslie," Zeke says, motioning to the dour little woman, who is standing with her arms folded over her chest. I offer my hand, and after a moment of consideration, she grazes my fingertips. When I walk with them across the foyer, though, her expression changes from impatience to interest. She flips on the light.

"What happened to you?" she asks.

Zeke lets out a whistle of appreciation. "Looks like you tried to clean that up, Jack, but you didn't do a very good job."

I look in a little streaked mirror hanging in the hall, distracted for a moment when I see Iris's coat hanging among windbreakers and sweatshirts. I hear a clattering of pans from someplace as I lean close to the glass to examine my face. I remember falling on my chin earlier; I made a perfunctory attempt to clean the wound, but Zeke is right—it's a mess. The skin is split and discolored, and a line of dried blood runs down my neck. I'm appalled and faintly embarrassed to have showed up in such a state.

"We have to clean you up right away," Leslie says, reaching up to adjust the angle of my face.

"Jack, there's *stuff* in it," Zeke says disgustedly. "What did you do to yourself?"

I stare at myself in the mirror. There are bits of white material in the wound. Plaster from the wall, I think.

"Come on," Leslie says. She takes my hand, startling me with the warmth of her touch. I'm halfway down the floral-papered hall when Leslie gives me a little shove into a tiny bathroom with a spotless tub and a thick plastic shower curtain decorated with all kinds of aquatic life. The window is propped open with an old Sanka can.

"Sorry about the trouble," I say to Leslie.

She has the medicine cabinet open and is rooting around inside. She looks at me, decides something, and slips around to close the door.

"I've heard about you," she says, pulling out a tube of ointment and wetting down a washcloth. "You sound like a decent person. I sort of feel like I know you."

Leslie brushes her thick brown hair from her eyes. I sit on the edge of the tub, and she leans close to me. I get a smell of citrus. Her sweater is so thick that I can't imagine how she stands it.

The sink is as spotless as the bathtub, a sure sign of female inhabitation. There are six toothbrushes in a coffee cup to the side of the tap, along with two tubes of off-brand toothpaste.

"Hold still now." Leslie hovers over me, gently pressing the washcloth to my chin. I wince in pain, but when her elbow brushes my chest, and I see her tongue pressed against her upper teeth, I have to will away a wave of sexual arousal. Leslie wets a cotton ball with hydrogen peroxide and, without warning, presses it against my face. It lets out a hiss, and I give a yelp of pain.

"You're a mess," she says, almost appreciatively.

I hear a polite knock on the door. Leslie takes my face in both hands and moves in close. I smell her hair and can tell that it was recently washed. She presses her fingers against my jawbone and temple. She's a lot stronger than she looks.

"Dinner's almost ready," says a male voice from the other side of the door.

Leslie runs her hand down my face and, for a fleeting second, touches my shoulder.

"You can open the door," she says, pulling away.

I thought the guy outside was young from his voice, but when he opens the door I see he's about forty, maybe older, with a ratty beard and a hippie knit hat. He's dressed in clean but astonishingly unfashionable slacks and a button-up shirt with a creased collar. He makes me think of a small-town minister. I nod at him, and he gives a neutral smile.

"I'm David," he says. "You got a nasty cut there."

"Jack Wright," I say.

"I know," he replies softly. "How'd you do that?"

"Tripped and fell."

David's brow wrinkles. "Well, I'll let Leslie finish. Then we can eat."

Leslie gives David a look of impatience. The door closes. "It's not so bad now that I cleaned it up," she says with satisfaction. She applies cream over the wound with quick, fussy movements.

"Come on, you can tell me," she says, focused on her work. "How'd this happen? You get in a fight?"

Her voice has softened and is almost husky. Her tiny torso is so close to mine that I am almost holding her by default. I feel very uncomfortable.

"I fell. In my bedroom." I tell her. "I . . . wasn't feeling well. I sort of fainted."

Leslie makes a little clucking sound, either of reproach or of sympathy, then takes out a square bandage and presses it lightly to my chin. I hear music from somewhere outside—jazz, soft, quiet. Lionel Hampton, maybe. Iris and I had one of his CDs.

I feel the synthetic pad attached to my face, and my eyes wander to a shelf and the space allotted there for tampons and sanitary pads. For a second I wonder whether, as a joke, Leslie has put a feminine hygiene product on my face.

Her hand moves through my hair, making sure she's cleaned out all the debris. It stops at the top, and her fingers explore.

"What's this?" she asks.

I know what she's talking about. It's been aching.

"Nothing much," I said. "Just an old injury."

"You've got a knot here," she says, pressing and making me hurt. "Feels like a lot of old scar tissue."

"Please stop doing that," I tell her. "It hurts."

"You hurt yourself a lot, don't you?" Leslie asks. "Where'd you get this one? Someone hit you with a baseball bat or something? Do you get in fights all the time?"

"Almost never," I say, tilting my head away.

"Well, whatever," she says with a theatrical expulsion of breath. "You're done. All cleaned up."

"Thanks. I guess I didn't know how bad it was."

"You're not taking care of yourself very well," she tells me. She puts her hand on my face again, touching my ear where my hairline begins. She leaves it there too long.

"I guess we should stop holding things up," I say. I stand, and the difference in our height destroys the unsettling intimacy. I edge my way past her.

Down the hall are two closed doors. Six people, two bedrooms. No wonder there are sleeping bags on the porch. I open a swinging door with light on the other side. The kitchen. Zeke calls my name from over the sink, where he holds a colander of pasta and a dishtowel over his arm. There's a tall guy next to him, watching the clock wind down on the display face of an old microwave oven. He's about six feet five, with thick lips and a frame devoid of muscle. Our eyes meet and he looks away as though he's too frail to make any kind of spontaneous contact.

"That's Jack," Zeke says to the tall guy. "Go on. Introduce yourself. You know what we talked about. Self-confidence, man."

The tall guy comes over slowly, as though he's walking into the wind. When we shake hands, he flinches away from making eye contact. He's so thin that he could carry water in the hollows of his clavicles.

"What's your name?" I ask.

"Mark," he says in a deep voice, then, with palpable relief, he scurries back to the safety of his vigil over the microwave— safety being a relative term, because the oven is oversize and ancient. I can't imagine the radiation it must be shooting into Mark's lower torso.

Still no Iris. I look around and wonder what kind of rent they might be paying. The fridge is old and noisy. The linoleum is of a vintage that it apparently defies attempts to clean it. The kitchen utensils splayed across the range and countertops are mismatched and old, looking like the bounty of yard sales and secondhand shops.

I wonder who does what here. Zeke works, but Iris is incapable. Mark looks fit for little more than hiding in a quiet room with his head in his hands.

Leslie comes in, ignoring me, our interlude in the bathroom forgotten. Zeke puts the pasta in a big bowl on a table by the window. I can't believe we're going to eat there—it's barely able to bear the weight of the bowl—but a set of folding chairs around it confirms my apprehension.

"So there are six of you?" I ask Zeke. He's got my wine in one hand and a rusted corkscrew in the other.

"We've had folks come and go," he tells me. "Right now there are six of us."

I resist the impulse to start searching the place for Iris. She's here somewhere. I can feel her.

Six toothbrushes for six misfits. I see no apparent signs of a Heaven's Gate meltdown waiting to happen here. Instead it looks like a poor, postcollegiate slacker household. It's not my thing, but it's hardly sinister.

"Is everyone here?" I ask.

Zeke gives me a small smile that I immediately recognize as false. Again I can tell he's waiting, or looking, for something.

"No," he says. "Cheryl isn't here. She works at Blockbuster and couldn't get off. She's also training for a marathon, so she'll probably go on a run after work."

I try to imagine someone winning a marathon and giving thanks to her inspiration: a brain-damaged woman who has trouble temporalizing and expressing abstract thoughts.

Leslie looks up as the kitchen door opens. It's Iris. She comes into the room as though her feet aren't touching the floor. Her hair is pulled tight from her face and stuffed into a black knit cap. Her face is clean, and her mottled skin has recovered some of the glow I remember. She wears all white, from a billowy blouse to an equally spacious skirt that hangs down to her bare feet. She hasn't noticed me in the corner; it's as though it takes her an inordinate amount of time to comprehend the coordinates and axes of each new space she enters.

Iris looks from face to face with blank serenity and benevolence that makes me breathe hard. The whiteness of her clothes absorbs the light and sends it back to me in a wave of unsettling grace. She looks older. She looks beautiful. Her slender body is erect, and a playful suggestion of a question crosses her lips when she sees me. She says nothing, instead acts as though my presence here is perfectly ordinary and natural. I can't account for the way I'm feeling. My former relationship with Iris was suffused with intense love, but it was a worldly relationship even at its best; we were no strangers to firestorms of temper or the blunt force of crossed purposes. Such things seem impossible now. She stands among us like a ghost, yet she is somehow *more real* than any of us.

I put my hand against the wall to get my bearings.

Iris's gaze lingers on Mark until he is forced to look up and acknowledge her. She has saved a special look for him of wordless complicity and affection. I see him relax, the air around him more clear and easy. He returns her smile, and I can see that he is a sweet soul torn up inside.

"Let's set the table," Iris says. Everyone mobilizes. David emerges from the back of the house with bustling efficiency, wiping plates with a cloth and arranging them with effortless care. Zeke and Mark start moving chairs. Leslie brings the rest of the food to the table—chicken breasts, plain white rice, snow peas. It's simple, but it looks good.

"Can I help?" I ask.

Iris comes over and lightly kisses my cheek. She moves cautiously, as though remembering recent mishaps wrought from her neurological impairment.

"You've done enough," she says. "You came to visit."

She moves to look into my eyes, and I feel a wave of warmth. She says my name and traces my face like a blind woman. She pauses on the bandage.

"You're hurt," she whispers.

"I'm going to be all right."

She has just washed; her tangy body odor of recent days is gone. I look into her blue eyes and feel pulsing radiance that is apart from, and unrelated to, anything I've ever known. She's not the woman I almost married. I feared I would feel like a pretender and a renegade here, but I am more at home than I have felt in years. She seems deeply grateful I'm here. I feel all the masks and illusions slip away, and I now know that we can be together if I want it to happen.

I look away. I don't deserve to feel this way.

When I look back, I reach up without thinking and wipe away the tears that have slid down her cheek. I take one of her hands. We sway together, as though in a slow dance.

I remember the first time I saw her. Her beautiful face and perfect black hair, her youthful body and the purposeful way she moved. I remember the first time she looked at me, her interest sparked beneath what I took to be sophisticated indifference. I remember her in the morning, sleeping while the sun shone through the curtains, her mouth open in the innocent breathing of sleep.

She looks at me. I know she remembers.

I put my face to hers. Her cheek is rough, but I hear the softness of her breath and know that I will never be absolved or forgiven. But I can *live*. She has just given me a gift. I don't know how she does it. There are no words for it. I have made her into this person.

We pull away slowly, each of us unwilling to sever the connection too quickly. There are tears on her cheek, but she is smiling with love and recognition of what I am.

I see her for what she is now. I love her so much I could die from it.

"Come to the table," Zeke says quietly. He squeezes my shoulder with brotherly respect, tacitly acknowledging my reaction to the power of her presence. I feel too sensitive, almost desperate, with every nerve in my body and every receptor in my brain opened wide up.

Everyone at the table is waiting for us so they can start eating. I don't know how long I was with Iris. I sit between Leslie and Mark. Iris sits next to Zeke across the table. We are complete.

A candle burns in the middle of the table, and someone has turned off the ceiling fixture. Each place is set with a small cup of wine. The chicken and rice are steaming, and I am ravenous.

Everyone is waiting. Iris stares down at her lap, her lips moving slightly. She looks up, and a stir of excitement passes over all of us.

"We've come a long way to be together," Iris says. She stares at the flame. Everyone at the table is looking at her. Zeke casts a glance at me but quickly averts his eyes when he sees me looking back.

"When we were young," she says haltingly, "we fantasized about the years ahead, about the shape our lives might take. But none of us knew what the years would do to us, we didn't understand . . . the things that would happen. We don't—I don't know. I don't really pretend to know what it means."

She laughs softly.

"But it happened. Life," she says with renewed determination to finish her thought. "And now we're here, today, at this table inside this house. What I'm saying, is that we're together tonight. The best we can do is for us to love each other. And that's what it all means. That's what it was all for."

I close my eyes and listen to the refrigerator humming. I treasure the cadence of her voice.

"Bad things happened that changed me," she continues. "You've let me share that with you. Now, Jack, we can start to share the things that hurt us both."

Her voice gains strength, and she gives me a conspiratorial look.

"When you found me . . ." She looks at Zeke, then Leslie. "I could barely talk then. I didn't know my name, or what had been done to me. But you were my friends. You respected me, and you love me. And you are . . . now you are my life."

David gives her a smile of unabashed devotion. Mark stares

at his interlaced fingers with rapt concentration. Next to me, Leslie nods and whispers to herself.

Why? Why?

I crave her approval, the benediction she bestowed upon me minutes ago. If it means befriending these strange people, then that's what it will take. I am willing.

I begin to feel dizzy.

"We talk and talk. Sometimes that's all we do." Iris wrinkles her nose indulgently. "About the stuff we probably used to laugh about. Peace and compassion. How some of us suffered yesterday . . . and today, still. And God. Then one of you remembers to pay the rent. It's so selfless, the way you work for all of us. For me. It makes me so very grateful to you."

I understand all at once that this is for my benefit. I sit back and take a deep breath.

"We've all lost things," Iris continues. "And we can't . . . get them back. But I don't want to. I have brothers and sisters now. Still, we all remember. I remember a lot of . . . a lot of things. I remember more things every day. You, Jack. I got so excited when I saw you. Remember?"

A surge of collective excitement passes over the table. I am now the subject of fond looks and appreciation.

"It's the way things happen," David says like a fond older brother. "We moved here not knowing why. But Iris had been talking about you, and when she came home a few days ago saying she saw you, then everything made sense."

"We were brought here to find you, Jack," Leslie tells me.

"Iris always told us how much you loved each other. Sometimes it's all she can talk about," Zeke adds.

Everyone is looking at me, waiting for me to say something.

"I . . . I really couldn't believe it when I saw you," I tell Iris. "Here, after all the time, and after all the . . . uncertainty. I wondered every minute of every day where you were. And it was such a shock to see how much you . . . how you changed."

I stop. I have been speaking without thinking. *How you changed. How I changed you.*

"I know," Iris says quietly. Her hands are shaking, and she rests her head in one open palm.

"I'm sorry," I say.

"You knew me better . . ." She lets her mouth hang open, and her eyes scan the room as though she thinks the words she seeks are hidden there. "Better than anybody. You loved me . . . before. I remember. I hope. I have hope."

"It's okay," Leslie says softly.

"I hope you still love me," Iris says to me softly.

I close my eyes and feel my head drifting.

"I do love you," I tell her. "I love you so much."

Iris smiles.

The first time I told her I loved her, we were walking across a bridge over the Charles River on an autumn night. We had been walking for hours. She was wearing my leather jacket and a green scarf that caught the wind and blew behind her like a flag. She had begun the walk irritable over something or other related to school, but the motion had calmed her and she had traced the breezes with her fingertips. I stopped her on the bridge, held her, and told her what she already knew.

"I'm sorry I ruined everything," I tell her. "I don't know how things went wrong. But I want to help now."

"Jack," Iris says.

"All I want to say is that I'm sorry for everything and that I'm going to do better. I'm going to *be* better."

My voice sounds hollow and formal. I fear that these people are going to suspect my crime. Instead they turn to Iris; she is far away, remembering something.

"I forgive you," she whispers.

I've been crying without realizing it, and her absolution stings like acid. I let her redemption beat against the petrous barricade of my guilt. It isn't right. I can't feel right, I don't deserve it. But there's no other hope for me.

I can't continue like this.

I look up. Iris has been watching me.

"I know," she says. "Do you really remember now?"

"I think I do. Please forgive me," I say, my voice breaking.

"I love you," she replies.

I'm looking down, and I feel like a lost boy. I nod vigorously. I can sit at this table. I can be in her presence.

"Do you know where your mother is?" Iris asks.

I look up, glance around the table. I'm not sure who she's talking to. "Jack," she says, her voice clear and strong. "Your mother. I just remembered. She was lost. Where is she?"

"I know where she is," I tell Iris. "I just found out."

Iris's face in the candlelight catches shadow, and her expression flickers with sorrow and some unfathomable knowledge.

"Go to her," she tells me.

"I can't," I say. "I just can't."

She just keeps looking at me. I can tell I'm hurting her, which is the last thing in the world I want to do.

"Iris, it's been too long," I say.

"You need her," Iris replies.

The mood at the table is suddenly uncomfortable; I can tell I'm saying the wrong thing.

"You don't understand," I plead. "It's complicated. I don't know how I can—"

"Please," Iris says. "For me. It's important. You have to know who you are."

I sit in disbelief over how the conversation has shifted. Still no one has served the food, and I can tell that no one will eat until this matter is resolved. *Go see my mother?* The notion is riddled with impossibility and obstacles too painful to surmount. But part of me knows Iris is right. I've dared to ponder resolution and to entertain the notion that my life could resume from its terrible stagnation.

"Go be John," she says, her eyes shining and powerful. "Then you can come back and be my Jack. Then you'll understand everything."

"All right," I say. I can barely believe what I'm hearing from myself. "I'll go to her. All right."

Iris forgives me. Iris still loves me.

SATURDAY

25

The Next Afternoon.

I ARRIVE IN CINCINNATI AT FIVE IN THE AFTERNOON. It took an eternity to haggle at the airport in Minneapolis to buy same-day tickets for cash—not so easy these days, just try it—then waiting to be screened by airport security. I had to empty out my bag and turn all my pockets inside out before I was allowed onto the concourse. At the gate I had to take off my shoes and stand in my socks while a man waved an electronic wand over my abdomen, lingering long to apply a hefty radiation dose to my genitals. I am traveling light, with a single change of clothes, some cash, and my photographs in my bag. Tucked inside the back pocket of my suit is my mother's address and phone number. I am bound for Tree Hill.

I was able to pack for this trip only because the apparition in my bedroom has disappeared—and gone with it, for the moment, is the fog that so often drapes itself over my mind. I feel vital, clear enough to make plans. I am also giving serious consideration to never entering my bedroom again.

And in that spirit, for reasons I don't quite understand, I brought all my money with me to the Minneapolis airport, where I stashed it in a duffel bag inside a locker in the outer terminal. The key jingles in my pocket when I walk.

"The phones are over there, Jack," says Kim.

Oh, and Kim. I brought her, too. I woke up this morning grasping at fragments of the night before—the mundane oddity of it all, the devotional simplicity of Iris's friends that had infected and swept me away. I promised Iris I would see my mother. When I return, she has promised me that I will be brought close to her again. I can neither argue with her nor let her down. So I packed, called Northwest Airlines to see what flights were available, and got in my car.

Then I went back in my house and called Kim on her cell phone. I can't face my mother on my own, and whatever the conditions of my renewed relationship with Iris, I doubt that spontaneous interstate travel is included. I could think of only one person whose role in my life approximated friendship.

"Weirdo. Jack." Kim is pointing at a big bank of phones clogged and congested by business travelers and families.

"Sorry," I tell her.

Kim gives me a "What have I gotten into?" look. This is the first time I've seen her away from the office, and the effect is unsettling. We're an odd couple: me dressed in my brown suit and light green shirt, Kim in a short red dress that exposes the bony lines of her neck, red-and-white striped tights, and black cowboy boots stitched with scorpions and cactuses. She was eager to accept my offer of a short trip with all expenses covered, but I can see in her expression a dawning realization that she knows precious little about me.

For my part, I'm chagrined that I dragged her into this. I've revealed the barest details about my mother and the reasons why I haven't seen her in so long. Nor have I made it entirely clear that this journey we're taking together isn't a prelude to a shift in our relationship into deeper intimacy.

I pick up the phone and look for the coin hole. There isn't one, so I fish in my pocket for my credit card and slide it through the slot. I get out the piece of paper and call the number for the assisted living facility where Karl's investigator found my mother for me.

The phone picks up on the second ring. It's a recording, a young woman's voice with a whisper of Appalachia.

"Thank you for calling the Tree Hill Assisted Living Facility. If you know the extension for the individual you're trying to reach, please press it now, followed by the pound sign."

I look down at the piece of paper. There's just my mother's name, an address, and the main number. No extension or room number.

"Weekend visiting hours are from nine A.M. until four P.M. Visitors will not be accepted after that time unless a prior appointment has been—"

I hang up the phone. I could have stayed on the line and seen if I could make special arrangements. But no. It can wait until tomorrow. I'll take any excuse to put it off.

"What's wrong?" Kim asks.

"Nothing," I tell her. "We're too late. We'll have to go in the morning."

Kim shifts the weight of her old canvas bag. I reach out and take it from her, grunting a little.

"Well, what now?" Kim asks me.

"I'll buy you dinner and we'll get two rooms at a hotel," I say. "We can go see my mother in the morning. If that's all right with you."

"I'm just along for the ride," Kim says. I can't tell whether she's relieved or disappointed that I don't expect us to share a room.

"One more call," I say. I slide down onto the metallic bench next to the phone, run my credit card through again, and call the number for Iris's house that I extracted from Zeke before leaving last night. It rings and rings, but no one answers. I should have known they wouldn't have voice mail.

Kim is standing by a window watching a big Delta jet creep across the tarmac toward a gate. Everyone is looking at it.

"Come on," I say. "We'll take a cab downtown. I want to buy you a nice dinner."

"Okay," Kim says. "Then you can tell me why we're really here."

We find a taxi, and soon we are sliding through traffic toward the center of town. Kim looks out at the still-green hills and picturesque topography of this river city. Each dot on the hillside, each far-off building revealed by another curve in the highway, leads me to the inescapable thought that my mother is out there somewhere. And I am going to see her in the morning, for the first time in almost seven years. She will be nearly fifty-five years old, far too young to be living in a nursing home or whatever Tree Hill is. I suppose she could have had a stroke, an accident, anything. I wonder what she looks like, and I wonder what I will look like to her.

The downtown is small and feels cramped; I allow myself to sit back and take in what to my eye is an architectural mix of Midwest utilitarian and southern Gothic. It feels like a place that isn't quite sure where it should be, which side of the river to hunker against. I have the taxi driver take us to a good hotel, where I rent adjacent rooms for Kim and me. I drop her off at her door, then go to my room to have a cigarette. I am looking at my face in the mirror, trying to see with my mother's eyes, when there's a knock.

"Hello, sir." Kim has changed her entire outfit; now she's in an old lady's flowery dress topped off by a bright crimson scarf. She steps past me into my room, finds the pack of cigarettes, and lights one for herself.

"No wonder your bag's so heavy," I say. "You have a lot of costume changes in there."

As soon as I speak, I regret it. My banter with Kim has always been vaguely antagonistic within the safely demarcated territory of the office. Now we're alone in a hotel room in southern Ohio.

"What I mean to say is that you look nice," I tell her. Kim flops into the chair by the window, gives me a sweet smile. I join her, and we look out on the dark waters of the river for a while. Kim breaks the silence.

"Why did you bring me here?" she asks.

I can tell by her voice that she apprehends that the reality of this trip is far more unsettling than the capricious idea I sold her on the phone several hours ago.

"I need a friend," I tell her.

"A friend," she repeats.

"I haven't seen my mother in a long time."

"And why is that?" Kim asks, puffing on the cigarette. Her nose is a little too big for her face, but it draws attention to her eyes, which are so dark as to be almost black.

I pause. "It's hard to explain."

"*You're* hard to explain, Jack." Kim sits up straighter in her chair. "I think you're a nice guy, but—"

"I'm trying to be a nice guy," I say.

"Let me finish. I think you really *are* a nice guy. Which is why I dropped what I was doing when you called to invite me on this trip. But I can't read you. I mean, I've been hitting on you for how long? I'm starting to feel embarrassed. Now you're bringing me to meet your *mother*. Aren't we supposed to date first or something?"

"Kim." I kneel down on the floor next to her chair. "I guess I called you because you're the only person I could think of who I trust."

"That's sort of pathetic, Jack," Kim says.

I laugh, and it sounds forced. "Maybe so."

"You didn't bring me here because you wanted to ask for my hand in a nonconfining but mutually satisfying relationship. Did you?"

"No," I say.

"Give me another cigarette."

She lights up and stares out the window for a while. I sit quietly, stealing a glance at her from time to time. In my usual myopic fashion, I haven't really put much effort toward trying to understand Kim. She's pretty, but not pretty enough for it to be the first thing I think about her. She always jokes and jabs at me so that I'm on the defensive. I've seen her do the same with other people. But I think her aggressive front has worked too well, and I can see how lonely she is.

I reach up and take her hand. She pulls it away. "Don't," she says. She seems to be close to tears.

"I'm sorry, Kim," I say. "I called you this morning because I like you. That's all there is to it."

"You can't deal with your mother on your own," she says with a hint of bitterness.

"That's right," I admit.

Kim still won't look at me. I get up and sit on the edge of my bed.

"Still want dinner?" I ask.

"You're in trouble, aren't you?" she asks.

I let the question hang. "You could say that."

"Is that what you were talking about the other day, when you were asking me about spirit possession and all that horseshit?"

"Sort of," I say. "I didn't realize you thought it was horseshit, though."

Kim finally lays eyes on me, and to my surprise, her expression reveals a sort of indulgent approbation. It feels as though she's seeing the real me, as though she really is my friend.

She goes over to the phone and reads the laminated card next to it. She picks up and dials two digits with her long fingernail.

"This is 327," she says. "I want you to send up two bottles of wine—a Chardonnay and a Bordeaux. Do you have a vegetarian salad, dinner-size? . . . All right, give me one of those." She looks up at me. "Let's see, we're kind of in the South. Send up a plate of fried chicken and mashed potatoes for my husband here. Charge everything to the room. All right? . . . All right. Thanksalot."

She hangs up the phone. "We're staying in, hubby," she says. "You're going to tell me what's happened to you."

The food arrives and we spread it over the table, which I drag right next to the window so we can watch the sunset and the city lights coming on. I feel a stirring of attraction for Kim after her performance on the phone, and when she takes off her scarf she reveals her figure under her form-fitting dress. I remember the bathroom last night, the strange moment of sexual charge between Leslie and me. I haven't been with a woman in two years, and probably won't be for a lot longer. It's another thing about myself I've lost touch with, and it's almost surprising to feel a heaviness growing between my legs.

"Where are you from, anyway?" I ask her.

"I'm from Minneapolis. My mother's a farm girl and my

dad's Lithuanian. They met at college and had me by accident."
She slices at her lettuce with startling energy. "It's a fascinating
story. But not as fascinating as yours, I'll bet. So come on,
tell me."

I finish off a glass of red wine and think. After I see my
mother and decide what to do with her, I'm going straight back
to Iris. That's my future, and I can't do anything to endanger it.
But I have a feeling that Kim might be able to help me understand what's happened.

"Tell me the whole thing," she says. "Don't censor."

I tell Kim about meeting Iris in Cambridge, then about
Frank, then about our months in Los Angeles. Despite her com-
mand for me not to censor, I find it impossible not to slightly
alter events, and their interpretation, in my favor. I omit the
depths of my social striving, the unflattering extent of my petty
jealousies, my indefensible disregard for the welfare of others.
Instead I accentuate my love, my loyalty, my deep-seated need
for those around me to be happy—even if I have no idea in the
world how to make them so. I can't help but edit here, embellish
there. I want her to like me, to understand that I regard myself
as a basically benevolent man. It isn't easy, to recast events of
the past without resorting to outright lies. She listens without
saying anything, drinking her wine and demolishing the salad.
I start to tell her about what's gone on in my house—the every-
day items inexplicably disappearing and reappearing, feeling a
presence, the flickering lights and strange sounds, the martinis
and the rearranged fridge contents. I finish by telling her about
the woman in my bedroom yesterday and how much the apparition frightened me.

When I'm done, I feel strangely light.

"This is all connected to your mother somehow?" Kim asks.

"No, not really," I tell her.

"Bullshit," Kim replies. "It's all linked. Remember what I told you about identity flux?"

"Sort of," I say, although in fact the expression had cut into me as an apt description of the source of the unremitting despair that has underlined my life since I was a small boy. Had I ever felt at home with anyone, anywhere, then perhaps I would have had a chance to make Iris happy and keep her safe. Instead of leaving her for dead and running away.

"You haven't seen your mother in seven years. Have you seen any other family?"

"No, I don't really have any other family."

"You're cut off," she declares. "You don't know who you are."

"Who does?" I ask.

She pauses, looks at me sadly. "*I* do."

I frown and slip off my jacket, trying not to touch it with my fingers. My hands are greasy from fried chicken, and I've gone through the napkins brought by room service. I go in the bathroom and wash. I wonder if I've told Kim too much.

When I return, she's smoking a cigarette over the ruins of her salad. She's leaning back at a slant and nodding to herself. She can never simply sit correctly in a chair—it's one of the most fabulous things about her.

"What?" I say, sitting across from her. I pour more wine. I have a feeling I'm going to need it.

"What happened to Iris?" she asks. "You left out that part of the story. You haven't seen her in two years, and now she's back in your life. What happened in the meantime?"

I stand there, hovering over her, blinking and thinking.

"She was injured," I say.

Kim shifts in her chair, just a degree, enough to suggest that she might be a little scared of me.

"Did you do the injuring?" Kim asks.

"It was chaotic," I say, then stop for a moment.

"What was?"

"That day," I tell her. "Like I mentioned, our business failed. A lot of money was at stake, and a lot of people were going to be angry."

"And this was enough to make someone injure your fiancée?" Kim asks, reaching for another cigarette.

"No, there was more to it than that."

Kim takes a puff and looks outside. The lights stretch out to the darkness of the river, and the lines of the streets look like sinews and veins in an anatomical sketch. It feels as though the mounting darkness will continue to intensify, deepening until it engulfs every flicker natural and man-made, until there is nothing but the void from which all things are said to have originated.

"What reason is there to hurt anyone?" Kim asks, still looking out there. I see her profile reflected in the window glass. "What *good* reason, I mean."

"None," I reply.

"Then what are the bad ones?" She paused. "Revenge, self-defense. Rage, jealousy."

I don't know what I have done, but Kim stops and looks at me. I slide back down into my chair.

"You were jealous."

She stares at me, and suddenly all the conditions of our previous interaction have been rendered null and void. She has just begun to see the vaguest outlines of who I really am. I feel naked and pale.

"*You* hurt her?" Kim asks. It's an accusation, although a surprisingly gentle one.

"I don't remember. I . . . probably did. Yes, I did."

"You don't remember what happened?" Kim asks, her mouth

dropping into a half-smile. Hers is the expression of someone being told an improbable story.

"No, something happened. I don't remember what."

"And yet you assume your guilt," Kim says.

"I have to." I make a gesture at the past, both warding it off and inviting it back. "I thought terrible things. I was very angry. I attacked my best friend."

"And then Iris."

"And then Iris."

"But you don't remember that part," she continues, "the part where you attacked and hurt Iris?"

"No," I say softly.

"What does she have to say about all this?" Kim asks. "You saw her last night, right? What did she have to tell you?"

"I know she remembers," I say. "I think she didn't for a long time, but she does now. She told me so. She said she forgives me. She said she still loves me."

"And you still love her?" Kim asks.

"Very much."

It seems like a lot of time passes, but I can't be entirely sure. I smoke another cigarette, I stare at the anonymous textures of the hotel room until their contours blur and I could be looking at them through a veil of gauze or lace.

"This is what I think," Kim says.

I look up. I realize that she's been staring at me for a long time.

"Something's fucked you up," she says, in a way that connotes no offense. "I've always known there was something different about you. This day you talk about, when everyone got hurt. Did you get hurt, too?"

I open my mouth but choose not to say anything.

"What about that bump on your head?" she asks.

Startled, I look up at my reflection in the window. My hair

has parted in an unusual place, and even in my indistinct reflection I can see the ridge of scar tissue by my scalp.

"I don't know how I got it," I say. "I think my friend gave it to me when we were fighting."

"Was it bad at the time?"

"I guess so," I reply.

"As for the stuff happening in your house, that could be a ghost, a classic haunting. It could be connected to your house, or it could be a spirit you're dragging around with you."

"Come on," I say. "Shit."

"I said it *could be*," Kim says. "I'm into this stuff. I have a spirit guide, Jack. You probably sensed something like that, and that's why you called me in the first place."

"Because—"

"Because you were entertaining the idea that something supernatural was happening to you." Kim finishes another glass of wine. "You were even asking me about spirit possession, remember? Is that what you were looking for? A reason to explain what you did?"

I can't tell. It's too difficult to remember. How am I to describe the world in which I have been living, with its disappearing time, its inexplicable sights, the memory loss, the intermittent fear that my hand has been guided from without?

"Head wound," Kim says.

She reaches out and touches my scar, and although I recoil for a moment, I let her keep her hand there. She closes her eyes, her fingers tracing the old injury the way she would caress the nape of a lover's neck.

"You've seen a ghost. So what," she says, her eyes still closed. "That doesn't make it real. You're hurt. Your mind isn't right. It doesn't surprise me that you've been seeing things."

"It doesn't?"

Kim shakes her head. "And you should listen to me. I believe in everything, but I don't believe you've been controlled or influenced by ghosts or spirits. I think you've been driven half-crazy by guilt, and that you have an untreated injury that needs medical attention."

I need help?

"Have you been trying to change your life?" Kim asks.

The question is so sudden, so direct and guileless, that I can do nothing but answer it honestly. "I have. There's nothing I want more."

Kim runs her hands through her dark hair. "Well, that's my diagnosis. You think you hurt Iris. Maybe you did. I don't think you're going to hurt me, or else I'd be out of here by now. I'm not really sure you have the capacity to hurt anyone, Jack."

I remember Frank on the floor. She's wrong.

"I want to come to your house. It would be great if it really is haunted. I want to feel the vibrations myself."

"You're strange," I tell her.

"You should talk."

We sit in silence for a while. We can hear the low roar of traffic as though we were at the seaside. The night is overcast, devoid of stars, though I can see the faint outline of the moon through a bank of clouds.

"What do you think?" Kim asks, her voice shattering silence.

"About what's happened?" I ask.

"No," she says, lighting another cigarette. "About who's going to win the Super Bowl."

"I think . . ." My voice trails off. "I think I've had blackouts and hallucinations. And that there's been something wrong with me for a long time. I'd like to think you're right, that I couldn't have hurt Iris. But it feels so much like wishful thinking."

Kim cares for me, I realize, and she wants to see something good in me. I share the impulse, but she cannot begin to comprehend the power of my thoughts the day I hurt Iris and

Frank, the depravity of the voice in my head. Even if I had never laid hands on either of them, I would have been guilty still of an intent that can only be called evil. It came from my weakness, the same weakness that I know I must vanquish in order to help Iris live the best life she possibly can within the constraints of her current condition.

And although Kim wants to open a tempting door toward absolution of some nature, it doesn't work. I think now, I think clearly. So I don't remember. What of it? No one else was there. It was me, Iris, and Frank. And Frank was in no condition to hurt anyone, even if he laid the blow that left the deep scar.

Or Iris. Iris could have done it.

"Maybe it's just a matter of perspective," Kim tells me.

"Maybe," I say.

We sit quietly for a minute, then Kim looks up at me with alarm.

"Are you all right, Jack?" she asks.

"Fine," I tell her.

"Oh, baby." Kim comes over to me and rubs my face with her hands. "It's not so bad. It's over. You said she forgives you."

I can't reply, so Kim takes me into an awkward embrace, my face pressed against the warmth of her breasts, and holds me that way for a while. I hear her heart beating, slow and regular.

"Come on," she says, leading me to the bed.

"I can't," I say.

"Lie down. We'll keep our clothes on."

I lie down next to her, and she puts her arm around me. I do the same, pulling her close. As I'm about to fall asleep, Kim puts two fingers to the back of my head and starts rubbing the base of my skull.

"What are you doing?" I ask in a dreamy voice.

"Massaging your yuzhen points," she tells me. "It shifts your focus from the cortex to the medulla. You need all the help you can get."

"You're crazy," I tell her.

"So are you," she says, and then I am alseep.

I wake in the night with a vision of Iris that takes several seconds to dispel. I extricate myself from Kim's embrace—she sighs in a husky voice and whispers something I can't hear—and go to the phone. In semidarkness I manage to dial Iris's number. It's almost one in the morning, but something drives me to check on her. I inhale sharply when the phone picks up on the first ring.

"The *line* is busy," says a woman's recorded voice. "For one dollar, we will ring you back when the person you are calling is free."

I ponder this for a second, then decide to do it. I punch in the number code for the ring-back service.

I lie down next to Kim and listen to the tranquil rhythm of her breathing. Soon I am asleep again, a good, sound sleep. I forget all about the call-back service I requested and how it didn't happen. How it never called me back.

SUNDAY

26

The Next Morning.

I AWAKE TO BLUISH EARLY MORNING LIGHT THAT WHISPERS
THROUGH THE GAUZY CURTAINS. I push off the blankets and feel
a burst of body heat escape, the room's cooler air against my
neck and chest. I pull my arms tighter around Iris, feeling the
slope of her belly and her soft fingertips. She's wearing a thin
silk camisole, and my hand wanders down to discover that she
didn't wear underwear to bed. I can't remember where we went
last night, but I slept so deeply that my mouth feels thick and
gummed up. My hand moves down to the patch of soft hair between her legs; I linger there, then move up the slope of her hip.
I will go brush my teeth, I decide, and then see if Iris wants to
make love.

I sit up, rub my cheeks. I'm dressed in pants and an undershirt. My morning erection presses against the light brown wool of my slacks. My jacket and shirt are on a chair by the window.

This isn't the apartment I share with Iris. I start, my body jerking. I look back at the bed. *Iris?*

She turns over and I see her face. I remember. Kim. Cincinnati. I shake my head. It's almost eight.

In the shower I trace lines in the steam with my index finger. While I'm shaving I begin to think about my mother.

The way she used to listen to me talk when she was putting on her makeup, absorbing my little-boy prattling with infinite patience. How we would go for weekend car rides with the windows down and the radio playing. The trips to the supermarket, where she would indulge my whims and buy me toys she knew I would discard within the hour. Her shyness and circumspect pride when she attended parent-teacher conferences and listened to how gifted her Johnny was.

These are the things that escaped me and went away when I decided to forget the other things.

I somehow got fried chicken grease on my pants last night—not to mention the fact that I slept in them—so I opt to wear my light green linen suit with a blue shirt. I spend a lot more time than usual in the bathroom fussing over my appearance, drying my hair, and flossing my teeth. I want my mother to see me healthy and happy. I don't want her to worry about me.

Kim has vanished to her room, but soon there's a knock and she enters in a surprisingly demure cardigan sweater and skirt.

"How do I look?" she asks.

"You look great."

Kim examines the room like an archaeologist inspecting

ruins. My fingers tingle in memory of the feel of her body, and she turns away.

"Are you excited?" she asks.

"I think I am," I tell her. I go through my bag and hold up a couple of my best ties, left over from the Lee-Leonard days.

"Wear the purple one," she tells me.

I go to the mirror and hold the tie up to my shirt, then flip up my collar and begin to knot it. Kim gets on the phone and orders breakfast. Maybe this will be a good day. My mother is in a nursing home, but her condition might be temporary. It occurs to me that maybe Tree Hill is an alcoholic rehab facility. Maybe my mother is getting her life together.

I remember her easy laugh. She always laughed when I was trying to be funny. We spent so many years together.

I still have a lot of money. Maybe I can make a down payment on a condo for her. I could arrange to have her brought to Minneapolis, or wherever Iris and I decide to settle down together. I imagine her taking me in an embrace, the tears and smiles of our reunion. I will apologize for being gone for so long, and we'll talk about the future. It's not impossible any longer for me to talk about the future.

"Look at you," Kim says. She sits very primly by the window, her hands folded and pulling her skirt down over her knees.

"What do you mean?"

"Jack, you're smiling at yourself in the mirror."

"I am?" I say, genuinely astonished.

"Don't get self-conscious," Kim tells me. "It's nice to see you happy for once."

Breakfast comes. We have coffee, orange juice, and croissants with jam. We smoke cigarettes. Finally, I get up and fetch a little yellow plastic bag.

"What's that?" Kim asks.

"My photos." I smooth the bag with both hands. "All I have left from when I was a boy. And some from later. I want to show them to my mother."

"Is there a picture of Iris in there?" Kim asks.

I put the bag on the table between us.

"Don't look so surprised." Kim smiles and puffs on her cigarette. "You said her name last night. When we were together."

"Did we—"

"No. But it was nice anyway. You have a very tender side, Jack. I thought so all along." I must look embarrassed, because Kim gives me a disarming laugh and points to the bag between us. "So, is she in there?"

I open the bag and take out the mishmash of pictures in all shapes and sizes: old matte photos, Polaroid instant snapshots, even a few tiny photo-booth images. I see myself as a boy, straight haired and smiling; my mother in a dress, holding an old mutt who died years ago. And a picture of Iris from college: She stands on a street corner in Cambridge in a light snowfall, framed by a brick building in the background. She's wearing a navy surplus coat buttoned up to the neck, and her black hair spills out over the collar. I hand the picture to Kim, who inspects it for a long time.

"She's beautiful," Kim says.

"Well, that was taken about four or five years ago," I say.

I carefully take the picture and replace it in the bag, which I fold over.

"She's the one you're been waiting for," Kim tells me.

"Yeah."

Kim nods slowly. "People change, Jack," she says. "Even though she's back in your life, she might not ever be the person you remember."

I think of Iris's shaking hands, the delicacy of her shoulder blades through her sweater. I see her in the kitchen, floating, her community gathered around her like her children.

"I know," I tell Kim.

I stop in the lobby and buy a bouquet of flowers. I'm on the way out when I tell Kim to wait. I rush back into the gift shop—the doorman is flagging a cab for us—and buy a little white carnation. When I come back outside, I give it to Kim.

"What's this for?" she asks.

"For being with me."

When we get in the cab, I give the driver the address for Tree Hill. Kim is wearing a shy smile as she pins the carnation to her cardigan. She reaches out and gives my knee a squeeze.

"You look good," she says. She pushes my hair from my forehead in a wifely manner, then brushes some imaginary dust off the lapel of my suit. "Your mother is going to be so happy to see you."

We take the highway out of the city past industrial parks and apartment complexes and shopping malls. I'm gently buffeted by the cab's motion, but I feel clearheaded. I hold on to the bouquet for the whole ride; I don't want the flowers to get creased.

Tree Hill, it turns out, isn't on a hill, and there aren't very many trees around. We're on the edge of the city, on a winding access road just a few minutes from the freeway. We pass a couple of nondescript office buildings and a condo community called Willow Falls set around an artificial lake. When the driver stops at the edge of a cul-de-sac, I think he might have made a mistake.

"This is it?" Kim asks.

We're in front of a squat institutional building with rows of rectangular windows that reflect the overcast morning. I had expected fences, grounds, paths, and walkways where my mother and I could meander and talk.

"Maybe there's more in the back," Kim says.

I pay the driver and we get out. The morning is cool, and there is a damp mist in the air. We watch the taxi pull away, then Kim hooks her arm in mine and executes a nervous little hop.

"Who cares what it looks like?" she asks. "We're here. I'm getting excited myself. I can't wait to meet her."

We walk up to the front door, and I see the sign:

TREE HILL ASSISTED LIVING
VISITING HOURS 9–4
Hamilton County

I'm a little surprised that my mother is living in a county facility—and I feel guilty when I think of my money. But I realize that Mom probably wasn't working when she got sick, or she had a job that didn't provide benefits. It doesn't matter. I'm here, and I can help.

Kim and I stop in front of the glass door, looking at our reflection. I stand up straighter, press down on the pictures in my pocket. Kim looks tall and pretty.

"Do you want to tell her I'm your girlfriend?" she asks.

"Why?"

Kim fusses with her hair, staring at herself. "Trust me. It'll make her happy to think someone's taking care of you."

"Okay. But don't start talking about your spirit guide. I don't want her to think I've gone off the deep end."

Kim pokes me in the ribs, but she laughs. "You *have* gone off the deep end. I pulled you back a little. Weirdo."

Then her expression turns serious, as though she has remembered something urgent and it might be too late.

"What is it?" I ask.

"Last night," she says. "The things you told me about. Don't think about them while you're here. Leave it all for later. I don't know if you're ever going to understand what happened to you and your fiancée, but this isn't the place for remembering."

I hold the door for her and put my hand on the small of her back to guide her in. She's right. I can stop being Jack the murderer for a couple of hours. I like the idea of pretending Kim's my girlfriend. We look like a happy young couple. I decide we should tell my mother we're engaged—I can make up a story later to explain why we didn't get married—but it's too late. We're already in the dimly lit lobby, where there's a circular desk and a freestanding ashtray full of old butts.

"Can I help you?" asks an older woman. She has a computer and a multiline phone in front of her, but her real attention seems focused on her coffee and newspaper.

I don't say anything. I'm incapacitated by the reality that Mom is in this building somewhere. I want to hear her voice. I want her to hear mine.

It's me, your son. I've come back for you.

"He's here to visit his mother," Kim says.

The woman looks at me over her glasses, takes in my suit and the flowers. "I don't recognize you," she says. "You been here before?"

"No, never," I say. "This is my first time."

The woman blinks with mild disapproval, or distaste, or something I can't quite identify. Then she flips on her computer.

"You'll have to wait a minute," she says. "I just got here. Have to wait for my computer."

"No problem, right, Jack?" Kim says.

When the computer has finally booted up, the woman puts her hands on the keyboard expectantly.

"Your mother's name?" she asks.

"Sandy. I mean, Sandra Ruth Wright."

The woman types, glances at the screen, then looks up at me.

"There's no one by that name here."

The flowers rustle in their cellophane. "I know she's here," I tell her. "Maybe you typed it in wrong."

The woman raises her eyebrows. "Maybe I *did*," she says, mildly indignant. She types in Mom's name again, with the same results.

"Who told you your mother's here?" she asks me.

"Jack, maybe your mother remarried since you saw her," Kim says quietly.

I snap my fingers. "That has to be it," I say, though the thought is oddly disturbing.

The woman behind the desk purses her lips. "How long since you saw your mama?" she asks me.

"About seven years."

She levels a stare at me but doesn't seem surprised. She must see and hear all kinds of things.

"Chief of staff's out today, since it's Sunday," she says. "But I can get you one of the doctors. Maybe they can tell you something."

"Please," I say. "Do that."

The woman gets on the phone, and Kim stands square to face me. She tugs at the ends of both my coat sleeves and smiles.

"Don't be nervous," she says.

"You can sit over there," the woman says, indicating a worn sofa. "Someone'll be out for you."

I thank her, and we sit together. Kim crosses her legs; I can tell she's every bit as worked up as I am. I listen to my breath, trying to imagine whom my mother might have married. Where's her husband today? Living here in Cincinnati, coming to visit daily? I imagine an older man, living alone, waiting for Mom to recover her health and come home again. Maybe he's *here*.

After what seems too long, a harried-looking woman in a white coat and glasses perched on top of her head comes into the lobby. She casts a questioning glance at the receptionist, then spots Kim and me getting up from the sofa. I compose myself and smile at her. She wears a metal nameplate I have to squint to read in the half-light: CHRISTA DOUGLAS M.D.

"Dr. Douglas," I say, extending my hand to shake. The doctor seems not to want to but acquiesces as I tell her my name and introduce Kim.

"You're looking for your mother?" Dr. Douglas says. She's about forty and has the air of someone thinking of several things other than what she's doing right now.

"I received word that she's here," I say. "She's apparently not in the computer."

"We think her name might have changed," Kim suggests.

"Yes." I pause. "It's been several years since I've been in touch with her. She might have remarried."

"What's her name?" Dr. Douglas asks.

"Sandra Wright," I say. "She goes by Sandy sometimes."

Dr. Douglas squints doubtfully. Her skin is pale, and her hands are lightly bruised.

"I can't think of anyone here by that name," she says. "But we have more than a hundred patients. I guess we should go inside."

"Yes. Please."

Dr. Douglas leads us through a door marked AUTHORIZED PERSONNEL ONLY, and we're in a long, brightly lit hallway that smells of bleach. There are doors—some open, some shut—lining either side. Dr. Douglas turns away, expecting us to follow, I shift the flowers, and Kim takes my hand.

"Come on," she says. "Don't just stand there."

All sound here is muted. I hear the drone of Sunday religious

TV shows coming from most of the rooms. No one seems to be doing much of anything. I glance in a doorway, and an old man looks up at us. He's propped up in his bed, his mouth hanging open. His TV isn't on. He's staring at a plastic plate of food on a tray in front of him. It's only when he uses his left hand that I notice his right arm is missing.

We reach a cordoned-off area with several desks piled high with files and papers. There's a coffeemaker and a box of doughnuts. Along one wall is a row of television monitors; I look closer and see that they're used to watch over patients. An empty bed fills one screen; on another, an old woman is moving slowly toward a sink with the assistance of a walker. A third screen shows someone leaning close over a bedridden patient who puts his hand out and turns his head to one side with a tight-lipped grimace.

I have to get my mother out of this place.

Dr. Douglas sighs heavily and puts her glasses on the nearest desk. She takes out a computer printout and hands it to me.

"These are all our current patients," she says. "You can look it over while I get one of the nurses. They might know more than I do."

The doctor stops to look at me. I'm wearing an expensive suit, holding a bouquet, trying to seem cheerful. Something in her eyes tells me I don't belong here.

"Let's see," Kim says, smoothing out the pages on a waist-high modular barrier. "We'll just find the name Sandra, and then we're in business. She has to be here somewhere."

I scan down the list. There are so many names. George Upton. Mary Jenkins. Bertha Coleman. Andrew Glass. Jane Robinson.

"I don't see her," I say.

Dr. Douglas returns with a stout nurse dressed in an over-size smock adorned with a floral pattern. Her cheeks are fleshy and rose colored. She holds in her hand a plastic bag containing some kind of tubular medical device. Dr. Douglas explains my situation to her; the nurse looks at me as the doctor talks.

"What's your mother's name?" she asks. I tell her. "I don't know anyone here by that name."

"Her name might have changed," Kim says. "That's what we think. That she might have remarried."

"Did you look at the list?" Dr. Douglas asks.

"I've looked at some of it," I say. "But it's so simple. Sandra Wright. Or Sandy. Don't you even know your own patients?"

Dr. Douglas stiffens. "There's no need to take that tone."

"But she's *here*," I say.

Kim looks over the printout with obviously increasing anxiety. "Look, I'm sorry," I say. "It's been a long time since I saw my mother, and I can't understand why you aren't helping me."

"We *are* helping you, sugar," the nurse says softly. "You just relax."

Another nurse appears, a slim older black woman who begins rearranging files on the desk with precise, self-contained movements.

"Becky," the first nurse says. "We're trying to help this man here."

"Becky will know," Dr. Douglas says.

"She's been here the longest," the first nurse explains.

"We have a lot of turnover," Dr. Douglas tells me in a conciliatory tone. "I've only been here a few months."

"I don't know why people keep leaving," the first nurse says to the doctor. "It's so *cheerful* here."

Dr. Douglas stifles a laugh, then nods discreetly at me. Kim is still furiously going through the list, moving back to page one.

"Sorry," the first nurse says.

Becky has been watching all this with impenetrable calm. "You looking for someone?" she asks me.

I feel relief and a tremendous sense of well-being in Becky's hands. Obviously she is going to fix this situation.

"I'm looking for my mother. I was told she is a patient here. Her name is Sandra Ruth Wright."

Becky eyes the flowers, looks at Kim. Then she reaches out and takes my elbow in her hand.

"Wait a minute, don't do that," I say.

"Honey," Becky begins.

"Maybe she was transferred or something," I say. "I can live with that. You must have a record of her transfer. Give it to me, and I'll go. Is she still here in the city?"

"Jack, calm down," Kim says, her eyes widening.

"I *am* calm."

"Honey, I remember your mother," Becky says. "Sandy Wright. She came here after having a stroke."

"A stroke patient?" Dr. Douglas asks.

Becky turns to the doctor. "Ruptured extracerebral artery," she says. "She was a long-term alcoholic."

"Just tell me where she is," I say.

"Jack," Kim whispers.

Becky looks at me sadly. "She had lost most of her speech and motor function when she came here," she says. "She rehabbed for a couple of months, but then she suffered heart failure. I'm sorry, honey, but your mother died about two years ago."

"No," I say. I put the flowers on the desk and rub my eyes. "It's obvious you people don't know what you're doing."

I move away and start down the hall. I'm calling for her. I feel for the photographs. Mom is going to want to see them, all of them. I can tell her all about Iris.

"Jack, no!" yells Kim.

I look in a room and see a woman lying back in her bed with breathing tubes in her nose. Her eyes meet mine.

"Sorry," I say. "Wrong room."

Kim puts her hands on me, but I pull away. I'm still calling Mom, going from room to room. I'll have to go back for the flowers because I left them on the desk. But Kim is here. She can get them for me.

"Mr. Wright!" Dr. Douglas calls, and looks around, not knowing what to do with me.

I go into another room, where a woman is having blood drawn. She's not much older than Mom, but it isn't her.

"Sorry to bother you," I say. "I'm looking for my mother."

Now Kim is holding on to my waist from behind, almost pulling me off the ground. She's saying my name over and over again. Dr. Douglas is standing in front of me, looking panicked and angry.

"Sir, I'm very sorry for your loss, but I have to ask you to leave," she is saying. "You're disturbing the patients."

All at once, I realize my ears have been roaring. The sound stops with an audible pop, and I relax. Kim slides around to my side and puts her arm around me.

"I'll leave," I say. "Okay."

As I'm walking out, Becky stops me. "I'm sorry," she says. "She seemed like a nice woman. She didn't suffer much when she died. I hope that makes you feel better."

I start to say something but realize that I cannot control my voice and I might start to yell. Instead I nod at Becky, and we leave the way we came in. In the lobby, Kim quietly confers with the receptionist and asks her to call us a taxi. I step outside into the morning air and loosen my tie. When Kim joins me, she frames my face in her hands.

"You're going to be all right," she says. "I promise."

"Do you have your cell phone?" I ask her.

Karl knew. He knew the whole time. He wrapped my mother's

death in a package, disguised it as a gift, and sent me here to open it.

Kim takes her phone out of her purse and gives it to me. I fish around in my pockets until I find Iris's phone number. Zeke answers on the second ring, and I move toward a row of bushes in search of privacy.

"Jack, is that you?" Zeke asks, fear in his voice. "Are you at home? Did you have anything to do with what happened?"

He sounds accusatory and terrified.

"What do you mean?" I ask. "I'm out of town."

"Some big black guy broke in the house last night and took Iris," Zeke says, his words coming out in a rush.

Solomon.

I remember the call-back service now, how it didn't call me back. The phone must have been off the hook all night.

"He said he worked for her dad, and that he followed you here Friday night. He threatened to hurt us if we tried to stop him. I think he had a gun." Zeke's voice breaks, and I hear him sob. "He just *took* her away, Jack. Did you know this was going to happen?"

"No," I say.

"I was trying to control the situation," Zeke says, sobbing. "I thought I could manage it. I never should have talked to Karl."

I change hands and put the phone to my other ear.

"You talked to Karl? When?"

"A couple of months ago." Zeke's voice is quiet, broken. "I knew he was looking for us, but we managed to lie low and not get found. It was my stupid fucking idea to call Iris's father. I didn't even tell the others."

"Why, Zeke?" I ask. "Money?"

"I thought I could *manage* the situation," Zeke says, his voice like a bawling child's.

"What situation?" I ask. I look over at the nearest window. Dr. Douglas and Becky are watching me.

"Calling Karl. Finding you. I thought I could grab some money and we could get set up comfortably somewhere. We could stop struggling and live like a real family instead of a bunch of fugitives. I'm the only one who knows how serious the situation is, man."

"You mean you found me in Minneapolis on purpose?" I ask.

"Of course, Jack. You think it was an *accident?*" Zeke demands. "Iris thinks it was, of course. I've protected her from all this."

"No, you haven't, Zeke," I yell back. "You haven't protected her at all."

Zeke begins crying again.

"Karl knows you found me? He knows I've seen Iris?" I ask.

Zeke sobs something that sounds like yes.

"And he used me to find Iris?" I say.

Zeke doesn't even have to answer. I start to press the button to disconnect the call, but I stop myself.

"One thing," I say to Zeke. "You get the fuck out of that house. I'll come back for the others, but not for you. Don't ever come near me or Iris again."

Then I hang up. When I turn around, Kim is standing next to me with a distressed look.

"What happened?" she asks.

"Nothing," I reply. "Nothing I can't take care of."

"Oh, God. Something's happened and it's my fault," she says. She puts her hands over her mouth.

I turn to the window. Everyone's looking.

"Oh God, oh God, Jack," Kim is saying.

"What?" I ask her. I feel strangely calm.

"Oh, Jack, please don't hate me. Don't hate me, please."

I hand her the phone.

"About a week ago this guy came to the office and asked how often you came in. I didn't think anything about it, but now something awful has happened."

"Big guy? I asked. "Solomon Ford?"

"You know him?" Kim slaps spastically at her sides, practically hopping up and down.

"What did he want?" I ask.

"He gave me his number and sort of, I don't know, asked me to call him if I had any information. He said you were in trouble."

"I see."

"Oh, Jesus, Jack, I wasn't thinking."

"It's okay. I understand."

"Jack, he gave me *money* and I took it!" Tears are running down her cheeks and her nose is turning red.

"Money?" I ask.

"Oh, God, Jack, and yesterday I *called* him after you invited me to come with you. I don't know why. I didn't think there was anything wrong. I thought I could help. I was *worried* about you, Jack. You know I care about you."

I could be angry with Kim, but what's the point? She wraps her arms around me and crushes her white carnation into my jacket. Over and over she's saying she's sorry, that she was only trying to help, that she was worried about what was going to happen to me.

I believe her.

The taxi comes, and I help her in. I give the driver the name of our hotel, then tell him we're going to the airport after we pick up our bags.

"Are you coming home?" Kim asks me.

"Maybe," I say. "There's someplace else I have to go first."

27

Tonight.
LOS ANGELES.

FROM THE AIRPLANE WINDOW, THE LIGHTS OF LOS ANGELES ARE
BLURRED BY HARD RAIN BLOWING IN FROM THE SEA. It looks
as though someone has smeared Vaseline over a camera lens.
By the time the plane touches ground, it's nearly dark out. I
breathe deeply and evenly while I wait for the aircraft to pull up
to the gate. Rain pelts my window. In this weather, it's going to
be a hard drive up the coast.

I secure a rental car within forty-five minutes, then take the
shuttle to the remote lot to pick it up. I smoke a cigarette under
a plastic awning advertising cigarettes, inches away from water
streaming from the sky, running down gutters, making puddles
of potholes. It's a sea storm, and I can smell salt in the air. The

smoke I exhale catches a draft of air and accelerates out, out there, where I have to go.

This city has changed since I've been gone. Nondescript strip malls in Playa del Rey have been razed, and in their place have sprung up posh-looking housing developments. I drive as fast as I can, going with the traffic flow up Lincoln Boulevard through Venice. Nothing seems familiar. Maybe it's the rain. I spot Ocean Park, where I would always take a shortcut back from the gym to our apartment.

I only remember it raining like this once. I lay in bed and listened to the rain with Iris beside me. The streetlight outside projected a rectangle of yellow on the ceiling; in it I could see the acrobatic play of raindrops. I thought Iris was asleep, but when I turned to look at her, I saw that her eyes were open.

I nearly miss the turnoff to the Pacific Coast Highway; I have to swerve and change lanes, and a chorus of horns honk behind me. I tense at the wheel and turn the windshield wipers up to the highest setting. They pound out a rhythm: One-*two*, one-*two*, hit the second beat hard. My headlights are barely able to cut through the sheets of water.

Frank said, *What happened to her, Jack? You don't remember.*

Jesus Christ, how my head hurts. I reach up and rub the scar on my head. I can't black out now. I have to drive. I have to *think*.

I almost lose sight of the road. PCH curves along the coastline, and I have to navigate by the other cars' headlights, hundreds and hundreds of white lights proceeding into and out of the darkness. A single driver could lead us all into the ocean.

Frank, with his arm dripping blood. *I could have helped you.*

More speed. I glance in the mirror and see countless headlights. There's no road divider, just two lanes in either direction snaking north. I reach a curve and ride the brakes, doubtful that my tires can maintain traction on the rain-slicked pavement.

Houses crowd one side of the road, a cliff edges the other. A cloud bursts somewhere in the sky, and big drops pelt the thin sheet of metal separating me from the elements.

I don't remember much more. That's what I told Frank before I sent him away.

I think of Karl sending me to the place where my mother died. Me in my suit, flowers in my hand, grinning. I hold the wheel with anger in my heart, thinking of what I might have to do tonight. Karl has finally found her, with my unknowing help, and surely dragged her back home. I know they won't be alone. I don't know what I might have to do in order to take her back. My teeth grind together. Everyone is driving far too fast, in a hurry to get home.

In the end, it could be just me and him. I can pay Karl back for everything he's done.

I shake my head and steer through a curve.

I think of the afternoon when my violence destroyed our lives, the way the golden afternoon light belied the panicked jealousy that exposed my every weakness and fear about myself. I was capable of anything that day.

God*damn,* my head hurts. I'm not well. I'm really not well at all.

Something's fucked you up, Kim said.

Karl said to me, *You really don't remember, do you?*

The traffic slows for a traffic light, then picks up again. I know the way to Karl's house. I remember every landmark along the way. Now I'm out of Malibu; to my left, the ocean is infinite darkness, with no moonlight to illuminate the water. My windshield wipers beat out one-*two,* one-*two.* I have to turn on the defroster; my breath is clouding up the glass.

My mother stood outside the big old schoolhouse with me on my first day of kindergarten because I was afraid to go inside. She held on to my hand until I gathered the courage to face the other children, the teacher, the prospect of being on my own.

Kim said, *Head wound.*

My car is part of a great wave that seems as though it is never going to break. My body is tensed. I can barely see what I'm doing. Why is everyone going so fast?

My heart is beating hard in the center of me. It can't keep going like this. I'm going to explode.

Sometimes I would wake up in the morning, feel Iris's presence beside me, and look at the clock. She always had a terrible time getting up in the morning, and she overslept all the time. If I knew she needed to get up to be somewhere, I would caress her cheek or her shoulder with my mind, and she would stir. I didn't even have to physically touch her.

You have *to know*, Karl said. He looked into my eyes. He searched my eyes. There was something I was supposed to know.

I remember what I need to remember, I told Karl.

But was that entirely right?

My head.

I pass a form on the right side of the road so quickly, I can't be sure what it was. But I tap the brakes, and the car horn behind me erupts with sound. I slow down, put on my signal. I must look crazy. There's no place to turn, nowhere to pull over.

What was—

I slow down more and edge the car off the highway, grinding to a stop flush against the hillside. I'm trapped between a sheer rock face and the onrush of traffic. I switch on my hazard lights and wait, panting for breath. Then I put my hand on the door handle and look back, waiting for a break in the traffic. I have to wait for a very long time.

Do you really remember now? Iris asked me. She was open and vulnerable. She held something out to me then, I just didn't realize it. *Come back and be my Jack. Then you'll understand everything.*

Now I have a chance. I push open the door and throw my body out, just as a flurry of vehicles speeds down the incline. I have to press my body against my car; the traffic that passes is just a couple of feet from me. More honking, the warm breeze of motion and exhaust.

It was—

I edge my way along the length of the car until I reach the back bumper, then press myself against the cliffside edging the highway. I've pulled the rental car right into the rock, and I get a glimpse of bent metal in the oncoming headlights. The rain has already soaked through my clothes, and I have to wipe at my eyes to see anything.

Do you really remember now?

I think I do, I told her.

But I didn't.

Please forgive me. I love you.

I start walking south, into traffic. I keep one hand on the rock face, feeling the earth tilt and gravitational pull luring me into the cars rushing toward me. My pants and jacket hang from my body, soaked, and I wrap my arms around myself when I feel the onslaught of a bone-racking chill.

When the wind picks up, I start to run. I try to picture what it was I saw that made me stop. A form, a glimpse of a face.

I turn around a bend in the road, running as fast as my shoes will allow. I slip, my shoulder grinding into rock. I might have cut myself, but I can't stop. The traffic is so close that I can hear the distinctive note that each engine makes, every whine and hum. I'm wiping sheets of rain from my hair.

I run faster when I see her up ahead. I scream out her

name, and the sound is lost in the rush of wind. She's walking hard, with her arms wrapped tight around herself. She's wearing only a T-shirt and jeans, and her clothes are darkened black with water.

When I catch up with her and try to take her arm, she shakes me away and tries to run. She won't look at me. She just wants to keep going. I have to grab her and restrain her. I say her name over and over. I thrust my face into hers and force her to open her eyes.

That day. My head. I *did* hurt Frank, I could have killed him. I let him drop to the ground. And then I went looking for Iris. She was hiding from me in the bathroom, and then she was in the room with Frank and me.

And *someone else?*

Finally she recognizes me. She lets me hold her and allows me to drape my soaking jacket over her shoulder. I motion back, and we begin walking together to my car. I keep my arm around her, and by the time I can see the car, I'm practically carrying her.

I had that club in my hand, that stupid club. Iris was crying and saying my name over and over.

And then I let it drop. I was surprised.

We wait for a pause in the traffic—sixty seconds, at least—and edge around the side of the car. I open the back door and push her in. I join her, then slam the door behind me an instant before a truck that would have taken it off passes.

"Jack Jack Jack," Iris says over and over again. She's shivering. Her hair is plastered to her forehead, and her eyes are wide and hollow with fear. I open up my bag and find yesterday's clothes. I strip her out of the jacket and T-shirt, dry her as best I can, and dress her in my dirty shirt and chicken-greasy jacket. I peel her out of her jeans, and she helps me get her into my slacks. She looks ridiculous, but soon her shivering begins to subside.

"I'll get us out of here," I tell her.

Traffic barrels down the slope. The car rocks in the wind. The rain sounds like thousands of fingers tapping on the roof.

"Jack. My father," Iris says.

I hold her, even though I'm wet. I press her face into my chest and comfort her as much as I can.

"I ran away," she says.

"I know," I tell her.

"I can't ever go back," she says. She looks up at me, and in the dark of the car, I see the face from my dreams. "Not after what he did to us, Jack."

"You don't have to," I tell her. "I'm going to take care of you now."

She reaches up and grabs my face, so hard that I cry out. She frames me in her hands and draws me close.

"Do you understand now?"

Try to remember. The gauze is thick. My head is pounding. I am shivering. I put down the club. Then someone picked it up. Someone struck me, hard, on the side of my head. Iris cried out, ran to defend me.

You really don't remember, do you? You have to know.

Karl. And then he hit her, too.

"I know." I run my hand along the slope of her cheek.

"Don't you understand?" Iris says. "I can never go back to him."

"I know," I say.

"Don't you understand?" Iris repeats. "You would never have hurt me. No matter what you think."

I remember being in my car, going home alone, waiting through the hours for the police to come, to tell me they had found her body. It was the only explanation my mind could have allowed.

I rub the ridge on my head, the repository of secrets. Karl injured us both, in a rage of his own. My crime was against Frank, and my crime against Iris was of the heart.

"You couldn't hurt me," Iris says.

But Karl let me believe that I could. To prolong my suffering, to divert blame from himself. His guilt must have been beyond fathoming. And he would have blamed me, once he found Iris, in the hopes that she wouldn't remember.

But she does. And now I do, too.

The weight hasn't lifted. But it doesn't press as hard as before. Of course I would never hurt her. I have that, it is mine.

"It can't . . . we can't ever be like before," she says, looking into my eyes sadly—more sad, I think, for me than for herself.

"Nothing has to be the same," I tell her. "We'll just have to see how it goes."

"Oh, Jack, I really like that." Iris smiles. She finally smiles.

I still have the money hidden in Minneapolis; the airport locker key is in my pocket. Karl can't touch us again, now that we both know. We'll go get Iris's friends—*my* friends—and we'll find someplace new to live. I have a family now: Iris, Leslie, David, Mark, even Kim if she wants to join us.

"You came back for me," Iris says, her voice choked with gratitude.

"I'll always come back for you," I tell her. "Every time. Until the end."

And the rain beats down, and I start the car and edge out into traffic, and Iris sleeps in the backseat, and soon we have blended back into the main. I drive and drive.

Today.

WHEN I REMEMBER ALL THAT NOW, ALTHOUGH IT HASN'T BEEN
VERY LONG AT ALL SINCE IT HAPPENED, IT COMES TOGETHER IN MY
RECOLLECTION ONLY TO SWIFTLY FALL APART AGAIN. Memory is not
a block of concrete. It has warmth and comfort, but little shape.
It's as fragile as a single old photograph. It's there, then gone
again. It's a handful of wind.

Should time collapse, and everything happen at once, then
the tragedy of life disappears. For change is what we take for
tragedy, the loss of what once was, the conditions that can
never be duplicated. But perhaps I am as I once was and shall be
again, and again. Maybe my birth and my death, and everything in between, and before and after, have already happened.

In the hum of silence I remember, and because I remember, nothing is really lost.

This room is small, but I'm warm and safe under a generous pile of blankets. I'm alone, but there's someone beyond the closed door. I hear the sound of things being moved and straightened. It's early morning dark in here, with only a sliver of pale yellow light intruding through the blinds. I smell an ashtray on the nightstand next to my side of the bed.

Another thing about remembering: Sometimes we remember only what we want to remember. Memories are like dreams, free of meaning save for that which we choose to impart.

I remember a man on a beach somewhere, sitting on a wooden bench next to his wife. The day is sunny, warm, summer. I am a boy walking slowly past him. He wears only swim trunks, and his body is tanned, muscular, hairy. His face is contorted in a grimace.

Here, come with me now. Look. Look at his foot. He's stepped on glass. He holds his sole up to examine it, and it drips blood on the sand.

I can choose to remember this in the context of my mother (surely I was on vacation with her at the time), or my fear of blood and violence (no matter how much I may or may not have caused). I can choose not to remember it at all. Maybe tomorrow it will be gone, a scene never to be played again in the theater of my mind. The players cannot be reassembled. Or else I will make a new connection, a new meaning that will erase all the ones that came before.

Someone hums in the next room. It's a woman's voice. I stir in my blankets, my head soft with sleep.

I remember, then I pass it on. It's my way of trying to understand what happened. And if, for the sake of piecing everything together, I've had to change a thing or two, it's only because it's taken me so long to begin to comprehend. Maybe I never found Iris on that rainy highway that night, and maybe I never had the chance to put things right. Maybe Karl finally succeeded in taking her away from me. But what kind of story would that be? What would my life have meant then?

And now, lying here in bed, listening to her hum, I can really believe that she's come back to me after all. Never what she was but, again, mine to treasure and hold. And whether she's here or not, I will always be hers.

Here in this dim morning light, as I sit up slowly and let out an involuntary sigh, the truth is that I can't be sure. I've just remembered who I am after a night of sleep, and I've just told you nearly everything that happened to me, and to her.

I might barely know who I am, but I am not entirely convinced that you have a significantly firmer grasp on your own identity, your own story.

But I am not concerned about you. The only thing that matters is that you have listened. I love her so that it pains me. I must have convinced you of at least that much. I no longer worry about the shadowy copses. I think of her constantly. I get up and go to the door. I hear her move. She has to be on the other side. She *has* to. This has been, and will remain, that kind of story.

PHOTO: © SARAH WALTER

QUINTON SKINNER is the author of nonfiction books on father-
hood and popular music. He lives with his family in Minneapolis.
Visit the author on his Web site at home.earthlink.net/~qskinner.